PRiNCESS
PRIVATE EYE

PRINCESS
PRIVATE EYE

EVELYN SKYE

DISNEP • HYPERION
Los Angeles   New York

First Edition, May 2023
1 3 5 7 9 10 8 6 4 2
FAC-004510-23076

Printed in the United States of America

This book is set in Atheneum Pro, FCaslon Twelve ITC Std, Teethreedee Std. Front, Clairvaux LT Std/Monotype; Adorn Roman, Goudy Trajan Pro, Jenson Recut/Fontspring

Designed by Alice Moye-Honeyman

Library of Congress Cataloging-in-Publication Data

Names: Skye, Evelyn, author.
Title: Princess Private Eye / by Evelyn Skye.
Description: First edition. · Los Angeles : Hyperion, 2023. · Audience: Ages 8–12. · Audience: Grades 4–6. · Summary: Twelve-year-old Gen, a foster child living in New York, discovers she is a long-lost princess of the Kingdom of Raldonia, and must solve the mystery behind a threat to the crown.
Identifiers: LCCN 2022031362 (print) · LCCN 2022031363 (ebook) ISBN 9781368078023 (hardcover) · ISBN 9781368096232 (ebk)
Subjects: CYAC: Foster children—Fiction. · Princesses—Fiction. Detective and mystery stories. · LCGFT: Detective and mystery fiction. Novels.
Classification: LCC PZ7.1.S5845 Pr 2023 (print) · LCC PZ7.1.S5845 (ebook) DDC [Fic]—dc23
LC record available at https://lccn.loc.gov/2022031362
LC ebook record available at https://lccn.loc.gov/2022031363

Reinforced binding

Visit www.DisneyBooks.com

To Clark, Sylvia & Mabel—
May you always be clever and curious

TABLE OF CONTENTS

GOOD DETECTIVE TRAITS

Know exactly who and what is around you.
At all times.

Never draw attention to yourself.

If you're going undercover, the best disguise
is one that the crooks will never suspect.

Remember—*everything* is a piece
of the puzzle.

Put others before yourself.

Gather as much information as possible.

Be as invisible as a ghost.

Always establish clear, nonverbal signals with your squad in case you can't talk to each other during an operation.

Utilize the element of surprise.

Never shy away from a situation just because it's unfamiliar.

Always use leverage when you've got it.

SOMETHING'S FISHY

Genevieve Sun limped into Frying Nemo on her crutches, sat down in the booth closest to the door, and picked up a menu like she was going to order. She didn't have any money, and most waiters might ask a twelve-year-old where her mom was, but Gen had learned over many years of basically being on her own that if you acted like you belonged somewhere, people didn't question you.

That's how she snuck into movie theaters, carnivals, and zoos. You just found a group of kids or a big family and tagged along at the edges. Then you ducked deeper into the group so the usher didn't realize you never had a ticket. The other method involved making a huge commotion and slipping in when all the grown-ups were distracted.

But that other method wouldn't work today. The toy thieves were here in the restaurant, and Gen didn't want them to notice her.

Kenneth Friedman, her eleven-year-old foster brother, sat down across from her and also picked up a menu, just like she'd told him to do.

She quickly took in their surroundings. That was Good Detective Trait Number One:

Know exactly who and what is around you.
At all times.

Frying Nemo was a small diner that smelled like greasy seafood and potatoes. It had a counter with eight barstools and four booths along the window.

The restaurant was only a third full. From Gen's seat near the front door, she had a clear view of the three other booths behind Kenneth.

Closest booth: empty.

Next booth: a group of teenagers with skateboards.

Farthest booth in the corner: three adults dressed up like the Hulk, Captain America, and Black Widow for the New York Comic Con that was starting later today.

Out of Gen's peripheral vision, she could also watch the counter. The barstools had been empty until thirty seconds ago, when a man and woman wearing black suits came in. The woman looked queasy as she sat down, but the man didn't seem to notice.

Gen caught a faint whiff of something out of place in a fish and chips restaurant. . . . Was that peanut butter, bacon, and pickles?

Weird.

"Which ones are the toy thieves?" Kenneth whispered, holding the menu over his mouth like he was a spy in a movie.

"You're being too obvious," Gen said, smiling while gently grabbing his wrist and lowering the menu back onto the counter. Good Detective Trait Number Two:

Never draw attention to yourself.

"Sorry," Kenneth said. "I'm just really excited."

Her eyes gleamed. Gen loved a good mystery, and this one had presented itself fifteen minutes ago, while she and Kenneth were in the nearby park. Gray-haired Mrs. Popper, who always pushed a dingy souvenir cart to try to sell Statue of Liberty keychains to tourists, had sprinted on wobbly knees toward them, the souvenirs on her cart jangling like alarms.

"Gen! Gen! We need your help! Some thieves just ran by. They knocked Jimmy's crutches out from under him and stole some of the neighborhood boys' backpacks full of action figures. The crooks were gone before we knew what happened, and the boys are crying, and I don't know what to do!"

Which is how Gen and Kenneth ended up here at Frying Nemo. With Gen borrowing crutches she didn't really need. Good Detective Trait Number Three:

If you're going undercover, the best disguise is one that the crooks will never suspect.

"The thieves are the skateboarders behind us," Gen whispered.

"How do you know?" Kenneth asked.

"There were skateboard skid marks right next to where the action figures were stolen," Gen said. "Then I noticed there were skateboard tracks in the dirt heading east. When we followed them, I saw flyers on the lampposts for Comic Con, so I deduced that the thieves stole the action figures to try to resell them at the convention."

Kenneth frowned. "If it's related to Comic Con, wouldn't the bad guys be the people dressed up like the Hulk?"

Gen shook her head. "Those costumes are custom-made—way above normal Halloween quality—which means they're superexpensive. The cosplayers don't need extra money. But since we've been here, the skateboarders have been talking about how much they want to buy the new virtual reality system that's coming out soon. That's why they're going to resell the action figures." Good Detective Trait Number Four:

Remember—everything _is a piece of the puzzle._

"How can you possibly listen to them and talk to me at the same time?" Kenneth's eyes went wide as dinner plates, super-impressed. "And also, how'd you know the skateboarders would come here?"

"The flyers said the doors to Comic Con open at two. It's only twelve thirty now."

A waitress came by to take their order. Gen's stomach growled.

But there were more important things to worry about right now, like getting those kids' toys back to them. Grown-ups often thought of Gen as a girl who got into too much mischief, but she knew the truth—she was guided by her big heart, and if there was any injustice that Gen could fix, she would do it. Good Detective Trait Number Five:

Put others before yourself.

"We need more time to look at the menu," she lied to the waitress.

The woman looked annoyed and grumbled under her breath, but she went away.

"So," Gen said, continuing to answer Kenneth's earlier question, "I figured the thieves would want to eat lunch before they headed over to the Comic Con. And there was a man on the last street corner holding a big wooden fish sign advertising fifty percent off meals for Comic Con ticket-holders. And voilà." She nodded her head discreetly toward the skateboarders' booth. "There they are."

Indeed, two small backpacks lay in the aisle, on top of skateboards. The backpacks were exactly like Mrs. Popper described—bright red and covered in Avengers patches.

"Well, butter my butt and call me a biscuit," Kenneth said. (His grandma was Southern and he was always saying random things like that.) "You're brilliant."

Gen grinned. "I know." That's one thing the foster care system had gotten right. Her case file description said, "Genevieve Sun is very smart but has a bit of a problem following rules because she thinks she can make better ones." (Gen had snuck a peek at her file once, when a social worker from Child Protective Services came to visit one of her foster families. During the meeting, Gen purposely burned some toast to set off the smoke alarm, and when the adults evacuated the apartment, she stole her file and had fifteen minutes alone with it on the fire escape before the firefighters said it was fine for everyone to go back inside. Gen snuck it back onto the coffee table, and the social worker never knew any better.)

"Okay," Kenneth said. "We found the thieves. What do we do next?"

Gen picked up her menu, leaned across the table, and began whispering the plan she'd hatched within the last few minutes, all while pointing at the menu to pretend *that* was what they were discussing.

When she was finished, Kenneth practically bounced on the vinyl seat of the booth in anticipation. Gen glanced at the four souvenir shopping bags she'd gotten from Mrs. Popper—two empty, two full—and she smiled at Kenneth.

"Now we spring the trap," Gen said. "It's time for Operation Rock 'n' Roll."

TIME TO ROCK 'N' ROLL

Kenneth ran past the thieves' table to the last booth, where the trio dressed up like the Hulk, Captain America, and Black Widow had just received their lunches.

"Whoa!" Kenneth shouted, throwing his arms in the air and making a commotion, just like Gen had instructed. "You're the Wrecking Ball Three, aren't you?"

The Hulk looked up with his face pinched. "The what?"

"From YouTube! The video game streamers with, like, twenty million followers. Oh man, I almost didn't recognize you with those costumes on!"

(There was no such thing as the Wrecking Ball Three, but Gen figured having celebrities in their midst was a great distraction. Plus, the skateboarding thieves had been talking about a virtual reality system, so they were obviously interested in video games.)

In fact, the thieves had already turned around at

Kenneth's fanboy yelling. Then, after he mentioned "twenty million followers," the nearest thieves hung over the seats and the farther ones leaned against their table to get closer to the supposed YouTube stars.

"Uh, sorry, kid," the woman dressed up as Black Widow said. "I think you got us mixed up with someone else."

"Oooooh." Kenneth put his index finger in front of his lips. "I get it. You don't want to get crushed by fans. Don't worry, we'll keep your identities on the down low, right?" He turned to the skateboarders, who started nodding vehemently.

As one of the middle children in his family, Kenneth was really good at talking about nothing for a long time, because that was the only way he could get attention.

As a foster child, Gen, on the other hand, had more experience with stealth. When you're an orphan whose life is in the hands of others, you learn how to move silently and hide in plain sight, becoming virtually invisible. That's how you eavesdrop on what the grown-ups have planned for you. Good Detective Traits Numbers Six and Seven:

Gather as much information as possible, *and Be as invisible as a ghost.*

Now Gen used those honed skills to slip soundlessly into the booth next to the thieves, with Mrs. Popper's souvenir bags carefully cradled to her chest and the crutches in her other hand.

"Can I get your autograph?" Kenneth was saying to the Wrecking Ball Three. "It doesn't have to be fancy. Like, on that napkin is fine. Even though it's dirty. I mean, what am I saying? I would be *honored* to have your ketchup stains on an autograph! So what do you say? Yes? Autographs for all of us?" He fired questions like he was at a shooting gallery at Coney Island, but Kenneth didn't give the costumed trio even a second to answer. He just kept talking. Very loudly.

Which is exactly what Gen needed. Using Kenneth's voice as cover, she reached out with one of the crutches, planted it on top of the closest skateboard, and rolled it (with the first backpack) along the aisle until it was next to her.

Before she picked up the backpack, Gen double-checked that no one was watching. The skateboarders were all begging for autographs and selfies with the Wrecking Ball Three. The waitress was talking to the man in the suit at the counter, and the suited woman was still trying not to puke. Kenneth kept blabbering.

Excellent.

Gen unzipped the backpack.

Jackpot! It was filled to the brim with action figures, just like Mrs. Popper had said. Gen quickly transferred the toys into one of the empty souvenir bags, then put a different souvenir bag—this one full of small rocks—into the backpack.

At the far booth, one of the faux celebrities finally managed to interrupt Kenneth's monologue. "Look, kid, I don't know what to tell you, but we're *not* the Wrecking Ball Three. So if you don't mind, we're trying to eat our lunch, okay?"

Shoot. Gen had better hurry. Kenneth could probably talk for another minute before the skateboarders stopped believing him, but once that time was up, she would be left without any cover. She still had another backpack full of toys to replace with rocks, plus she had to get the skateboards back where they belonged.

"Oh, yeah, I totally get it," Kenneth said. "I was thinking about getting some lunch, too. Gotta power up for Comic Con and all your fans, huh? What do you guys recommend? Are the fish and chips good? Or maybe fish sticks? Or maybe something more adventurous, like the Fried Squid Tentacle Delight. I mean, I've never been here before, so . . ."

Gen used the crutch to roll the second skateboard and backpack over to her table. She poured the action figures from that backpack into another empty souvenir bag, crammed the last bag of rocks into the backpack, and just finished zipping it when the man dressed as Captain America said to Kenneth, "Move, kid. I have to pee." He tried to slide out of the booth, but Kenneth threw himself in his path and shouted, "Please give me an autograph first and then I won't bother you anymore!"

Yikes! Gen had fifteen seconds, at best. She rushed to set the rock-filled backpacks onto their skateboards.

With the closest crutch, she pushed them one at a time back down the aisle. The first one rolled too far and bumped into Kenneth's ankle bone, and he winced a little when it hit him.

He nudged it back toward the thieves' table.

Gen held her breath. Would the skateboarders notice?

Luckily, they seemed more focused on whether Captain America was going to give Kenneth an autograph.

Whew, that was close. *Too* close.

"Seriously, kid," the Hulk said. "Beat it!"

Gen scooted out of the booth and back into the one closest to the door, bringing the crutches and souvenir bags of action figures with her. Then she pretended to yawn and stretched her arms far over her head.

That was her "Time to Go" signal. Good Detective Trait Number Eight:

**_Always establish clear, nonverbal signals with your squad
in case you can't talk to each other during an operation._**

Kenneth saw her signal out of the corner of his eye.

"You're right," he said loudly to the Hulk. "The Wrecking Ball Three is way nicer to their fans than you are. You know what? Now I'm not even hungry anymore. Thanks a lot for ruining a kid's day."

The skateboarders grumbled, too, disappointed as they settled back into their booth.

Kenneth pretended to sulk as he returned to his and Gen's original table, and together they slipped out of Frying Nemo.

"Stellar performance!" Gen said, high-fiving Kenneth when they were a block away.

He beamed. "Did you get the action figures?"

"Of course," Gen said, holding up the two souvenir bags proudly while carrying the crutches in her other arm. "Those con artists weren't going to foil me."

Kenneth frowned. "They weren't con artists. They were just grab-and-run thieves . . . Ohhh," he said, suddenly understanding Gen's play on words. "I get it. Comic *Con*, and *con* artist. Good one, Gen."

She was very pleased with how Operation Rock 'n' Roll had gone, but she felt even better when she returned the action figures to the boys at the park and saw the huge smiles on their faces. Jimmy and a couple others were foster kids like her, and Gen had an extra soft spot for anyone in the system. You just got bounced around a lot, and sometimes, all you really had were the few possessions you got to carry from place to place.

"I'm sorry I couldn't get the backpacks, too," Gen said as she handed the crutches back to Jimmy. (He'd been sitting on the grass while they waited for her and Kenneth to come back.)

"It's okay," Jimmy said. "The action figures are the most important."

One of the younger boys looked up at Gen, face beaming. "You know who my favorite superhero is?" he asked.

"No, who?" Gen said.

He threw himself around her legs and gave her a hug. "My favorite hero is you."

GEN HAS A TAIL

Kenneth had plans with a friend, so Gen headed back toward home alone. She replayed the last hour in her head and laughed as she imagined the con artists unzipping their backpacks at Comic Con, getting ready to sell the action figures, only to find a whole lotta rocks.

Justice served, and another victory for Detective Genevieve Sun, she thought, grinning.

But just as she rounded the corner, a mere ten blocks from her apartment building, Gen felt a prickling on the back of her neck, like something wasn't quite right. And she smelled peanut butter, pickles, and bacon.

Strange . . . She'd smelled that at Frying Nemo, too. It was out of place there and *definitely* out of place here on the street.

Peeking over her shoulder, Gen suddenly realized she had a tail—a man and a woman in suits.

She chewed on her lip. What did they want?

Gen whipped around, but the man and the woman spun on their heels and pretended to be very interested in the gossip magazines at the newspaper kiosk in front of them.

Okay, then, she thought. *We can play this the hard way.*

She turned back toward home and acted like she hadn't noticed the suspicious pair wearing too-thick black suits on a muggy summer day. Instead, Gen started whistling as she walked.

At the next corner, though, she ducked around a cart selling sunglasses. She held her finger in front of her mouth to the guy who owned the stand, a silent gesture to *please, please, please* be quiet.

The sunglasses vendor nodded once and continued polishing his wares.

There were skinny mirrors on the racks that allowed customers to check themselves out as they tried on sunglasses. Gen watched the reflection of the suited man and woman as they passed by.

"Where did she go?" the man asked.

"I don't know, but she couldn't have gotten far," the woman said. They both had light brown skin and spoke English with a soft accent that sounded like a burbling stream. Gen had never heard such an accent before, which was saying a lot, since New York was a huge melting pot of immigrants with accents and languages from literally all over the world.

"Maybe she went east," the man said.

"Or north," the woman said.

"Or," Gen said, popping up behind them and tapping the man in the suit on the shoulder, "maybe I'm right here."

He yelped and nearly jumped out of his pants.

The woman managed to keep her cool a little better, but she still staggered backward and accidentally stepped into the gutter full of litter.

Good Detective Trait Number Nine:

Utilize the element of surprise.

"Why are you following me?" Gen demanded, hands on her hips.

"Um, what? No, we weren't following you," the man said.

"Yeah you were," Gen said. "You were at the counter of Frying Nemo."

"You're mistaken," he said. "That must have been someone else."

"Nope," Gen said. "I remember seeing your fancy suits and wondering how you'd get the odor of grease and deep-fried batter out of the fabric. And you," she said, turning to the woman, "are pregnant, even though you haven't told anyone."

"H-how did you know that?"

"You're hiding a peanut butter, bacon, and pickle sandwich in your purse. I recognized the smell, because I had a nanny once who craved that same combination when she was preggers." (The truth was, there was no nanny, just another foster mom. But Gen wasn't about to let these two creepers know anything about her.)

The woman turned pale.

"So what do you want?" Gen said.

The sunglasses vendor got up from his chair and stood next to Gen with his arms crossed, like a bodyguard. She nodded her thanks for the backup.

"She's, er, feisty," the suited man said to the suited woman.

"Let me handle it," she said, recovering herself. "I'm good with kids." She crouched down to get closer to Gen's height. "You're very observant, sweetie. But don't worry, we were just wondering if you have any keepsakes from your childhood? We're, um, conducting a survey of New York City's kids."

Gen rolled her eyes. "Right, like that isn't sketchy at all. Why don't you drive around in an unmarked van and offer me candy, too?"

"Do we have any candy?" the man whispered to the woman as he started searching his pockets.

The woman let out an exasperated sigh. "She was being sarcastic."

"Whatever, I'm out," Gen said, holding both hands in the air and starting to cross the street.

"Wait!" the man shouted, lurching into the crosswalk.

Gen leaped out of the way. "You better back off, mister. I'm serious. My family is rich and powerful," she lied, "and if I catch even a whiff of your fish fry suit again, they'll call the authorities and have you thrown so deep in prison, you'll forget what the sun ever looked like."

Surprised, the man stayed frozen like a Popsicle in the

middle of the crosswalk until the sunglasses vendor hauled him out of the road and growled in a low voice, "You heard what the girl said."

Gen winked at the sunglasses vendor, and he grinned back. Then she ran off. Still, she couldn't help taking one last curious look at the man and woman in their now-wrinkled suits.

Because a good detective never completely turns her back on a potential mystery.

HOME STINK HOME

"And now, the lion tamer has returned home," Gen said as she stepped inside the apartment, joking with herself like she was the narrator in one of those nature documentaries. "The beasts that live here are nowhere to be seen, but evidence of their recent feast abounds."

The cramped apartment smelled of microwaved pizza pockets and old milk, because the oldest of the five sons was a hairy teenager who ate frozen pizza pockets by the dozen, and the youngest was still trying to figure out how to drink from a sippy cup. There was popcorn on the entryway floor—probably remnants of a food fight between the seven-year-old twins—and half-drunk juice boxes lay forgotten on the stained carpet.

"Hiya, Gen-Gen," Mikey, the toddler, said as he waddled over to greet her. Kenneth was Gen's favorite foster brother because he was closest to her age, but Mikey was a close second.

"You gimme snack?"

Gen smiled and scooped him up. "Sure thing. Whaddya want?"

"Super Choco Puff."

She laughed. "Nice try, buddy. I don't think your mom would be too happy with me if I gave you sugar cereal, though. How about some yogurt?"

Mikey faked a pout. But he was a good-natured little kid, so he got over it fast and just asked, "Wid nanners?"

"You got it. Bananas on top, coming right up," Gen said.

"I wuv you." He leaned in and gave her a slobbery kiss.

Gen melted.

This was the best foster family she had ever lived with, besides the Shens. They'd owned a dumpling buffet (!!!), and Gen helped out in the restaurant kitchen. She was lightning quick at making potstickers—maybe she had the talent in her DNA—and at the end of every night, she could eat as much of the leftovers as she wanted. (Scallion pancakes were like crispy, savory discs of ambrosia from heaven!)

Gen had been really upset when the Shens' grandfather got sick back in Macau and they had to sell the restaurant and all their belongings to move overseas. Living with the Shens was the first time Gen had felt like she belonged. Except it turned out that she hadn't belonged with them enough for them to be able to take her out of the country. There were laws about that sort of thing.

But the injustice of the whole foster care system is why Gen cared so much about making things right for others, like getting the action figures back from the con artists. Even if life couldn't be 100 percent ideal for Gen, she could try to make it better for other kids.

Gen carried Mikey into the kitchen and made him a bowl of yogurt with bananas. Then she went into the pantry and counted out ten crackers for herself. Her foster parents, Mr. and Mrs. Simmons, only got a certain amount of money from the State of New York for taking care of Gen, and she didn't want to overstretch their budget. (Especially since Teen Wolf Brother and his pals devoured burritos like they were free samples at Costco.)

Besides, Gen had had other foster families who put locks on the fridge and cabinets, and she'd only been allowed to eat when they unlocked them for her. This apartment felt like a downright luxury in comparison.

When Mikey finished his snack, Gen cleaned him up, and he wandered off to find out what his oldest brother and his friends were up to.

Gen took her remaining crackers (she liked to savor them slowly) and retreated to the old futon in the corner of the living room. There was a folding partition that separated this part of the room from the rest, and the ten-by-six-foot space served as Gen's "bedroom." The smell of pizza pockets and milk still permeated her space, as did the screaming of the seven-year-old twins as they fought over the remote control, but once she was settled on the cushion of her futon, it didn't matter, because she was in her "peaceful place."

She had a snack, a library book called *Advanced Computer Hacking Concepts* (she'd already mastered everything in *Ethical Computer Hacking for Kids* last year), and a pale-green baby blanket with the words *Genevieve Sun* and an embroidered sun stitched onto it with yellow thread. The blanket was her most prized possession—the only thing that made it out of the car crash with her over a decade ago, and Gen's only connection to her parents.

She knew nothing about her past, not even her real last name. Child Protective Services had been equally flummoxed by her identity, and they'd only given her the surname Sun because of the embroidery on her blanket, though it could've easily been a reference to the picture or a nickname. (Gen liked to tell herself that Sun *was* her real last name, because then she'd have more than just an old blanket to connect her to her mom and dad. Plus, Sun was a Chinese name, which would explain why she looked like Andi Mack.)

The one thing Gen knew for sure, though, was that every time she pulled the tiny blanket over her lap, she immediately felt a wave of comfort. But as Gen reached for the blanket this time, she froze. Because she realized what else it was—a keepsake from her childhood.

Exactly what the two creeps in suits had asked her about.

THE WAY THE CRACKER CRUMBLES

There was a nagging feeling in the pit of Gen's stomach, like when you drink milk that you *know* isn't good anymore but you just really wanted to have cereal for breakfast that morning. What was the deal with the man and woman who'd followed her? Was it related to the con artists? Like, maybe they had some supersophisticated friends who were after Gen because she'd embarrassed them.

But no, the Suits (she'd decided they needed a name as well) arrived at Frying Nemo *before* Gen swapped the action figures for rocks.

So she suspected there was something more behind that weird confrontation at the sunglasses stand. And the key to the mystery was probably her baby blanket.

Gen picked it up, looking at it more closely than she ever had before. She ran her fingers along the edges, sniffed it (ew—it smelled a little bit like overly steamed cauliflower and needed to be washed), and even tried shaking it. There wasn't anything obvious, though.

Time for more advanced sleuthing skills, Gen thought.

First, she brainstormed whether the colors—pale green and yellow—could be symbolic of anything. Green made her think of spring, nature, and maybe . . . new beginnings? Yellow felt like sunshine and happiness.

Or maybe Gen was totally overthinking this and her parents had just gotten her a green blanket because it was more gender neutral than blue or pink.

Humph.

Gen started tossing the blanket in the air while she thought some more. Every time the blanket came back down, she caught it before it hit the futon. But just then the twins started screeching about a video game on the other side of the partition—"It's *my* turn to play!" "No! You played twice in a row and it's not faiiiiir!"—and Teen Wolf Brother and his pack of friends all ran into the kitchen at the same time and started wrestling loudly over the last pizza pocket, and Gen missed her catch.

The blanket hit the metal bar on the edge of the futon, and she heard a distinct *clink*.

Gen held her breath. Blankets were soft. They didn't *clink*. Unless . . .

She snatched it from where it had fallen and tossed it again. This time, she watched carefully to see which part fell first. If there was a section of the blanket that was heavier, then that would mean—

Yes! The section embroidered with her name hit the

futon a split second before the rest. Gen pressed her fingers into the stitching, feeling for something hidden inside. *Anything.*

Gen gasped as she discovered a tiny lump in the blanket. It was flat and had been concealed by the raised embroidery of her name and the sun, which is probably why she'd never noticed it before.

She ran to the bathroom and rifled through the drawers for nail clippers. Then she ran back to the living room, hurdling over the twins, who were now on the ground fighting over the video game controller. Gen flung herself back onto her futon and began to snip at the edge of the blanket closest to her embroidered name.

When enough of the stitching had been snipped open, Gen wriggled the little lump toward the blanket's edge.

Wiggle, wiggle, wiggle . . .

"Aha!" she cheered to herself as the secret fell into the palm of her hand.

It was a silver-colored pendant, about the size of a nickel but a lot thinner and lighter. The pendant must have been made of a really valuable precious metal like platinum (whoa!), because it wasn't tarnished at all. (Gen knew that silver turned a dull, brownish color if it wasn't polished, and this pendant was too shiny to be silver that'd been stashed inside a blanket for more than ten years.)

But what gave Gen even more of a jolt was when she turned the pendant over.

There was a strange crest on it, the kind that looked like a medieval coat of arms. There was a shield covered in stars, and an enameled purple fox flying out of the night sky like a celestial spirit. The fox was wearing a crown.

"Holy cow!" Gen exclaimed. (Although, technically, she supposed it should have been "Holy fox!")

But what did this pendant and crest mean?

There was only one place she knew of that held all the information in the world.

Gen stuffed the pendant and blanket into her pocket, forgot all about her crackers, and sprinted out the door.

PHISHING FOR CLUES

The local library was a squat cube of chipped bricks, like a quiet nerd who'd had its teeth busted by a bully. But even though it looked timid and beat-up on the outside, the library's insides were amazing.

Okay, fine, the walls and carpets and furniture were actually unimpressive and worn, too, but what mattered to Gen was all the books—especially the detective series—and the computers.

Ah, computers. Humankind's greatest invention yet. With a *tap-tap-tap* on the keyboard and a few quick searches, Gen could find answers to anything she needed. Or, at the very least, clues.

She found an unoccupied computer away from the others (not that she was going to do anything bad, but, you know, just in case), and Gen pulled up a search engine and began to type.

Fox coat of arms.

The browser spit out a bunch of images of foxes on shields, but they were all red and mean-looking, not like the fantastical purple fox on her pendant.

There were also questions like *What does a fox on a coat of arms mean?* (Answer: faith, sincerity, and justice). And *What is the name of a fox's house?* (Answer: a den. Duh.)

Gen chewed on her bottom lip. While she liked the idea that faith, sincerity, and justice might be part of what her family was known for—*if* this pendant was related to her family at all—that clue still didn't get Gen any closer to figuring out where the pendant came from and what it was doing in her blanket.

She tried typing in another search.

Purple star fox.

That brought up search results for a video game.

Genevieve Fox. (What if she had, like, a secret identity?)

Nope. Just a lawyer, an author of adventure books who died in 1959, and a journalist.

"Rats," Gen muttered. She'd kind of been hoping to discover a secret identity. Maybe the little boy calling her a superhero this morning had gone to her head.

Still, that got her thinking. The pendant had been hidden deep inside her blanket, which probably meant it *was* a secret. Like, her parents sewed it up to hide it in the most ordinary-looking thing possible so that no one but Gen could find it.

Why?

Maybe her mom and dad hadn't wanted to be found?

Or they didn't want anyone to know who they really were?

"Interesting . . ." Gen said to herself.

She typed furiously as she did more research about coats of arms and learned that they were mostly European. So Gen started researching European crests, especially the lesser known ones. After an hour and some pretty serious digging, a strange search result finally popped up:

Kingdom of Raldonia.

"Yes!" Gen said, pumping her fist. She clicked on the Wikipedia link.

The kingdom of Raldonia is a small country in Western Europe, measuring only 438 square acres. Due to a confidential diplomatic "incident" in the past, Raldonia is not officially recognized by the world's superpowers, including the United States.

There was an image of the Raldonian royal crest, and it was a shield of stars with a purple fox on it.

Gen's eyes almost fell out of her head. This was more information than she'd ever had on her family. She had no idea *which* side of her family, but still! Gen scrolled to read more.

But there was no more. The page just stopped.

"Seriously? That's it? No!" Gen shouted.

A librarian on the other side of the room shushed her.

Gen glared at the computer screen.

Any other kid would have quit right there. Heck, any other adult might have, too. After all, if web search after web search netted nothing but one pathetic little Wikipedia page, maybe there was nothing else to find.

But Genevieve Sun was not a quitter. She was a fighter, a sleuth, and . . . a hacker.

A mischievous grin spread across Gen's face.

To be clear, she was an *ethical* hacker. There were evil hackers who tried to break into things in order to steal identities or demand ransoms, but there were also honorable ones who used their skills for the forces of good. Like those who volunteered to test for security flaws in voting machines or who worked for banks to make sure their software was safe from cyber crooks.

Gen checked to make sure the librarian wasn't watching her. Some grown-ups had a really hard time understanding the moral differences in hacking. All they would see is a kid "breaking" the computer and typing a bunch of gibberish into it, and then Gen would be kicked out of the library and never allowed to return. Which could *not* happen. So she stayed obediently quiet for a few minutes to make sure the librarian was otherwise occupied before diving back in to the computer.

Finally back at it, Gen scoured the Raldonian Wikipedia page, letter by letter. Maybe there was some kind of code hidden here, a way to access more information for those in the know. A phrase? A purposeful misspelling? Even the spaces between the words and punctuation were scrutinized.

And then Gen saw it. The fox on the Raldonian crest was winking.

Gen fumbled in her pocket for the pendant. She held it up with shaking hands next to the computer screen.

"I was right," she whispered, hardly daring to breathe now. The fox on her pendant had wide-open, curious eyes. It was identical to the image on the screen, except for the winking.

She clicked on the fox.

Nothing happened.

Gen tried clicking specifically on the fox's eye.

It took her to a page that was blank except for *This Content Is Not Available In Your Country* written in bold and accompanied with a frowny face.

For a second, she frowned, too. Gen remembered learning in school that some internet content was accessible only from certain parts of the world. Something to do with licensing rights and *boring, boring, etc., etc.*

But a *Raldonian* computer would certainly be allowed to see Raldonian content, right?

Gen grinned.

Her fingers flew over the keyboard. It took her less than a minute to set up a VPN—virtual private network—which let her library computer pretend it wasn't in the United States but actually in Raldonia.

A few more commands later, Gen's screen lit up with all the search results she'd originally wanted.

"Victory is mine!" she said (quietly so the librarian wouldn't shush her again). "I'm in."

THAT'S AN AWFUL LOTTA NAMES

N ow that Gen had access to Raldonian internet content, she could read anything she wanted about it. So she started devouring all the information about this mysterious kingdom she'd never heard about before.

The government website was pretty boring. Raldonia was currently ruled by Queen Michelina Eleanor Avalyne Leire of the House of Claremont, Queen and Sovereign of the Realm, Defender of Faith, Sincerity, and Justice. (Yep, that entire mouthful was her full title.) It was a small island nation in Europe. The official language was English (although a few people did speak Raldonian), the population was just around 40,000 as of the recent census, the primary natural resources were lavender flowers and a special kind of extra-large shrimp, blah, blah, blah, blah, blah. . . .

Gen's eyes started to glaze over. Sure, lavender was pretty and smelled nice, but who cared if some country far away had a lot of flowers? And Gen definitely didn't care about shrimp, even if they *were* the size of lobsters.

What she really cared about was who her family was. Were they scientists? Bakers? Firefighters?

She decided the best clue to start with was her fox pendant.

Gen found a legend about the first king of Raldonia being a fox that came down from the heavens. Okay, so that explained the crest.

Then she found a picture of the country's flag. It was purple, with the same star pattern as the crest, but it didn't have a fox on it.

Why not?

Gen clicked on a link about the history of the flag. She figured it would be boring, but . . .

She gasped.

It is illegal to possess the symbol of the Raldonian Fox unless you are a direct descendant of the king and queen. Even siblings of the monarch are not permitted to wear, carry, or otherwise display the fox. Anyone found in violation of this centuries-old law is guilty of subversion of the throne and shall be punished accordingly.

Gen looked goggle-eyed from her pendant to the words on the screen to the pendant again.

Her first thought was if anyone saw her with the fox, she'd be arrested for treason.

But then logic kicked in and Gen realized, *OMG. I have a Raldonian Fox.*

At that exact moment, the Suits burst into the library.

They sprinted over to the bank of computers but skidded to a stop when they saw what Gen was holding.

"It's true!" the man shouted in awe. He fell to his knees and bowed.

"Not here," the woman hissed, yanking him back up to standing.

"Why is it so hard for people to be quiet?!" the librarian snapped. She and the rest of the people were staring at Gen now.

So much for not drawing attention.

Gen swiftly shut down the pages of source code and other evidence of hacking on her computer screen. (Even though, as a reminder, it was 100 percent ethical.) "Um, do you mind telling me what the heck is going on?"

The suited woman smiled like she wanted to eat Gen. (The woman was definitely not as good with kids as she thought she was.)

The man started to bumble with his words. "Fox! You! Car! Purple!"

Gen blinked at him, confused. (Kenneth's grandma would probably say, "That guy's cornbread ain't done in the middle.")

"What he means," the woman said, lowering her voice so that no one else in the library could hear, "is that your mother was Princess Adrienne of Raldonia, and that makes you Genevieve Illona Caliste Aurelie of the House of Claremont, Princess of the Realm, Defender of Faith, Sincerity, and Justice."

Gen squeaked. "Uh, can you say that again?"

The woman smiled, but this time Gen could see that the hungry look on her face wasn't Big-Bad-Wolf hungry. It was the expression of someone who'd finally found what she was looking for and couldn't believe her eyes.

And it confirmed what Gen suspected.

"Ms. Sun," the woman said. "You are the missing princess of Raldonia."

WE'RE THE GOOD GUYS, HONEST!

The librarian kicked them out for causing a ruckus.

"We're so sorry, Your Highness," the man said once they were outside.

The woman whacked him in the arm. "Shhh! Don't call her Your Highness in public!"

"Um," Gen said, "you realize that you both seem kind of nuts, right?"

They stopped their bickering to stare at her.

"You don't believe us?" the woman asked.

Gen scrunched up her face. "I'm not denying that my research led to a similar conclusion, but it didn't say anything about a missing princess. . . . And I have to say, this is all pretty out there."

"It's the truth, Your—" the man paled as the woman glared at him, and he whispered "Highness" so quietly, it disappeared into the sound of New York traffic.

"Let me explain," the woman said. "We're part of the Raldonian Intelligence Agency."

Gen actually squeaked in surprise. The Raldonian equivalent of the CIA was here to ... to what?

She pulled herself together and led them to a bench near the side of the library, set off from the street and away from people. "If you are who you say you are," she said, "show me your badges."

"Oh, yes, official credentials!" the man cried. "Of course, Your High ... Of course, Ms. Sun."

Huh. Gen wasn't used to grown-ups who acted deferential around her; usually, it was foster parents or teachers or social workers yelling at her for doing any multitude of things wrong. So the man's nervous bumbling was actually kind of endearing. It seemed like he wanted ... Gen's approval?

He fumbled in his suit jacket and presented a gold, star-shaped badge emblazoned with *Raldonian Intelligence Agency* across the top and *Faith, Sincerity, and Justice* below. There was also an RIA identification card with the man's photo and *Agent 34* printed on it. The woman's credentials looked identical except for her agent number.

"Where are your names?" Gen asked.

"Names?" the man blinked in confusion.

"You do have names, don't you?" Gen asked. "Why aren't they on the ID cards?"

He frowned. "Oh. I'm Ahmed al Dabbagh. And this is my twin sister, Maryam."

"We usually just go by our numbers," Maryam said.

"Part of a longstanding RIA tradition. He's Agent 34. I'm Agent 43."

"They got a kick out of giving us mirror digits," Ahmed explained with a laugh. "A twin thing, I guess. Though I pushed hard for the higher number. Maryam has always done better than me at everything, and I wanted to beat her for once."

"His final score on the entrance exam actually was just one point less than mine," Maryam added with a fond smile at her brother.

These two definitely don't act *like criminal master-minds*, Gen thought, so this was unlikely to be some big evil trap. And their burbling brook accent, which she'd also noticed earlier, was kind of soothing.

Besides, the Suits were as close as Gen had ever been to finding out who her own family was. She decided that she'd listen to what else they had to say.

But Gen would call them Agent 34 and Agent 43, respectively, per their tradition. That also made it sound like she was in a spy movie, which, to be honest, was kind of a fantasy of Gen's. Not that she would tell *them* that, though. She needed to keep the upper hand, and that meant keeping her childhood fantasies to herself.

Instead, Gen pointed at the bench. "Why don't we sit? And then you can tell me the truth about what's going on, not the made-up nonsense you tried to pull at the sunglasses booth earlier. Why have you been following me?"

Agent 34 sat down and shook his head sadly. "The truth is . . . we're not supposed to tell you the truth. It's nothing personal. Queen Michelina forbade anyone to speak of it."

Gen furrowed her brow. "What could be so big and so bad that the queen wants it buried in the past?"

He shrugged in that what-can-you-do kind of way. "If we tell you, we could lose our jobs. We could even be put in jail."

But Agent 43 spoke up. She was looking down at her stomach when she said, "I think, though, that Ms. Sun should know at least some of the history. It's *her* past, too. She deserves to hear it."

"Wait. So Sun really *is* my last name?"

Agent 43 nodded. "Your father was Lucas Sun from South Mallanthra. It's a small kingdom near Brunei. The population is made up mostly of immigrants from all around Asia, much like Singapore," she added, probably in response to Gen's blank look. (Gen had never been good at world geography.)

But the real reason Gen was so thunderstruck was because, up until a few minutes ago, she'd no idea who she was. And now she knew not only her own name with 100 percent certainty, but also her parents'. And where they were from.

Wow. I really am *Genevieve Sun. And I am half Raldonian and half South Mallanthran.*

I have a history.

She took a moment to let it sink in.

Of course, Gen desperately wanted to know more about this mysterious past of hers. There's nothing worse to a detective than a mystery about herself. It's like an itch in the middle of your back that's just out of reach to scratch. But at the same time, she felt bad about putting the agents in this position. Gen definitely didn't want them to get fired or arrested. And at the end of the day, she didn't want to be the one to create more suffering in the world. Good Detective Trait Number Five:

Put others before yourself.

"It's okay, I don't need to know," she said. "I'd like to. I mean, I'd *love* to know why you're here and who I am and why this is all such a huge hush-hush deal. But not if it means you'll get in trouble."

The agents glanced at each other. As siblings, they seemed to be able to communicate with looks and eyebrow raises alone. Then Agent 43 nodded, and Agent 34 cleared his throat. "No, no. My sister is right. You deserve some answers."

"How about this?" Gen said, going into problem-solving mode. "I only want you to tell me what you can without technically going against the queen." She was a master at the art of evading rules—there were plenty of creative ways to interpret what you were and weren't allowed to do. For example, her most recent foster parents had a rule about screen time: only thirty minutes a day, unless it was for homework. But what about all that time Gen spent teaching herself about hacking and writing an artificial intelligence program—her beloved Hopper—that would help her hack more efficiently? (Only for the forces of good, of course! To help her solve mysteries!) That screen time wasn't assigned by the school. But Gen decided it fell into a technical gray area of "independent study"—kind of like self-assigned homework. And voilà! A screen time loophole was born.

She figured that if the Suits could do that, it would be a win-win. Gen could get more information about her past, and they wouldn't get in trouble.

Agent 34 nodded. "Good idea. All right, let's see, where to begin? Well, a few months ago, an insurance-claim adjuster in the United States began following up on a loose end and made a startling discovery about a potential survivor in a car crash. That accident—which took place nearly twelve years ago—involved your father and mother, princess and heir to the Raldonian throne."

Agent 43 took over the story. "Until now, communication between our countries had been . . . shaky. So everyone believed that all three of you had died tragically in the crash. We had no idea you were still alive and that Child Protective Services had taken you under their jurisdiction. But as soon as the queen found out, she dispatched Agent 34 and me to New York City to confirm whether it was true. Queen Michelina is getting on in age, and she'd like to retire in a few years and pass on her crown. The king passed away two decades ago—a heart attack, rest his soul—and the queen has no children or grandchildren other than, possibly, you."

"Which is why you wanted to know if I had any family keepsakes," Gen said, opening her fist to again reveal the fox pendant.

They nodded. "No one but the royal family—direct

descendants—can even touch the imperial fox crest, let alone carry it," Agent 43 said.

Gen swallowed the lump that had formed in her throat. After close to twelve years of fending for herself, she was afraid to believe that she'd really found her family. Or that they had found her. If Gen thought about it too hard, this all might disappear. She'd probably wake with a start on the futon at her foster family's place and realize she'd imagined the fox, the RIA agents, everything.

Besides, as an amateur detective, Gen also knew you couldn't act on just a single piece of evidence. You needed to gather more facts to be sure. It was Good Detective Trait Number Six.

Gather as much information as possible.

"S-so how are you going to confirm I didn't just steal or find this pendant somewhere?" Gen asked, her voice shaky. She closed her fist over the medallion as if that could keep two grown adults from wresting it from her if they wanted to.

"Well," Agent 43 said, "Agent 34 and I just need a couple more pieces of proof."

"Like what?"

Gen swore that Agent 34's face turned a little green, and then Agent 43 spoke again.

"Ms. Sun, are you scared of needles?"

BLOOD IS THICKER THAN SALIVA

Gen didn't particularly like needles, but she wasn't squeamish about them either. It turned out what the Suits wanted wasn't some weird Frankenstein experiment; they just needed blood for a DNA test to confirm that Gen really was a member of the royal family. Sure, there were DNA tests that used saliva, but blood was the most accurate.

After the quick test, they went to a nearby park to wait for results. (The agents had a connection with a lab headed by a former Raldonian, so it would only be an hour or so.) Once they'd settled on the concrete edge of a fountain, Agent 43 opened her wallet and pulled out a worn photo. She showed it to Gen. It was of a woman with chestnut-colored hair, in a chic sweater and long skirt, a man with Donnie Yen movie star looks wearing a blazer and jeans, and a chubby hapa baby with a gummy smile.

Gen suddenly felt warm and quivery. Her *parents*. She touched the photo gently.

When she looked at herself in the picture, though, she noticed the pale-green baby blanket draped over her tiny legs. "Th-that's my blankie! It's the only thing I have from before the car accident."

Agent 34 leaped up. "You have another keepsake? Besides the imperial fox pendant?"

She nodded. "It's at my foster family's apartment."

"If you could retrieve it," Agent 43 said, "that would be further proof that you're the missing princess." She gazed at the photo while touching her stomach again, as if the family portrait was making her daydream about her own baby.

Thinking about Agent 43 as *both* an international spy and a mother made Gen like her more. Agent 43 was the kind of real-life superhero Gen wanted to grow up to be: busting espionage rings by day and playing board games with her family by night.

Her *own* family. Not one she temporarily lived with, courtesy of Child Protective Services.

And it sounded like that family was in Raldonia.

In Raldonia, Gen would have a grandmother. *Maybe the queen bakes cookies?* Gen always loved the idea of a grandma who would bake, her whole house smelling like butter and sugar and chocolate chips. She and her grandma would sit together to decorate cookies at the royal table—or maybe they'd sit in their thrones, ha!—all while her grandma told her stories about her mom and dad. What her mom was like as a kid. How she met her dad. Why they left Raldonia, and how much they loved Gen.

The last part got Gen a little choked up.

Stop thinking about all that! Gen said to herself. There were no guarantees any of this would work out. The DNA test could be negative. Or the queen of Raldonia could decide she didn't want a New York City urchin as a granddaughter. Or a million other reasons this could fail. As an orphan and a charity case, Gen was used to being forgotten or discarded. She knew better than anyone how to steel herself for disappointment.

The best option was not to get her hopes up at all.

Still, she frowned at Agent 43's comment that the RIA would need more proof than a DNA test. "I'm confused. Isn't it case closed once you have genetic evidence?" DNA was always the main evidence in mystery novels and detective shows.

"Scientifically, yes," Agent 34 said, furrowing his brow. "But if you have the same blanket as the one in this photo, that's even better. We have to show the Raldonian people as many forms of authentication as possible, because a lot of them believe in a—"

Agent 43, eyes wide in alarm, whacked him so hard, she almost knocked him backward into the fountain. Then, immediately realizing what she'd almost done, she grabbed his arm with big-sisterly concern and said, "34, are you all right? Did you get wet?"

Gen felt a pang of jealousy, the same kind she always felt whenever she saw siblings together. What would it be like to grow up with a brother or a sister? With people of your own blood?

Maybe Gen would get to find out soon in Raldonia. Maybe she had more family there, beyond her grandma? Cousins her age? Uncles, aunts?

"I'm sorry," Agent 43 was saying to her brother. "I was just worried you were going to tell her—"

Agent 34 shook his head gently. "No, I wouldn't, but don't you think she should know . . ."

Gen again felt bad for both of them for being stuck in this bizarro situation where they were bound by secret rules about what they could and couldn't say. But at the same time, she couldn't tamp down her curiosity. "Don't you think I should know what?"

"Nothing to worry about," Agent 34 said.

"Just some superstitious nonsense," Agent 43 added. "No big deal." She smiled the kind of smile adults gave when they meant *This topic is now closed, end of discussion.* You couldn't get a grown-up to budge once they smiled like that.

So Gen didn't press the issue. But that didn't mean she wouldn't investigate later. Gen would most definitely investigate later.

At that moment, Agent 43's phone rang. She answered immediately. "43 speaking. Yes? Uh-huh. Uh-huh. Ninety-nine point nine nine percent accuracy? I see. All right. Thank you." She hung up.

Gen could feel her heart pounding like it was trying to beat its way out of her chest. She hadn't realized how nervous she was—and how much she wanted the DNA test results to confirm her identity—until Agent 43 just sat there, chewing on her lower lip and not saying anything.

For once in her life, Gen was actually shocked into inaction.

Slowly, Agent 43 rose from the fountain ledge. She didn't look at Gen, and Gen's heart stopped pounding furiously. Instead, it began to sink. The phone call was probably negative results. The agents were going to walk away and leave Gen here, where she belonged to nobody. Her life in New York City had been fine up till today, when the hope of a real family had been dangled before her. But now that the agents were about to yank that future away, Gen suddenly felt unbearably empty.

Agent 34 walked over to 43, and they conferred with each other quietly.

Gen got up and trudged away.

Suddenly, everything around her looked gray, the color of disappointment. The birds in the trees sounded flat when they sang. Even the churros from a nearby street cart smelled like nothing.

But a minute later, Agent 34 yelped behind Gen. "Hey!" He jogged to catch up. (She hadn't gone far, since she could hardly motivate her feet to move.) "Where are you going?" he asked.

"Back to my foster home," Gen said sadly.

"To get your blankie?" Agent 34 asked.

Her head snapped up. "What?"

"Your blanket. To bring with you to Raldonia."

Gen stared at him. "Wait. You mean . . ."

"The lab confirmed it, Your High—" Again, he stopped himself just in time. A few people feeding pigeons nearby had paused to watch them. After all, two suited agents and a kid were kind of a spectacle.

Agent 34 bent down to Gen's ear and whispered, "The DNA test confirmed you are our lost princess. Agent 43 and I were just working out logistics on how to get you home to your family."

Princess? Home? Family???

"Oh my god!" Gen shouted, startling him as she began to jump and whoop. She grabbed his hand and started dancing in circles, which he gamely joined in on. Then they looped back to the fountain where Agent 43 stood, talking on her phone and looking very serious. But when Gen offered her hand, Agent 43 grinned, hung up, and took Gen's outstretched hand.

"Do you want to know what 34 and I always did as kids when there was something to celebrate?" Agent 43 asked.

"What?" Gen asked eagerly.

"We stuffed ourselves full of candy, then did cartwheels over and over until we threw up."

"See?" Agent 34 said. "I *knew* I should have brought candy in my pockets."

Agent 43 and Gen both laughed. Then they sprinted together toward a grassy patch of the park and did cartwheels over and over until they fell down. (Gen was super impressed that Agent 43 even attempted cartwheels, being queasy and all.)

Afterward, Agent 34 bought Gen a necklace chain from a street vendor so she could wear her family crest pendant proudly. (Her family crest!!!) And Agent 43 bought them each a celebratory churro. They didn't have them in Raldonia, and she and 34 loved them so much, they ended up buying all the churros from the cart and gorging themselves.

"No more cartwheels, though," Gen said when she'd finished her fifth churro.

"No more cartwheels," Agents 34 and 43 agreed, groaning happily at their full bellies. "Besides, we have to get you to the airport to fly home to Raldonia. Your grandmother is excited to meet you."

"Home," Gen said quietly, trying the word on for size.

Grandmother, she thought even more quietly, still afraid the idea was too fragile to say out loud.

Gen would miss Kenneth and Mikey, of course. But foster placements were never permanent, and Gen had learned to move on when she had to. Besides, she could always send postcards from Raldonia.

And princesses ought to be able to afford small gifts, right? Gen would definitely mail them something Raldonian as a present.

She laughed to herself as she bit into another warm churro. *I hope this country has something cooler to buy than extra-large shrimp.*

YOU CAN'T WEAR A BABY BLANKIE

Gen had never been on a plane before, let alone a *royal* plane. She and the agents didn't have to go through a security check or X-ray machine or anything. They just waltzed onto a private tarmac at LaGuardia Airport, because even though Raldonia and the United States had a shaky relationship, the Americans weren't such giant jerks that they'd deny a foreign dignitary's plane a runway.

"Hey, I was wondering," Gen said, "why was it so hard for me to find information about Raldonia on the internet?"

Agents 34 and 43 looked at each other uncomfortably for a long moment, but finally, Agent 34 cleared his throat and said, "Well, er, for political reasons, the United States refuses to officially recognize Raldonia as a country. It, um . . . it has to do with a diplomatic disagreement from more than a dozen years ago. But anyway, that's not important. Are you excited about this plane ride?" He pointed at the red carpet that was rolled out in front of the staircase that led up to the shiny silver private plane. "We've got it stocked with Raldonian snacks!"

But the agents' secretiveness about the Raldonian–US relationship meant there was a real mystery here, and Gen wouldn't be shaken off its scent with a simple, inelegant subject change about snacks. (Even though Gen was also super curious about Raldonian snacks.)

"A dozen years…" Gen said. "*I'm* twelve years old. Would that 'diplomatic disagreement' have anything to do with me? Or my parents? I mean, only if you can tell me without getting in major trouble," she added.

The agents exchanged looks even more uncomfortable than before. Agent 43 seemed a little ill, and Gen was pretty sure it wasn't the morning sickness. She didn't answer until they started climbing up the steps to their waiting plane.

"How to best explain this?" Agent 43 said over the noise of the engine. Gen had to stick to her heels in order to hear. "Your mom," Agent 43 said, "was supposed to be the heir to the Raldonian throne. But after her wedding to your dad there was some, uh … *fallout*, and then she and your dad left the kingdom soon after. It was viewed as a huge insult to Queen Michelina that your mom would turn her back on the royal family like that.

"Duke Charlemagne—that's your mom's cousin—tried to convince them to come back, but when that failed, the queen blamed the US for not forcing her daughter to go home, and ever since then, relations between the two countries have been chilly."

Then Agent 43 stepped into the plane, and despite the tension of the story she'd just told, being on the jet seemed to relax her immediately. Agent 43 let out a contented sigh. Gen followed her.

"Whoa," she murmured, momentarily distracted from the mystery surrounding her parents' departure from Raldonia. "This plane is like the fanciest hotel in New York City, but it *flies*."

There were deep leather seats and gilded tables, purple velvet drapes, and Raldonian flags. Classical music swelled from the surround-sound speakers, and chandeliers glimmered from the ceiling. (Chandeliers! On a plane!)

That's when it really hit Gen that she was on a private royal plane, belonging to a kingdom that she might be queen of someday, if all went well.

Mind. Blown.

"Welcome to Raldonian luxury, Your Highness," Agent 43 said.

Gen knew it was another attempt at changing the subject from her parents' past, but as before, Gen let it go, because that meant Agents 34 and 43 had reached the limits of whatever loophole they were using to be able to tell her this stuff. Besides, Gen would find ways to fill in the gaps later. After all, she'd actually be in Raldonia, and if nothing else, she could unleash Hopper, her artificial intelligence program, on the Raldonian internet to collect info.

"It *is* all for you," Agent 34 said with a kind smile. "Your Highness." He bowed, and Agent 43 joined him. The pilots and the flight attendants came out and bowed, too. Gen was too stunned to say anything, so she just giggled nervously. "Did you say there were Raldonian snacks?"

An hour later, Gen was strapped into one of the huge leather seats while scarfing down something that was sort of like small flower-shaped soft pretzels stuffed with jam made from raldonberries, grown only in Raldonia. The pretzels were, apparently, a seaside treat, and if beach treats were a Raldonian specialty, Gen was definitely looking forward to it. It was only too bad that she couldn't share them with Kenneth and Mikey at her foster home. She felt a pang of sadness at leaving them behind. Life for her in New York had been hard, but there was a lot she loved, too. It was the only city she'd ever known, and the only people she'd ever known.

But this is an adventure, she told herself. Good Detective Trait Number Ten:

Never shy away from a situation just because it's unfamiliar.

So Gen tried shifting her thoughts to elsewhere. She played with the different controls at her seat for a while, changing the TV and radio stations, dimming and brightening the lights, accidentally dialing someone random in Australia (oops). Whenever there were gadgets around, Gen couldn't help but explore them. When she was older, she wanted to join a hackerspace, which was basically a tech playground for adults where they could build robots and program video games and anything else they wanted.

Where had she gotten the techie gene? Was it her mom? Or her dad? Her grandma or grandpa?

Maybe this was a good time to bring up her parents again. But Gen changed her mind after one glance at Agents 34 and 43, who seemed happy and calm in their seats across from her (the cabin was set up like a living room, with spinning chairs around gold-edged coffee tables). The agents had finally loosened up, and Gen didn't want to put a damper on the rest of the long flight.

But she could still ask other questions, right? That was the thing about Gen's mind—there was never a shortage of curiosity.

"When we were in New York," she said, "you didn't want to let people know I was royalty. But what did you tell my foster family and Child Protective Services?"

"RIA headquarters took care of it," Agent 43 said. "They made up a story about long-lost relatives—*not* mentioning the royal part—so that's what your foster parents believe. As for CPS and the insurance representative who stumbled upon your existence, we've sworn them to confidentiality."

"You can do that?"

Agent 34 puffed up his chest with pride. "Indeed. The RIA can definitely do that."

"Cooool," Gen said. This really was like being in her own personal spy novel.

Soon after, she yawned.

"We'll dim the lights and get you a blanket," Agent 34

said. "We've got another ten hours to go. You should rest, Your Highness."

She didn't protest. It had been a ridiculously eventful day. The flight attendant draped a soft purple cashmere throw over Gen, and in two seconds flat, she was asleep.

Gen woke as the plane began its initial descent. The pressure in her ears was discombobulating, and she didn't know where she was for a second.

"Good morning, Your Highness," Agent 34 said. He dipped his head respectfully, like a little bow.

Right. I'm a princess. On the Raldonian equivalent to Air Force One. Gen blinked the sleep out of her eyes and pushed aside the blanket. Agent 43 hurried over and folded it neatly. Oops, was Gen supposed to do that? She started to wonder what, exactly, would be expected of a princess.

"We'll be landing in about twenty minutes," Agent 43 said as she passed the tidily folded blanket to the flight attendant.

"Welcome to your kingdom," Agent 34 said, his voice a little gentler.

My kingdom . . . Gen reached under the collar of her hoodie for the fox pendant, thankful that Agent 34 had bought the silver chain so she could have the medallion close to her at all times. The necklace wasn't the best quality—after all, it had come from a kiosk on the street, and the clasp was a little wonky and had already come undone a few times—but Gen felt like it was a pretty accurate metaphor for her time in the Big Apple: occasionally dysfunctional but mostly totally fine.

Now, though, she touched the pendant not because it reminded her of New York. She touched it because she was headed toward a *new* home, and even though the whole Surprise!-you're-a-princess situation was exciting, it was also . . . nerve-racking. Would the queen of Raldonia—Gen's grandmother—like her? Gen wasn't exactly ladylike. She'd basically grown up like a stray alley cat.

And what about the opposite questions? Would Gen like the queen? And Raldonia?

All of this was why Gen held on to her fox pendant. It suddenly felt like a protective talisman—a gift from her parents—and as long as Gen had the medallion with her, she knew she could handle anything, even being flown away from the only country she'd ever known and into another one. (To be honest, if Gen could've clutched her baby blanket, she would have, but she was twelve, and a twelve-year-old carrying around a blankie in public was ridiculous. The necklace would have to be good enough.)

"Your Highness," Agent 34 said, interrupting her thoughts. "You might want to peek outside. Raldonia is coming into view."

Gen turned to look out the window. The sun had just risen, and below them, the ocean glimmered and the main part of the European continent stretched from its coasts in all directions as golden farmland and green hills. But that wasn't what caught Gen's eye.

"Is that . . ." she asked in a hushed whisper, pointing.

In the middle of the deep blue of the sea, an island stood out like a rare gem. It wasn't green or brown like the rest of Europe. It was purple.

The agents both sighed happily as they looked at the island. "Yes, that's our Raldonia. What you're seeing are the lavender fields in bloom. Lavender is one of our major exports."

"It's beautiful," Gen gushed. As she watched the island grow closer and closer, she smiled and let the pendant fall softly to her chest.

2 + 2 = TROUBLE

The Raldonian Palace was majestic. Illustrious gates glimmered gold in the sunlight. Gigantic topiaries of unicorns and winged lions and dragons lined the long, winding driveway. Gen's eyes goggled as the chauffeured limo—shiny black, with tinted, bulletproof windows, of course—drove by an enormous hedge maze, which looked like a life-size 3D puzzle.

Most stunning of all, though, was the coral-colored palace. It might as well be descended from Cinderella's fairy tale castle: Saw-toothed parapets lined the top of the walls, conical towers soared even higher than that, and guards in rich purple uniforms with gold-tasseled epaulets on their shoulders marched the perimeter.

Gen's Spidey-Sense started tingling as soon as she and the agents pulled up to the entrance. How would Gen fit in a perfect place like this? It was almost, like, *too* perfect.

From her experience, anything that picture ready on the surface usually meant there was trouble brewing underneath. She reached for her pendant beneath the collar of her hoodie.

A sudden movement caught Gen's eye. As soon as their limo slowed near the palace steps, a bronze-skinned woman in an alarmingly bright yellow blouse and severely starched gray slacks hurried to greet them. She opened the car door before the driver even put the car in park.

"Genevieve Illona Caliste Aurelie of the House of Claremont, Princess of the Realm, Defender of Faith, Sincerity, and Justice?" she asked in a clipped, no-nonsense manner. She had a similar Raldonian accent as Agents 34 and 43 had—like a burbling creek—except whenever she spoke, *her* creek sounded like it was flooding. Genevieve spotted a headset resting on her ear and a clipboard with a pencil tied to it with string in her hands.

"Uh, yeah? That's me," Gen answered, still not used to the title. (Also, now that she'd heard it a few times, she noted that her actual last name, Sun, wasn't included. What was up with that? Maybe it was because it had just officially been confirmed, but Gen had a real soft spot for her last name. Like, did Raldonian royals just not have surnames, kind of like the royals in England? Gen added this to her mental list of things to investigate later.)

"Welcome to Raldonia, Your Highness. My name is Lee Jiménez, and I'm the palace chief of staff, in charge of all scheduling and logistics for Queen Michelina. Come with me. Everyone else has already assembled."

Everyone else? Gen turned to look at Agents 34 and 43. Maybe they would tell her what was going on.

But Agent 43 just smiled in her awkward way, which was probably her attempt to be encouraging, and Agent 34 got a little teary-eyed, like he was super-proud that Gen was all grown up now and striking out on her own. Except that she *wasn't* grown up and she had no idea what she was supposed to be striking out to do.

"Quickly now, Your Highness," Lee said.

"Go on," Agent 34 said. "You're gonna do great, Your Highness."

"Wait, you're not coming with me?" Despite their rough start in New York, Gen had grown fond of the agents. Plus, they were literally the only people she knew in this country.

Agent 43 shook her head. "The RIA's part is finished. Our mission was only to investigate and confirm your existence and then safely transfer you back to the kingdom."

"But if you need anything," Agent 34 said, "you can call me on my direct line, okay?" He found a receipt from the airport food court and scribbled his phone number on the back, then handed the receipt to Gen.

"34," Agent 43 said in her gentle chastising way, "that's a violation of RIA protocol."

He shrugged. "I think the RIA can make an exception to help our princess settle in." He turned to Gen. "Your secret code name can be . . . Sunbeam. And your pass phrase will be the name of the diner where you first spotted us."

Gen nodded eagerly, excited to have access to real-life spies. She stashed Agent 34's phone number safely in her ratty camouflage backpack, which carried her baby blanket, a lock-picking kit (a serious detective wouldn't be caught without one), and the few other things she owned.

Meanwhile, Lee tapped her bright yellow heels impatiently on the cobblestone driveway. "Your Highness, *please*," she said, as if being two minutes later to a meeting that Gen hadn't even known about was going to be the end of the world.

Gen, who'd never been good with authority, sighed heavily. But she was going to try to roll with it since she was new here, even if the palace welcome was colder than she'd been hoping for. She'd had foster families in the past who were similar. Gen could handle this.

"Bye, Agent 34 and Agent 43," Gen said as she scooted out of the car. Lee shut the door behind her before the agents' goodbyes even made it out. Sheesh, charisma was *not* this Lee lady's forte.

Gen cast one last glance at the car. She couldn't see the agents through the tinted windows, but she *could* see through the front windshield. There was a placard on the dashboard that announced who was in the car, except it read DUKE CHARLEMAGNE rather than PRINCESS GENEVIEVE.

Weird.

But as she turned to ask about it, she saw Lee already clip-clopping her way up the stairs. Gen scrambled to follow because she got the sense the woman might just give up on her entirely if she didn't hurry up.

"Baby Fox is on the move," Lee said into her headset.

Gen wrinkled her nose. Ew. Was "Baby Fox" her royal

code name? She'd have to have a talk with whoever chose that and get it changed. She much preferred the one Agent 34 had given her.

Lee led Gen through pristine marble hallways, where everything was four times what it functionally needed to be and polished to a reflective shine. Despite the early hour, palace staff bustled everywhere, all wearing what must be the standard uniform of a white tunic and loose purple pants. Whenever Lee and Gen got close to anyone, they would stop dusting or arranging flowers or whatever else they were doing and bow, murmuring "Your Highness," and not move until Gen walked past. For a kid who was used to being ignored by everyone, this was . . . unreal. Like Gen had stepped into an alternate dimension.

The one thing that felt familiar was that the staff seemed to be a melting pot of ethnicities, just like the people of New York. Different skin tones, different eye shapes, and plenty of people who looked multiethnic, just like Gen. She'd noticed the same thing on the drive from the airport to the palace, too. Even though Raldonia had the look and feel of a quaint European country—stone buildings and big, open central squares, clock towers, and wide, tree-lined parks, the citizens she'd seen had the same diversity as the Big Apple. It helped her feel a bit more grounded in an otherwise completely alien place.

"So, um, what is this meeting about?" Gen asked as she tried to keep up with Lee's speed walking.

"Plans for your coronation."

"Coronation?"

"The ceremony that will make you a princess."

Gen frowned. "But aren't I already a princess if my grandma is the queen?"

Lee sighed as if she hadn't wanted the job of answering questions from a clueless American girl. "You are a princess by blood relation, but under Raldonian law, a coronation ceremony is required to *officially* grant you the title of princess. And only those who have official royal titles can be eligible to rule the kingdom someday."

Ah, okay. So it was like a political technicality. Gen thought about it some more as they scurried deeper into the palace. It was pretty mind-blowing to think that this opulent castle was going to be her home, and that eventually she could be in charge of an entire kingdom.

Lee continued her brisk pace, although Gen wasn't sure how she managed to do it in heels. Gen practically had to jog, and she was wearing sneakers.

A couple minutes later, Lee glanced back at Gen, trailing, and said, "The queen's receiving room is just around the bend."

They turned the corner and almost crashed into a Black man in a chef's uniform (complete with embroidery of his name, Chef Brillat-Savarin, and a matching tall fancy hat) and a boy about Gen's age who shared the chef's friendly brown eyes. The boy wore the normal staff outfit of a white tunic and purple pants.

"Apologies, Your Highness," Chef Brillat-Savarin said, bowing. "For my son and I." Like everyone else here, he spoke English with that beautiful, lilting Raldonian accent.

"It's totally fine," Gen said. "It was our fault."

"No!" Lee snapped. "You must learn that it's *never* your fault, Your Highness. You are the heir to the throne and therefore never in the wrong."

Gen knit her brows skeptically. As much as she'd love being right 100 percent of the time, her sense of justice was stronger, and this seemed pretty darn unfair.

She caught the chef's son sneaking a peek at her. He was also bowing, but when he saw Gen looking, he winked. At least he seemed to understand that this whole scene was a little absurd.

"Come, Your Highness," Lee said, brushing past the boy and the chef as if they weren't even there. That really rubbed Gen the wrong way, so as she passed them, she mouthed, *Sorry.*

Guards stood outside two heavy gold doors. They pulled them open for Gen and Lee, but before Gen could step inside, Lee stuck out her arm to block the path.

"What're you—"

"Shh," Lee said. "You must be announced before you can enter a room. Remember, you're royalty now."

Oh, for goodness' sake. Gen barely restrained an eye roll. Just a few minutes into this palace and there were already so many rules.

In a sonorous voice, one of the guards said, "Genevieve Illona Caliste Aurelie of the House of Claremont, Princess of the Realm, Defender of Faith, Sincerity, and Justice!"

Lee nudged Gen, and Gen stepped into the room.

She let out a small gasp. Holy royal mackerel. This wasn't

a room. It was . . . a palace inside the palace. Crystal chandeliers hung from intricately painted ceilings. The plush carpet was the deep purple of the national flag, and white marble benches lined the walls, presumably places for people to sit while they awaited their audience with the queen.

The grandest part of the hall, though, was the raised platform with two gilded thrones on top. An elegant woman with coiffed white hair—Queen Michelina, Gen presumed—occupied one of them, while the other was empty. A gathering of people stood in front of the queen. Like the staff, they were a diverse group, except they all seemed to wear some sort of stuffy business suit.

A hush descended upon the receiving room at Gen's arrival.

I can do this, she thought, even though this was unlike any situation she'd ever found herself in before.

Gen touched her necklace briefly for an infusion of courage, took a deep breath, and approached the throne.

The crowd of business suits parted. Gen stepped up to the base of the raised platform and . . .

She looked around, unsure about what to do.

Was she supposed to curtsey to the queen? Run up and hug her? This was her grandma after all.

But the queen—in a prim wool skirt and jacket—didn't seem excited to see Gen. She didn't seem to have *any* feeling about her granddaughter's appearance. She just sat stiffly on her throne, a vacant expression on her face. If she hadn't blinked, Gen might have thought the queen was actually a statue.

"Uh, h-hi. I'm Gen," she said, her nerves making her stutter the most inarticulate introduction possible. She sank into the ugliest curtsey-bow combo. Her legs crossed at her ankles, and she sort of squatted with both knees sticking out in opposite directions. Behind her, Gen could hear Lee's audible sigh.

The queen's eyes darted over to a handsome man in his forties, wearing an expensive suit with satin lapels and a paisley silk handkerchief in the pocket. He had the same straight, long nose as Queen Michelina, but his skin was brown, not white like hers.

Someone else mixed race like me? Gen wondered.

He also seemed to have a twinkle in his eye that reminded Gen of herself whenever she was on a case.

"Duke Charlemagne," the queen said, her Raldonian accent tinged with a hefty dose of imperiousness.

Ah, so that's why he resembled her a little. He was family. And Gen remembered that the duke had been the one who'd reached out to her mom and dad in the US to try to get them to come back to Raldonia, which made Gen like him already.

"It's worse than I feared," Queen Michelina said to him while looking down her very straight royal nose toward Gen. "Duke Charlemagne, I am putting you in charge of doing something about *this*."

Gen frowned as she rose. "What's *this*?" she asked.

The adults in the room ignored her.

Duke Charlemagne dipped his head to accept the queen's command. "My pleasure, Your Majesty."

The duke had a calm, royal confidence in the way he moved, and he smiled kindly—almost apologetically—at Gen before he turned to the group of men and women in business attire. She now noticed all of their suits were a lot plainer than the duke's.

"I believe we shall have to implement Emergency Plan Orange," Duke Charlemagne said. "Normal plans A and B will not suffice." His accent was strong but softer than the others somehow, more . . . gentle brook full of velveteen waves than burbling creek. (Gen wasn't the greatest at nature analogies, but whatever.)

"Agreed, sir," one of the men said. "Rest assured, Hot Shots Incorporated is the best public relations firm you could hire for *this*. We won't let you down."

"What is *this*?" Gen asked again.

But they acted like she wasn't in the room. Gen had gone from being the center of attention in the palace to being completely invisible in five minutes flat. She was going to have whiplash at this rate.

Gen decided to use the moment to study the room. Good Detective Trait Number One:

Know exactly who and what is around you. At all times.

The space was awfully big, but she'd seen similar throne rooms in movies, where the king or queen received diplomats and other important visitors.

However, there were only ever enough thrones for the number of rulers. Like, if there was a king but no queen, then there was only one throne. If there was a king *and* a queen, then there were two thrones. But here, there were two thrones even though Queen Michelina was the sole monarch. Why did she still keep an empty throne around if the king died twenty years ago?

Interesting. Gen stashed away this observation in case it added up with something else later.

Meanwhile, the adults had kept talking about Emergency Plan Orange. Everyone talking over one another made it impossible for Gen to follow their conversation, other than when Lee asked loudly, "How are we going to address the rumors about the curse?"

The room went silent. Gen's eyebrows shot up. *Um, what?*

Queen Michelina snapped out of her impassive posture and said sharply, "Don't worry about the curse."

"What curse?" Gen asked, leaning forward.

There was a second of uncomfortable shifting of feet, and then everyone started talking again about Emergency Plan Orange, seeming to forget that Gen was still in the room.

But she'd had enough. It was fine that Gen's welcome home hadn't been full of adoring crowds cheering in confetti-covered streets. It was even fine that her grandma hadn't leaped up to hug Gen, because okay, they didn't actually know each other and you can't force affection. But what was *not* fine was Gen traveling all the way to the other side of the world to feel even *less* important than an orphaned foster kid in the middle of the giant city of New York.

So she climbed up the steps of the dais and onto the

empty throne. Standing, Gen put two fingers in her mouth and wolf-whistled.

"Hey!" she shouted. "If you're going to invite me to a meeting, at least have the courtesy to tell me what the heck we're meeting about!"

Every face swiveled to gawk at her, including the queen. Gen was suddenly very aware of the fact that she was standing in dirty old sneakers on a very gold, very expensive throne.

But Lee said I'm never wrong, didn't she? Gen was a princess, and therefore never at fault.

Based on the appalled stares, though, Gen began to think that maybe the rule didn't apply here.

No one said a word.

At that precise moment, the faulty clasp on Gen's necklace unlatched, and her imperial fox pendant clattered onto the throne she was standing on, bounced off her left shoe, then her right, and landed in Queen Michelina's lap.

Gulp.

The queen exhaled audibly.

Then she looked Gen right in the eye. *"This,"* she said, "means *you.*"

Gen gulped as she put two and two together. *This* was a problem that needed to be solved.

And the problem is me.

ONE SHEEP, TWO SHEEP, THREE SHEEP...ZZZZZZ

After the meeting, Lee led Gen to her room. As they wove through carpeted corridors and up and down winding staircases, Gen's mind raced over everything that had happened after her standing-on-the-king's-throne stunt.

Duke Charlemagne had been the first adult to cut the tension by chuckling, as if Gen's shocking behavior wasn't a big deal. Then he began to explain what all the hub-bub was about, which Gen felt really grateful for (although he didn't say anything about the curse that Lee had mentioned).

The duke did clue her in to the fact that the news of the princess being alive had already leaked to the Raldonian public, and the entire kingdom was clamoring to get a glimpse of Gen. That's why she'd traveled this morning in a car marked with his name, because no one thought the duke was worth getting worked up over. (He'd laughed humbly at that.)

However, there was certain, er, *education* that Gen would have to go through before she could be officially presented to the public. Namely, the Hot Shots PR team needed to transform her from Gen Sun, scruffy underdog foster kid from New York, into polished Genevieve Illona Caliste Aurelie of the House of Claremont, Princess of the Realm, Defender of Faith, Sincerity, and Justice. (Gen would have to practice memorizing that. Her title was So. Long.)

So Gen's coronation would be set for one month from now. Every day until then, there would be classes on Raldonian customs, as well as royal etiquette and elocution lessons. (Seriously. Princesses were expected to pronounce words in a certain "imperial" way.)

She'd also get a fashion makeover because princesses couldn't wear hoodies and torn jeans. It seemed that no one in the palace wore casual clothes. Gen hadn't seen a single pair of jeans or even sandals since she'd arrived. This did *not* bode well for her comfort.

Please, please, please don't make me wear a suit like everyone else, she thought. Then Gen glanced over at Lee, who was still striding ahead of her down the hallways like they were marching for their lives. Her yellow blouse was buttoned so tightly and high up her throat, it had to be uncomfortable. Not to mention the fact that it could have lit the path through an underground tunnel. *And please don't let Lee be in charge of my wardrobe.*

Finally, they arrived at a cream-colored door decorated with the imperial fox crest.

"Here we are." Lee turned the gold knob and opened

the door, revealing an enormous set of rooms. Gen's jaw dropped as she walked inside.

It was bigger than her foster family's entire apartment. There was a sitting area with a velvet chaise, mirrored coffee table, and a pair of overstuffed armchairs. Next to that was an ornate desk with a matching chair, so pretty and delicate, Gen wasn't sure she could trust herself to sit in it without scratching it or leaving smudgy fingerprints on its lacquered white surfaces.

Beyond that, there was a mini library with shelves full of books that lined the walls. Then there was the canopy bed, piled high with pillows and thick, luxurious blankets in Raldonian purple. And even deeper into the suite, there were two more doors: one that led into a walk-in closet and another that opened onto a gleaming marble bathroom.

Gen cleared her throat nervously. "So, um, I'll be staying here?" She was too afraid to ask outright if this was her room. Maybe it was just the temporary guest suite.

Lee didn't even glance up from the to-do list on her clipboard as she answered. "This is the Princess Suite, Your Highness. Formerly your mother's rooms when she was the heir to the throne, and now yours."

"My mom's room?" Gen whispered. Her bottom lip trembled. She'd been so overwhelmed by the discovery that she was a princess that Gen had temporarily forgotten *how* she was a princess. Her mom had once been a girl in this palace, too.

She'd studied at that desk. Looked out that window. Slept in that bed.

Gen reached into her hoodie and clutched the pendant tight. This was closer than she'd been to her mom in twelve years.

Lee, however, didn't seem to notice that Gen had gotten a little wistful. She checked something off on her clipboard—it was probably the instruction to drop Gen off at her room—and gave herself a satisfied nod for accomplishing one of her tasks.

"Well, Your Highness, I'll leave you to get settled in," she said. "The RIA agents called in a guess about your clothing and shoe sizes, so you'll find a few outfits in your closet to hold you over until the royal tailor can create a bespoke wardrobe for you." Lee glanced at her clipboard. "He'll be here at 11:00 a.m. to take your measurements.

"After that, you'll have a quick lunch break—the kitchen staff will send a meal for you—followed by a five-hour introductory lesson on Raldonian history, politics, and trade."

"Five hours?!"

But Lee kept talking. "Formal dinner begins at half past six—"

"*Formal* dinner?" Gen interrupted again.

Lee sighed, clearly exasperated. "Yes, Your Highness."

"So it's, like, fancy?"

"Yes, Your Highness."

"I have to dress up, I'm guessing."

"Yes, Your Highness."

"And, um, how often do these formal dinners take place?"

Lee pursed her lips before responding. "Your Highness," she said in a way that managed to be both polite and impatient at the same time, "you are a princess now. *Every* dinner is formal."

Gen groaned.

Lee gave her a stern look that basically said, *Would you prefer to be an orphan again, bounced around from foster placement to foster placement with no family or place to call home?*

It was enough to chasten Gen. She could handle some boring lessons and stuffy dinners if it meant she got to live in the same rooms her mom grew up in.

She put on what she hoped was a reassuring smile and gave Lee a thumbs-up. "Formal dinners. Got it. Not a problem."

Gen tried really hard not to yawn during her afternoon lesson on Raldonian history, politics, and trade. But it was ALL CAPS B-O-R-I-N-G, and what Gen really wanted was a little downtime to herself, to explore the bedroom and see if there was anything in here she could learn about her parents. At one point, she at least tried to steer the lecture toward South Mallanthra, where her dad was from. Gen knew nothing about it except what the agents had mentioned on the plane—that South Mallanthra was a small kingdom made up of immigrants from Korea, Japan, Malaysia, and the rest of Asia. She was eager to hear more.

But the minister of finance and culture, her teacher

today, sniffed at her interruption. "First we are covering the must-know facts about *Raldonia*, Your Highness. Which is not a small list." And then he droned on and on about the Raldonian government's budget, the construction of the kingdom's roads and freeways, taxes and tariffs on other countries that traded with Raldonia, and the price of a pallet of lavender (they were different if the flowers were fresh or dried, of course).

In the fourth hour, Gen finally nodded off during a "riveting lesson" on the price of sheep. She jolted awake when her head hit the desk.

The minister looked over disapprovingly. "Princess Genevieve, I cannot emphasize enough how important it is for you to grasp these concepts. In a few years, Queen Michelina will officially retire as the head of Raldonia, and it will be up to you to lead our illustrious kingdom. Unlike most monarchies in the modern world, our queen is still very active in the politics of our country. If you cannot be bothered—"

"Oh, give Her Highness a little break, Minister Tallyho," a new voice cut in.

Duke Charlemagne bowed from the doorway—a quick show of respect, but not as deep as the staff's bows, since the duke was part of the imperial family. "The poor girl has been uprooted from her previous life, traveled all day, and is probably jet-lagged."

"Yes, but the queen said—"

Duke Charlemagne waved his hand. "The queen won't mind if her granddaughter has only four hours of lessons today instead of five. Let the princess rest, and I'm sure she'll be eager to learn more tomorrow. Isn't that so?" He looked at Gen and gave her a subtle nod as if to say, *Just play along.*

Gen confirmed enthusiastically. "I'm super excited for tomorrow, Minister Tallyho. I'm really looking forward to hearing about the, um . . ." She tried to think of what other subjects he'd mentioned but hadn't covered yet.

Behind the minister's back, Duke Charlemagne pantomimed someone with a fishing rod, throwing in the line and then reeling in a catch.

"The seafood industry!" Gen said. "Yeah, I heard we're really big on shrimp here."

The minister clapped his hands together, pleased. "Indeed! We are quite *big* on shrimp here, if you know what I mean."

Gen just stared at him for a second. But Duke Charlemagne let out a loud laugh. "Minister Tallyho, you are a clever one! What a joke!"

Ohhhh, Gen thought. *Right. Raldonia's known for its extra-large shellfish.*

"Ha-ha, good one, sir." She managed to chuckle.

"Well, this seems like a reasonable place to conclude our lessons for today," Minister Tallyho said. "It's always best to leave something to look forward to, I like to say!" He bowed to Gen and left her rooms. Too bad he didn't take his stacks of manila folders overflowing with charts and laws and other mind-numbing documents. Those, he'd said when he first arrived, were hers to study. Along with all the books on her shelves, which unfortunately weren't spy novels, but treatises on matters of Raldonian law, politics, and trade.

Joy.

Duke Charlemagne must have seen Gen's grim expression at the folders on her desk, because he came over and put a gentle hand on her shoulder. "Don't worry, Princess. Minister Tallyho isn't too bad once you get used to him. And all these subjects he's trying to cram into your head? It might seem overwhelming right now, but I can tell you're a smart one. After living in the palace for a while, you'll absorb all this information as if by osmosis."

Skeptical, Gen looked up at him and said, "I'm going to learn about the history of the national parks just by living here?"

The duke laughed, for real this time. "Well, perhaps not that. But my point is, don't stress too much. There is plenty of time to learn what you need to know to rule the kingdom, and besides, you will always have the ministers—and me—to help you." Then he pointed at the pendant that had fallen out from underneath Gen's collar. "And the good thing about Raldonia is that our traditions tend to stick."

Gen relaxed into her chair. It was a relief to be reminded she didn't have to do this all on her own, and even more of a relief to have a friendly adult here in the palace.

Gen remembered some of her questions from earlier. "Duke Charlemagne, did you know my parents? Could you tell me about my mom? Like, what happened that made her leave this?" Gen gestured to the gorgeous suite and the palace in general. "Why would she run away to New York?"

The duke frowned, thinking. "My dear aunt—that's the queen—has forbidden anyone from talking about the Incident."

"Oh. Right." Gen looked down at her hands. Agents 34 and 43 had told her the same thing. Then she perked up. "Are you allowed to tell me about my mom and dad *before* the Incident? I think one of the RIA agents mentioned that you and my mom were cousins. So that makes you . . . my uncle?"

"Technically," the duke said, "you and I are second cousins, once removed, but yes, you can just think of me as an uncle if it's easier. You see, my father was the queen's first cousin, twice removed—in short, it means your mother and I share the same great-great-grandparents. That side of the family can trace its roots to the great Charlemagne, king of the Franks, king of the Lombards, and emperor of the Romans. My mother's side is from the imperial family of Thoda, a small but regal kingdom near India."

"Whoa, so you're, like, super royal," Gen said.

Duke Charlemagne chuckled. "Something like that. But it doesn't matter. What matters is the line of succession—that's the official name for who will inherit the throne. And that line goes from the queen straight to you. And before your mom . . ."

He trailed off, but Gen was brave enough to finish the sentence for him. "Before my mom died, she was also in the line of succession."

The duke nodded sadly. "You know, your mother was

one of only four living people in the world who spoke Raldonian. Now there are only three—a professor of linguistics at the National University of Raldonia, the queen, and me."

"I could learn Raldonian," Gen offered.

Duke Charlemagne smiled, but Gen could tell he didn't believe her. "Raldonian is a dying language and very difficult. I think you have enough on your plate for now. And don't worry—I shall recite the traditional poem in the Raldonian tongue during your coronation. It is a ritual that has been performed at every crowning ceremony for centuries, and this one shall be no different."

Gen hadn't realized there was a Raldonian poetry recitation at the coronation, so it hadn't been on her radar to worry about it. But it was great that the duke was taking care of it.

"However," Duke Charlemagne said, "you wanted to know about your mother, not poems, right? Well, your mother—Adrienne—was a firecracker of a girl, full of a real zest for life. But Queen Michelina has always aimed to preserve the monarchy as it always had been—with Raldonian tradition and duty above all else."

"Sounds kind of stuffy," Gen said.

Duke Charlemagne laughed. "Imperial life *can* be restrictive. However, there are also incredible, wonderful things about being part of the royal family. I hope I can show you some of those things."

"I'd like that," Gen said. Then, after a moment, she asked, "So . . . the queen didn't like my mom?"

"Oh no, no, no, that isn't what I meant," the duke exclaimed. "They simply . . . clashed. Adrienne craved a life outside of the palace, away from all of the queen's demands. But ruling a kingdom is tricky, because there are so many citizens who need and want different things, and traditions exist for a reason. I may not always agree with the queen, but I respect her. It is through her leadership and firm adherence to Raldonian principles that our little kingdom has remained strong and stable in rapidly changing times."

Gen looked at the stack of manila folders on her desk that Minister Tallyho had left behind. Then she looked at the walls of the room, the very same walls that had sheltered her mom, but, by the sounds of it, also made her feel trapped. *Will I feel the same way, too?* Gen thought.

For a brief moment, she wondered whether it would have been better to stay in New York. Sure, she wasn't a princess there, but at least as an unimportant foster kid, Gen could come and go as she pleased. No one really cared where she went as long as she came home to the foster family every night, kept up decent grades, and didn't get into trouble.

But then she looked at Duke Charlemagne, with his kind, wide eyes and the soft brown wrinkles on his forehead. *He's family. Real, blood-related family.* Gen touched the chair she was sitting in, remembering that her mom once sat here. And her mom probably used to have a stack of manila folders to study, too.

Gen may have missed the familiarity of New York,

Kenneth's friendship, and making snacks for little Mikey, but New York didn't have a permanent place for her.

Raldonia did. As long as Gen didn't muck it up.

Her stomach rumbled as if deciding this was a good time to make an ultimatum. *Feed me if you want me to help fuel your brain to learn all of Minister Tallyho's facts.*

"Oh dear," Duke Charlemagne said. "Let's get you a snack. Listening to the minister pontificating takes so much energy, it would work up an appetite in anyone, let alone a growing girl."

"But isn't there a big formal dinner tonight?" Gen had gathered from Minister Tallyho that the dinners were usually eight-course affairs that lasted for three hours. Ugh.

Duke Charlemagne's eyes twinkled mischievously again. "Yes, but trust me, you'll enjoy this a great deal more. Has anyone mentioned the secret tunnels?"

A-MAZE-ING

"Secret tunnels???" Gen bounced out of her chair. This was *way* more her speed than lessons about taxes and trade.

"Yes," Duke Charlemagne said. "They're an architectural security feature. There are hidden panels in the throne room and every bedroom belonging to the royal family."

Gen's eyes lit up. "You mean there's a hidden panel in This. Very. Room?"

The duke nodded.

"Where?" Gen jumped to her feet and began scanning all the walls. There were no visible seams in the wallpaper or any little lumps or anything. But she supposed that made sense; if the royal family were in danger, they wouldn't want their escape route to be obvious.

Duke Charlemagne strolled over to the bookshelves that lined the far wall of the room and tapped a bronze sculpture of a man's head. "Your mother always hated this bronze bust of Leopold Schumfeld."

Gen gasped and leaned into this scrap of information about her mom. She'd already noticed that there were no portraits of former princess Adrienne in the palace, even though the walls were lined with gilded paintings of other members of the royal family going centuries back. The only picture Gen had seen of her parents was the one that Agents 34 and 43 had shown her back in New York. And the Princess Suite had been scrubbed clean of any personal touches her mom might have left—no loose panels with diaries hidden inside, or novels on the shelves, or even a stray doodle on the desk. Everyone was super careful about revealing details about Gen's mom—it seemed that the queen's rule about not talking about the Incident had made people cautious about *anything* related to Princess Adrienne. Gen, of course, wanted to absorb every possible tidbit about her.

"Leopold Schumfeld was one of Raldonia's most famous poets," Duke Charlemagne said, "but your mother thought the hollows in the sculpture's eyes were unsettling. Still, Adrienne couldn't just get rid of the bust, because—"

The duke twisted it 180 degrees so that the creepy eyes faced the back of the bookshelf. Immediately, something clicked as if it were unlatching. One of the bookshelves hinged forward, revealing a dimly lit passage behind it.

"No freaking way." Gen's jaw practically hit the floor.

The duke was already stepping into the tunnel. He poked his head back in between the bookshelves to look at Gen. "Well, are you coming, Your Highness?"

"Am I ever!" Gen zipped across the room and slipped into the corridor.

Duke Charlemagne pushed the door closed behind them. "That resets the Leopold Schumfeld bust so that it's facing outward again and your pursuers wouldn't see anything amiss."

Gen nodded and began taking in her surroundings. The only illumination in here was a trail of small lights along the ground, one every six inches or so. The floor was carpeted—probably to make sure the royal family could escape quietly—and the hallway itself was relatively narrow, maybe four feet across.

"How many times has the royal family had to use these tunnels to flee?" she asked reverently. Not that she wanted attackers to come to the palace, of course. But still, it was kind of exciting to think of life in this stuffy castle like the stories in books and movies.

Duke Charlemagne laughed. "I hate to disappoint you, but the answer is zero. The tunnels are rarely used nowadays, although your mother made good use of them when she was a kid, especially to sneak down into the palace kitchens for snacks."

"Cooool."

"Perhaps we could have a *little* more light, though," the duke said. "My middle-aged eyes aren't as good as your young ones." He pulled something out of his pocket that looked like a phone, except it had a blinking green battery indicator on the top. Though the intermittent green flashing didn't add a lot of visibility.

The duke tapped the device to wake it, and the screen lit up, bathing the tunnel in artificial brightness. "Ah, much better!" He began to lead the way down the corridors, which, it turned out, were not one single path, but rather branched out in many directions through different parts of the castle. Gen would definitely come back later to explore on her own. She wanted to make a mental map of this place.

For now, though, she skipped to catch up to the duke. "What *is* that?" she asked, pointing at the non-phone. It looked a lot clunkier than what she was used to seeing back in New York.

"Oh, this is my beloved PalmPad," Duke Charlemagne said.

"It looks, um . . ."

He chuckled good-naturedly. "I know, I know. The tech is outdated, but I've had this for twenty-five years, and the staff in palace IT—information technology—have been kind enough to keep it running for me."

"Do you mind if I look at it?" Gen liked tinkering with gadgets. While her first love was hacking software, she also enjoyed figuring out how any tech worked. In New York, she'd been part of a STEM (science, technology, engineering, and math) outreach program for underprivileged girls, and her favorite activity had been "gadget dissection," when the counselors would bring defunct stuff from tech recycling places and let the girls break them open to learn about all the circuits and chips inside.

Duke Charlemagne handed his PalmPad to Gen and

watched affably while she used the stylus on its screen to open and close windows, then browse the menu. It was slow and the user interface was awkward, but it was still fascinating to Gen to poke around on a first-generation device. She could hardly imagine what life must've been like without cell phones and iPads and superfast internet.

After a few minutes, Gen handed the PalmPad back to the duke.

"I could upgrade," he said, "but I'm quite attached to this dear old thing. I do all my work on it. Why, earlier this afternoon, I was drafting a new zoning law on it." He patted his PalmPad fondly.

That, Gen could understand. She loved the artificial intelligence program she'd written back in New York the same way (it was named after Grace Hopper, one of the first female computer scientists and a brilliant inventor). As soon as Gen could get her hands on a computer here in Raldonia, she would start working on Hopper again. There were some bugs in her code—Hopper's "personality" was a little sassy—but it was close to done. Gen dreamed of having a phone or other tablet that she could load it onto. That way, she'd be able to carry her AI with her and have it handy all the time.

She wondered when she'd be able to get online. There hadn't been a computer in her room, but Gen wanted to download not only Hopper's program but also all her old files from home.

"Duke Charlemagne?" she asked as he took a left turn

and then led her down a flight of stairs. "After we grab a snack, can you show me how to get online? I need internet access to get to my files on the cloud."

"I believe you'll be meeting with the information technology team tomorrow morning," he said. "I remember them telling me that the rest of Raldonia was 'in the clouds,' whatever that means. I'm sure they can show you how to be, er, 'in the clouds,' too."

Gen grinned to herself. Adults could be so clueless about technology, but the duke seemed especially oblivious. Case in point: He was using a PalmPad from the 1990s! Internet was barely even invented then. But she didn't poke fun at him, because he was the nicest person in the palace so far.

"Duke Charlemagne?" she asked again, hoping she wasn't annoying him too much with all her questions. "At the meeting earlier, Lee mentioned rumors of a curse. What was that about?"

He hesitated. It was only a split second, but Gen was an expert at catching the subtle body language changes in people's behavior, and she wondered what these rumors were that made him react that way.

The duke cleared his throat. "Just an old superstition, Your Highness, nothing to worry about."

Hmm. Earlier, he'd been upfront when there was something he wasn't allowed to talk about. But now he was actively evading Gen's question. Why?

At that moment, though, they turned into a new corridor and he said, "Aha, here we are!" In front of them stood a very ordinary-looking door. There was even a sconce beside it, lighting up the exit.

I guess if you're already inside the tunnels, you know about the doors in and out, Gen reasoned.

Then Duke Charlemagne pulled the door open. All the delicious smells of the palace kitchen flooded into the tunnel, enveloping Gen in wafts of chocolate, sugar, and butter. Exactly what she'd always wanted—a grandmother whose house smelled of baking cookies! Her stomach rumbled eagerly, and Gen rushed into the kitchen, promptly forgetting that the duke hadn't really answered her question.

HEAVY IS THE HEAD THAT WEARS THE CURSE, I MEAN, THE CROWN

The kitchen was the size of a house and full of every kind of fancy stainless-steel appliance possible. Pots clanged, mixers whirred, and a dozen cooks bustled around with pans full of sauces and baking sheets laden with pastries. In the center of the culinary whirlwind was Chef Brillat-Savarin, whom Gen had crashed into earlier outside the throne room, and the boy who'd winked at her. Gen immediately grinned at seeing another face she recognized.

The instant he saw her, he grinned, too. Everyone else in the kitchen noticed Gen about a half second later, and suddenly, all the banging and mixing ground to a halt, and every cook bowed. In unison, they said, "Your Highness."

And then they just stood there, still bent in half.

Gen grimaced as she turned to Duke Charlemagne. "Is this going to happen whenever I walk into a room?"

"Indeed," the duke said. "It's a show of respect and a

great honor. No one has ever held a bow like that for me. You should enjoy it."

She shifted uncomfortably. Seriously, all these grown-ups were frozen in place, unable to move because Gen was here. It seemed wrong that they had to be subservient just because of who she happened to be born as. "Uh, but what if I don't like it?"

"You're just like your mother." Duke Charlemagne chuckled.

Just like your mother. That phrase made Gen all warm and fuzzy inside.

"Adrienne hated all the royal pomp and circumstance, too," the duke continued. "She commanded the staff to dispense with bowing upon her arrival. In fact, as princess, you could issue a blanket order like that."

Gen perked up at the ability to let the palace staff off the hook from all this silly bowing. And to be like her mom.

"Okay," Gen said, turning to the cooks. "So, um, I hereby command you to dispense with bowing upon my . . ." She tried to remember exactly how Duke Charlemagne had worded it. "Upon my arrival. Forever!" she added, to clarify that it wasn't just a one-time exception.

Everyone rose. "Thank you, Your Highness," each cook said, giving her smiles and approving nods. Gen beamed, feeling like she'd made the right choice.

"Now," Duke Charlemagne said, "about that snack."

"I'll help Her Highness," the boy said, dashing around the steel countertop and stopping right in front of Gen. "Hi! My name's Hill. I'm the chef's son." Like everyone else, he spoke with a Raldonian inflection to his words, but it was peppier on him than on most.

"Hi!" Gen said, relieved to be talking to someone her own age. "Call me Gen."

"Uh." Hill glanced over at the duke.

She frowned but quickly realized the solution. "I *command* you to call me Gen."

Duke Charlemagne shrugged. "If that's what you wish." The green light on his PalmPad changed color to flashing orange. "Oh dear, my battery is running low. I'd better return to my office to plug it in. Hill, can you make sure the princess gets back to her room in half an hour so that she has time to change for dinner with the queen?"

"Yes, sir."

The duke nodded, and distracted by the urgent low battery light, he wandered out of the kitchen without another word.

Hill grabbed Gen's hand. "Come on! I'll show you where all the tastiest stuff is around here."

Thrilled to have a friend, Gen let Hill pull her through the kitchen and into a walk-in pantry that looked more like the aisles of a grocery store than a storage room. He took her to the back corner, where the shelves were lined with chips in every flavor Gen could imagine—from barbecue to dill pickle to Raldonian shrimp, to name a few—as well as bins full of a rainbow assortment of candy.

"Whoa," Gen said. "I've never seen most of this stuff before. You get to eat here every day?!"

Hill laughed. "Yep. And now you do, too! Awesome, right?" He passed her a paper plate from a different shelf, and they started loading up on everything they could get their hands on.

When Gen's plate was piled high enough with lobster-flavored crackers, cream cheese paprika corn puffs, lavender shortbread, and a sampling of candy, Hill took her to a plain wooden table and chairs in the main kitchen, away from the cooking area. It was where the staff ate their meals in between serving the rest of the palace.

Sitting at a normal table, not in a fancy room full of marble and gold, allowed Gen to truly relax for the first time since arriving in Raldonia. This unassuming setting was a lot more familiar to her than the rest of the palace. She would try her best, of course, to get used to all the fancy formality that Queen Michelina wanted her to learn. But for now, Gen was happy to have a short break from it all.

She and Hill gorged on their snacks. When they were finally full, Gen slouched contently in her chair.

"I thought finding out I was a princess would be the highlight of my week, but I think *this* is."

"Pretty hard to beat all-you-can-eat snacks," Hill said. "Is that right? Do you say that in America? I think it was in a show I watched."

Gen smiled. She'd just met him, but Hill was so easy to be around, he felt like a long-lost friend. She'd forgotten he was a stranger from another country. That *she* was in another country.

"Yeah, *all-you-can-eat* is right. But I meant that the best thing about today was meeting you."

"Oh wow, thanks." Hill looked down shyly. Then he thought of something, and he bounced in his chair. "Wait till you meet my friends Cara, Lilah, and Callan! We'll show you the video game we're into. It's called *Escape from Octopus Isle*, and it's an open world, which means you go on quests with your friends and—"

Unfortunately, Gen's time in the kitchen was quickly cut short by the arrival of none other than Lee. "Your Highness! You'll spoil your dinner! And the royal tailor is waiting for you in the Princess Suite."

"Why? I just saw him a few hours ago. He already took all my measurements."

"Yes, and he used those measurements to alter a sumptuous gown for your first royal dinner tonight with the queen, so you are required in your rooms at once. Quickly!" She clattered off in her heels, taking the normal exit, not the door into secret tunnel.

Quickly! Gen mimicked in her head. She had a suspicion this was a key word in Lee's vocabulary.

Hill shrugged, probably used to Lee's prickliness. "Guess I'll see you later," he said to Gen.

She sagged at having to leave him. She wanted to hear more about the *Octopus Isle* game, and the prospect of making more friends so soon—and being able to play with them online—was so tempting, it almost hurt physically that Lee was pulling her away.

"See you tomorrow?" Hill asked.

"Yes!" Gen was rejuvenated by the thought. "Tomorrow. I'll find time somehow, between all the lectures Lee has scheduled for me."

With that, Gen said goodbye to Hill and hurried to catch up.

As they walk-sprinted through the corridors of the palace, it occurred to Gen that she might be able to get Lee to tell her about the curse. Not in an outright conversation—that would make Lee clam up—but maybe Gen could trick her way into the information without making it obvious what she was angling for. Good Detective Trait Number Two:

Never draw attention to yourself.

Gen started raving about the snacks she'd just had, picking an invisible piece of lint off her hoodie. "Oh my gosh, that lavender shortbread was so delicious, it's like it was made by magic. I hope the curse wasn't what made it taste so good."

Lee snorted. "The curse doesn't affect food."

Excellent. She nibbled the bait. Now to make sure she takes it.

"Sure it does," Gen said, infusing her voice with confidence. "A lot of times, hexes make bad things happen by masquerading as good things."

Lee scowled. "You bringing an end to all of Raldonia doesn't *remotely* look like a hexed dessert."

Gen's eyebrows shot up. "Wait—everyone here believes that?"

"Not *all*, maybe fifteen or twenty percent according to the latest polls. But it's enough to be a problem. This obviously isn't the first time someone who's not one hundred percent royal blood might take the throne, but your arrival has stoked the flames of the fear."

Not the first time? Does she mean because my mom married my dad—a commoner?

And then Gen's thoughts shifted to the other part of what Lee had said.

Whoa, there are actually people who believe I'm going to destroy the entire kingdom!

Suddenly, Gen burst out laughing.

Lee stopped in her tracks, teetering on her ridiculously high heels. "What's so funny?"

"Seriously?" Gen asked when she finally caught her breath. "People think we're all going to fall over dead just because I'm only fifty percent royal? That's the most ridiculous superstition I've ever heard."

"Y-you didn't know what the curse was about?" Lee's cheeks reddened.

"No, but thanks for telling me," Gen said, still giggling. She didn't mean to make Lee feel bad about revealing something that the queen obviously hadn't wanted discussed, but Gen couldn't get over the absurdity of it all.

Lee huffed. "Well, you'd better take the curse seriously, or at least the damage the rumors can cause. Your mom and dad suffered because of it." She turned and fixed Gen with a frosty glare. "And if you don't watch your step, you'll suffer, too."

Then Lee stomped off down the hall, expecting Gen to follow.

But Gen didn't move. She wasn't even laughing anymore. Instead, icy chills ran up and down her spine.

Gen wasn't sure if the chills were because of the curse, or because of Lee.

IS A HACKER WITHOUT A COMPUTER EVEN A HACKER ANYMORE?

L ast night at dinner, Gen had managed to use the dessert spoon for her soup and the fish fork to spear her salad. She'd mistakenly eaten something that she thought was cheese but turned out to be a triangular wedge of butter, and then gagged as she spit it into the napkin. She also knocked Countess Elmendorf's wine onto Baron Schnegglebottom's lap, sent a bread roll flying halfway across the table as she tried to cut it, and got scolded for feeding the seafood delight appetizer to the palace cat, who'd snuck into the dining room.

All of this took place in the first thirty minutes. Queen Michelina had not looked at Gen again the remaining two-and-a-half hours of the meal.

Now Professor Règles paced in the Princess Suite. "It seems we must begin with the most basic of etiquette instructions." The professor was a petite Black woman who had perfect posture and wore very prim and proper glasses. She was also an expert in Raldonian culture and language (and one of the three people who spoke Raldonian, according to Duke Charlemagne), and she'd been tasked not only with teaching Gen a proper Raldonian accent but also teaching her some manners.

Gen winced as the professor went through all of Gen's mistakes from her first formal dinner. Apparently, Lee had been taking copious notes on every single one of Gen's transgressions. Why was it rude to put her elbows on the table? It was comfortable.

As she went through the morning etiquette lessons, another question formed in the back of Gen's mind: *Why does Lee dislike me so much?* Lee was obviously super-loyal to the queen. Did Lee somehow see Gen as a threat? But how would that be possible? Agents 34 and 43 had said Queen Michelina hoped to retire in a few years and have someone—presumably Gen—take over. If that were really the case, then Lee shouldn't have an issue with Gen being here.

And yet . . .

Something fishy was going on.

But Gen didn't have time to dig into it, because after etiquette lessons came an endless parade of sessions from a slew of guest lecturers. There was an hour on military flags and the meanings of their shapes and colors. Then another professor from the National University of Raldonia expounded on the history of economic development in the kingdom. And the harbormaster gave a lecture on the ongoing construction of the capital city's newest docks and the traffic rules for shrimping boats.

No one would change their lesson plans to address what Gen really wanted to know—what happened to her mom that made her leave the kingdom? Who was Gen's dad? What was South Mallanthra like and was her grandpa still the ambassador? Would he ever come to Raldonia so she could meet him?

Instead, Gen thought her head was going to explode from being stuffed with too much useless information.

When two members of the IT staff arrived, she practically leaped over her desk to hug them. Finally, techie people, here to talk about subjects she cared about!

In fact, Gen had written down a list of questions, and she began asking in rapid-fire as soon as they'd sat down.

"First things first—is there a computer room here?"

Trisha, a red-haired woman, shook her head like she didn't understand. "You mean the server room?"

"No, just a place where I can get online," Gen clarified. "Back in New York, the library had a bunch of computers that anyone could use. Do you have something like that in the palace, or can I go into the city to a library?"

Miguel, the other IT person, smiled. "The palace residents all have their own computers. One can be sent here to your suite."

Gen's mouth dropped open. She'd never had a computer of her own before.

"No way . . . C-can I get it today?" she asked hesitantly.

"Well . . ." Trisha said. "Technically, the queen has to request one for you."

"Why?" Gen asked, slightly disappointed.

"Palace IT guidelines."

"Oh. Okay." But then Gen had an idea. "Wait, can I just get around that by, like, commanding you to give me a computer?" She cringed as she heard her own words. Gen hadn't meant it to sound so obnoxious. She'd only thought of it because it'd worked to excuse the kitchen team from bowing to her.

Miguel and Trisha didn't seem offended, though.

"Unfortunately," Miguel said, "giving an order won't work in this case because you're under eighteen."

Gen frowned. "What does that have to do with it?"

"The palace IT guidelines section 4.07(b), subsection (iii) states that 'no minor may be allowed the use of technology without the explicit consent and request of their guardian.' In your case, that's the queen."

"Hmph." Gen crossed her arms. But okay, fine. She'd just ask the queen later today during their scheduled 3:00 p.m. stroll around the Imperial Lavender Gardens.

For now, Gen returned to her list of questions. "All right, *when* I get my computer, what kind of cybersecurity protocols do I have to be aware of? Obviously, I know to use a complex password. But are there firewalls? Do you have limits on the use of VPNs? What type of application security system does the palace use, and do you alert us when you might be engaging in penetration testing for vulnerabilities or other probes for viruses and malware?"

Trisha and Miguel stared at her with their mouths hanging open, like fish who suddenly found themselves on the deck of a boat and didn't know what to do.

Miguel chortled nervously. "W-well, Your Highness, those are excellent questions."

"I'm glad you think so." Gen poised her pencil over her notepad, ready to jot down the answers. "So? What do I need to know?"

"Um . . ." Miguel glanced at Trisha. "Well, you don't need to know anything. It's all taken care of. Everything is secure. I assure you that you need not be concerned."

On the contrary, Gen was becoming *very* concerned. She had the sinking feeling that the IT staff had no idea what she was talking about.

"Is there, like, a manager I can talk to?" Gen asked.

Trisha smiled broadly. "I'm the chief technology officer for the palace."

Egad. This was worse than Gen thought. She wondered what the computers here looked like. Would they deliver a bulky desktop circa 1996 to her rooms, along with a dial-up modem? Even Duke Charlemagne's PalmPad was more advanced than that.

Time to try a different tactic. "So . . ." Gen said, "what are you doing to modernize the palace?"

Miguel huffed. "We are very 'with it,' Your Highness. Just because bigger countries like the United States might have faster access to Silicon Valley technology than we do, doesn't mean we're still using quill and parchment here!"

Eep. She'd offended him, and Gen needed the techies

on her side. Without them, she'd never get access to her files and AI program.

"I'm sorry," Gen said, widening her eyes so she looked like a harmless Bambi-type. She'd used this look often with social workers in New York, and it worked nine times out of ten. "I'm sure Raldonia's just as innovating—if not *more*—than where I came from. After all, this is the royal palace, and the queen would only hire the best of the best."

Miguel flushed with pride, and Trisha nodded eagerly.

With that relationship salvaged, Gen thanked them for their help and ended the meeting early.

Gen arrived in the Imperial Lavender Gardens five minutes ahead of schedule. After yesterday's throne room meeting and the faux pas at dinner, she had a lot to make up for to get back into Queen Michelina's good graces. Gen hadn't known what to wear to an "afternoon stroll," but just in case it was something like speed walking, she'd picked the most practical outfit in her closet—a sky-blue blouse and loose navy trousers that were almost like jeans. If you squinted.

The queen arrived wearing a dark green wool suit and pumps, though, and Gen silently chastised herself for not asking about the dress code earlier so she could have worn something fancier. Oh well, she was here already. Better make the best of it.

Gen hopped up from the stone bench she was sitting on. "Hi, Grandma!"

Queen Michelina drew back sharply, as if Gen had bitten her.

Lee appeared from the hedges with her usual headset and clipboard, although today she'd traded her garish yellow top for something that made her look like a red-striped zebra wearing oversized brass buttons on her cuffs. "You should address the queen as *Your Majesty*," Lee said.

Gen gulped. Right. She and her grandmother weren't on friendly terms yet, and Gen was probably supposed to be using more formal speech, too. "Good afternoon, Your Majesty," she tried again. "The weather is, um, lovely, isn't it?"

"Too warm for my taste," Queen Michelina said, and Gen wasn't sure if her reply had been about the temperature or if Gen still wasn't being formal enough.

Regardless, Queen Michelina began to walk briskly into the Imperial Lavender Gardens with Lee close behind, and Gen had to scramble to catch up.

"Thank you very much for welcoming me to the palace, Your Majesty," Gen said, laying it on thick. "Everyone has been so kind and very generous in teaching me about Raldonia."

"Hmm," the queen said, keeping her gaze straight ahead.

"Out of everything here, though, my favorite so far has been the Princess Suite. I've never had a room of my own, and the fact that I get to live in the same place as my mom did is even more amazing."

Queen Michelina's posture stiffened further, and she quickened her pace.

Shoot, what did I say? Gen replayed the last two

sentences in her head. Was she supposed to declare meeting the queen as her most favorite thing? Crap, that was probably it, and now Gen had gone and insulted her royal grandmother.

All around them, the scent of lavender perfumed the air, and bees buzzed back and forth. It should have been the moment Gen had dreamed of all her life—walking with a family member in the beautiful gardens of their home— but instead she felt like she was treading water in Raldonia and could barely keep her head above the surface. At least in New York, Gen had understood the lay of the land.

I thought the queen wanted me here, Gen thought miserably. Maybe, though, she wasn't "princess-y" enough. She certainly hadn't given a sparkling first impression in their meeting in the throne room, and last night's dinner was no better. *Who am I, anyway?* A New York street urchin? An orphan who knows nothing about her family history? An unofficial princess who could be tossed onto a plane and shipped back to Child Protective Services, as if she were a piece of equipment the queen ordered online but decided she didn't actually want?

Gen's shoulders slumped, even though she knew she was supposed to be showing off her best posture.

Lee pursed her lips behind her headset, shaking her head in disapproval.

At least there was one thing Gen was sure of: Lee did *not* like Gen at all, and nothing Gen did would be good enough for her.

For some reason, that gave Gen a boost of resolve. She

didn't really care about being a princess, but she knew for certain that she wanted a family, and that meant getting in the queen's good graces. But to overcome Lee's influence on Queen Michelina, Gen would have to triple her efforts.

Maybe changing the subject of their conversation to something like IT would be a safer topic than the Princess Suite or Gen's mother. (As long as Gen didn't make the mistake again of asking about technological modernization.)

"Your Majesty," Gen said, "I was wondering if I might be able to have a computer? Trisha and Miguel in palace IT said they needed your okay."

The queen glanced over at Lee but didn't say anything.

Was that a yes? Or a how-soon-can-you-get-rid-of-this-pest-of-a-granddaughter?

A few uncomfortable minutes later, Lee said, "Your Majesty, if I may remind you that you had something else you wanted to bring up to the princess?"

Okaaayy. Gen had no clue what the answer was to her request for a computer. Apparently, they were just moving on to the next subject on Lee's agenda.

Queen Michelina sniffed as if she'd smelled something off-putting. "I have received word, Genevieve, that you issued a blanket command to the kitchen staff not to bow to you. While I will not undo that order, I *will* issue my own command to you now—no more excusing anyone from paying their respects to you. That means bowing, calling you by your title, etc. It is important for a princess to inspire at least *some* sense of wonderment in her subjects. Understood?"

"But Duke Charlemagne said—"

"I am the queen, and I do not care what the duke said. You obey *my* commands."

Gen gulped. She hadn't even been here for two days, and she'd already messed up so many times. "Y-yes, Your Majesty. I understand."

The walk continued. No one talked. A full ten minutes passed without a word.

The quiet was killing Gen.

"Where should we go next?" Lee asked when they'd reached the end of the lavender gardens.

"Oh!" Gen exclaimed. "I saw a hedge maze when Agents 34 and 43 first brought me to the palace. Can we go there?"

"No," the queen said curtly.

"Why not?"

"No!" the queen practically shouted. Even Lee seemed taken aback by the queen's sudden fire.

Sheesh. What is so wrong about wanting to go into a hedge maze?

Gen looked down at the tiny, polished stones that lined the garden paths. She'd thought the labyrinth would be fun, but really, Gen had just wanted to do something to try to bond with her grandma. They could sort these stones by color, if that's what the queen wanted to do. As long as they did it together.

Because there was so much Gen wanted to say. Stuff like how happy she was to be with family, to finally have a permanent (hopefully) home, and about wanting to get to know her new country.

Instead, Lee chose a new route for them through the royal roses, and uncomfortable silence descended once more.

Finally, unable to take it any longer, Gen blurted out, "I love Raldonia so far and can't wait to go into the capital city to explore more!"

Queen Michelina stopped in her tracks. Then she turned to Gen in what seemed like slow motion before she said, "You shall *not* be leaving the palace grounds without supervision until you learn to behave like a proper princess. Do I make myself clear?"

Gen shrank under the queen's intense glare. "Yes, Your Majesty," she squeaked.

"This stroll is over," Queen Michelina said to Lee, and without another glance at Gen, they marched into a different part of the gardens and left her standing there on her own.

RALDONIAN "BOBSLED" TEAM

"It sounds like you could use a break," Duke Charlemagne said after patiently listening to Gen unburden everything that had happened during her walk with the queen. "You are under a great deal of pressure, but you're still a kid. What can I do to help?"

"I don't know." Gen flopped backward onto her bed. "I wish I could run away for a few hours, you know? But the queen forbade me from leaving the palace grounds without supervision."

"It seems to me that, just like your mother, you aren't the type of girl who usually follows those kinds of rules," Duke Charlemagne said with a smile.

Gen happily sank deeper into her pillows. She loved every time the duke said she was "just like" her mom. The tidbits of information were small, but still, it was something to hold on to.

Also, did the duke mean it would be okay if Gen snuck out sometimes as long as she didn't get caught? Is that why he showed her the secret tunnels?

"Of course, if you want supervision," Duke Charlemagne continued, "I'd be happy to be your chaperone. The queen can't object to that. And I believe I know just the place to help you unwind." He pulled out his PalmPad and tapped on the screen. "There. I've informed Lee that I want to take you somewhere, so you won't be attending tonight's imperial dinner, and nor shall I."

Gen sat up abruptly in her bed. "B-but . . . won't the queen be mad?"

Duke Charlemagne shrugged. "Queen Michelina and I have had plenty of disagreements in my lifetime. One more won't tip the scales. And this way, you can't be blamed. My message to Lee made clear that this was all my idea. Now, come with me." He rose from the armchair he'd been sitting in. "Let's fetch your friend Hill from the kitchen and, as you Americans say, 'get the heck outta here.'"

Gen grinned at this refined, extremely well-dressed, middle-aged man trying to speak with an American accent. Maybe this was what it was like to have a dad, someone who was willing to get in trouble with the higher-ups for his kid's sake. The queen hadn't turned out to be the cookie-baking type of grandma Gen had imagined, but at least Gen had the duke to look out for her.

Duke Charlemagne offered his hand. "Well? Shall we?"

"We shall." Gen bounced out of bed, took his hand, and together they turned bronze Leopold Schumfeld's head and ducked into the secret tunnels, the duke's PalmPad lighting the way.

"My sister, Cleo, makes the best frosty cream," Hill gushed as their car turned onto the dirt road leading to the Brillat-Savarin dairy farm. Hill had been disappointed they couldn't ride in Duke Charlemagne's fancy limo—the driver was out on an errand, so one of the Imperial Guards took them in what looked like a purple police car. But it didn't really matter, because Hill was thrilled to get to ditch work, courtesy of Gen and the duke.

"What's a frosty cream?" Gen asked.

"I believe it's similar to an American milkshake," Duke Charlemagne said, "but with richer ice cream, sweeter sugar, and more toppings. The secret ingredient, however, is the Brillat-Savarin milk, which is, I daresay, the finest in Europe."

Hill beamed. "My family's been in the dairy business for so many generations, I can't count that far back. My great-great-great-great-great-great-great-grandpa bought the first cow. Or maybe there are eight *greats* before *grandfather*. Or nine? Whatever. Anyway, everyone in the family except my dad works here, and that's only because the queen discovered what an amazing cook Dad is, so she hired him away to be her head chef. And since I like cooking, too, I help him out in the palace kitchen whenever I'm not in school."

Wow, Gen thought. She couldn't fathom knowing that much about your family, going that many generations back. She'd only just found out about a single grandparent and was no closer to knowing anything about her mom or dad, or her dad's side of the family in South Mallanthra.

The dirt road curved, and before Gen knew it, they arrived at a small store painted a cheerful cherry red on the outside. Behind it, there were pastures as far as the eye could see, as well as several barns.

A tall Black girl with her hair in elaborate braids bounced out of the store. She was probably seventeen or eighteen, but she had the same bright eyes and open smile as Hill. Definitely his sister.

When she saw who it was getting out of the car, she gasped "Your Highness!" and dropped into a bow.

Gen blushed. "Please rise," she said, her voice cracking a little. The queen had prohibited her from allowing anyone else off the hook from bowing, but it was still embarrassing.

"It's an honor to meet you, Your Highness. I-I'm Cleo, and *someone*"—she shot Hill a look—"didn't call ahead to let me know you were coming. I apologize that we weren't ready for you."

"No worries, we're the ones who should be sorry," Gen said. "We just dropped in on you. By the way, please call me Gen. And this is Duke Charlemagne."

Cleo bowed again. "I can't believe I have two royals at our little farm."

"This is *little*?" Gen gestured at the fields of grass that just kept going and going and all the cows that milled around them, grazing to their heart's content. They had plenty of room to roam. Seriously, it looked like each cow had enough land to claim a farm of its own.

Cleo smiled. "We like to make sure our ladies are happy."

Hill snickered and fake-whispered to Gen, "Ladies— that's what she calls the dairy cows."

"They have better manners than you," Cleo quipped, "and they smell better, too."

Gen laughed, although as always, she felt a pang of longing at how comfortable siblings were with each other. Gen suddenly missed Kenneth and Mikey, and all her other past foster brothers and sisters. They were only temporary siblings, but it was the closest Gen would ever get.

Duke Charlemagne reached over and squeezed her shoulder, as if he instinctively knew how she was feeling. His touch helped Gen let go of her momentary sadness. She did have family now—and it was the duke who'd gotten her out of the stifling palace and out here into the fresh air. (Well, *sort of* fresh. There were a lot of cows, after all. But it smelled more like milk than cow, probably because the fields were far away and the grass to cow ratio was high.)

"Cleo," Hill said, "I was hoping you could whip up a couple frosty creams for Gen and Duke Charlemagne? Gen's never had one before."

"Never?" Cleo's eyes widened. "Well, you are in for a treat! Do you want extra sprinkles, extra chocolate chips, or extra cake crumbles on top?"

Gen jumped in place, too excited to stand still. "Can I have extra everything?"

"You got it. A Princess Genevieve Special, coming right up."

After wolfing down the frosty creams (which were INCREDIBLE), Duke Charlemagne asked Cleo for an in-depth tour of the dairy farm to see the entire process of how they made milk, butter, and cheese. Gen thought she'd have to go, too, but the duke waved her and Hill away, telling them they ought to go enjoy themselves before they'd all have to return to the palace.

"Woo-hoo!" Hill shouted as he and Gen ran off. "What should we do? Where should we go?"

"Ever been bobsledding?" she asked.

"Doesn't that require snow?" He looked around, pointing out the obvious fact that they were surrounded by grass and cows, not a snowflake in sight.

"Details, details," Gen said. "I've got a workaround, if you can find me a big box and some stairs!"

Hill took her to his house. On the outside it was identical to the other barns, but it had been converted into a two-story cottage. Inside, the house was full of family life—framed photos of Cleo and Hill on the walls, snow globes and other vacation souvenirs on every shelf, a partially completed jigsaw puzzle on the coffee table. Hill's computer—with an impressively huge screen for gaming—

filled a corner of the room. A whiteboard on the wall showed his team's progress on *Escape from Octopus Isle*, as well as assignments for each member of the online crew. Hill was commander, Cara was the muscle, Lilah was the sharpshooter, and Callan was the wizard. Gen almost forgot they were here for indoor bobsledding.

That is, until she noticed the pièce de résistance of the family room: the tall, straight staircase with carved cows on wooden posts of the banister.

"It's perfect," Gen said, smiling at it.

She told Hill what materials they needed—a gigantic cardboard box, strong scissors, rope, a very fluffy pile of pillows—and after he gathered them, they got to work.

"How does a princess know how to make a sled out of old cardboard?" Hill said as Gen cut holes into the front of what used to be a twenty-pound box of romaine lettuce.

"Before you met me, I was just Genevieve Sun, orphan in New York City who lived with whatever family would take me."

Hill dropped the rope he was unspooling, and his mouth dropped open, too. "How can they treat a princess that way? You didn't even have a family?" He glanced around at all the photos of him, Cleo, and his parents around them.

Gen shrugged sadly. "They didn't know I was a princess, remember? I was a nobody."

"Why were you all in America anyway?"

She looked at him, confused. "You don't know?"

He shook his head. "Nobody tells kids anything. Besides,

whatever happened to your parents? No one's allowed to talk about it."

"Huh," Gen said. "Weirdly, it makes me feel better that I'm not the only one in Raldonia who has no clue why my mom and dad ran away to the United States."

Hill touched her arm softly. "At least you know you're a princess now. And you're important."

"I guess . . . I dunno. Sometimes—*most* of the time—I don't think the queen even wants me in Raldonia. So why am I here? In New York, I used to be able to go out and do whatever I wanted, whenever I wanted, like solve mysteries for other kids and help them. But here, I'm just stuck in boring lessons all day at the palace, and I have to learn to talk a different way and wear fancier clothes and not ask too many questions . . . I'm a princess, but not even a good one."

If only she could find a way to still be herself while also being a granddaughter that Queen Michelina—and the rest of the country—could love.

Gen jabbed another hole into the box, maybe with a little more force than was necessary.

"For what it's worth," Hill said, "*I* think you're an awesome princess. Who wants a stuffy, stuck-up girl ruling the kingdom? Not me." He handed her the rope. "I'd much rather have a princess who can teach me how to bobsled on an island where it never snows."

Gen gave him a genuine smile. His friendship was a saving grace in what would otherwise have been a not-so-great start to her "new" life here in Raldonia, and she was glad for the way he steered the conversation back to the fun they were supposed to be having.

She looped the rope through the holes in the box. "This is how we steer," she said, holding up the "reins" to show Hill.

"Cool!" he said. "What do you think about adding Bubble Wrap? You know, to pad our butts."

Gen laughed. "Brilliant!"

About half an hour later, she put together the finishing touches: a fat pile of pillows on the landing at the bottom of the staircase. "Okay, I think this looks cushiony enough to break our fall. Is the sled ready?"

"Yup!" At the top of the stairs, Hill patted their gigantic cardboard box.

Gen ran upstairs and put on a bike helmet.

"Don't you think it's a little ironic that we're putting on helmets when we're about to fly down a stairwell in a box?" Hill asked.

"Safety first!" Gen chirped. "There's a fine line between genius and recklessness, you know."

He laughed, secured his helmet, and got his stopwatch ready.

They climbed into the box, with Gen at the front. "Raldonian Bobsled Team, run number one. Ready, set, go!"

She and Hill shoved their weight forward, and the box lurched down the stairwell.

"Ahhhhh!" they screamed gleefully, their voices bouncing with every step they careened over.

One point three seven seconds later, they smashed into

the bank of pillows at the bottom. Gen tumbled out of the box, and Hill landed on top of her.

"That. Was. Awesome!" she shouted, trying to catch her breath.

"Let's do it again," Hill said.

"Obviously!"

They scrambled to their feet, readjusted the pillows, and ran back up the stairs, carrying their cardboard sled above their heads.

"This time, let's try to center our gravity so the box doesn't wobble side to side as much," Gen suggested.

"Good idea." They climbed back in and huddled their bodies closer to the middle.

"Raldonian Bobsled Team, run number two," Gen said. "Ready, set, go!"

"Woo-hoooo!" they screamed on their way down. This run felt faster than the first.

Hill checked his stopwatch as he climbed up from the pillows and confirmed. "One point two nine seconds! We should try out for the Olympics."

Gen cracked up. "I can see the headlines now: 'Princess of Raldonia Wins Gold Medal by Being Inappropriately Un-Royal.' I think Lee would have a heart attack if I were a member of the bobsledding team."

"Do we actually have a bobsledding team?"

"I dunno. I'm new here, remember? But if we don't, we should definitely petition to start one. It'd be worth it for Lee's reaction alone."

The front door of the house creaked as it opened.

"What would be worth it for my reaction alone?" Lee stood with arms crossed, scowling at Gen and Hill. She wore a red-yellow-and-green jumpsuit like a traffic light, but the dominant color—and mood—was definitely red.

Gen and Hill froze.

"Uh . . ." Gen didn't have a snappy comeback ready. She'd had permission to leave the palace. Duke Charlemagne was here with them to supervise. She had zero expectation that Evil Lee would suddenly show up to ruin her fun.

How did Lee always know exactly where Gen was?

"You're going to have to be a great deal quicker with your retorts, Your Highness," Lee said. "If you're officially crowned as the heir to the throne, the media will constantly pepper you with questions you don't expect. You must always be prepared. For example, in this instance, you could have said something like, 'As princess, I truly believe that occasional pushing of limits is beneficial to Raldonia. A monarch who is willing to take the less-traveled path is one who can see unorthodox solutions to her kingdom's problems.'"

Gen sighed. Lee had the uncanny ability to ruin even the most innocent of moments. Like turning a cardboard sledding experiment into political strategy.

And it hadn't slipped Gen's notice that Lee had said "*if* you're officially crowned." Not "when."

Gen shuddered. Lee was up to something. Gen just didn't know what.

Yet.

"Speaking of acting like a princess, you are late for the nightly imperial dinner."

"What? No," Gen said. "Duke Charlemagne—"

"Is going to have some explaining to do to the queen," Lee said curtly.

Gen wilted like a cut flower left out too long in the sun. Now the duke would get in trouble just for trying to do something nice for her. She felt awful.

Lee shifted her attention to Hill. "As for you, your father needs help with the dinner prep. Clean up this mess here, and when we return to the palace, report to the kitchen immediately."

"I'll start putting the pillows back." Gen sighed.

"Absolutely not!" Lee snapped. "You are a *princess*. Hill will clean up while you return to the car."

"But—"

"Let's go. Quickly."

Gen turned to Hill. "Sorry . . ."

"Don't worry about it." He winked, just like he had the first day she met him. "It'll only take me a few minutes to clean up." Then he lowered his voice to a whisper. "You'd better go before Lee decides to punish you more, like give you extra pronunciation homework."

She winced. Gen already had to "practice" talking for an hour every day. Evidently, princesses were supposed to speak with the elegant lilt of the Raldonian accent, like Duke Charlemagne and the queen. Their words were supposed to *glide*. Not rush and skitter "like rats in a New York City subway."

Lee escorted Gen back to the car. On the way, she said,

"If I may offer some advice, Your Highness. You may want to spend less time with the staff."

"What?" Gen stopped abruptly in the middle of the grass. "Why?"

"You may not have noticed, but there is a certain hierarchy within the palace. It would be best if you respected it. Trying to be friends with the staff could complicate their roles and would be confusing if it ever got out to the press."

Gen's stomach twisted. There was no way she was going to stop being friends with someone because of some made-up hierarchy. "And what about you?" Gen asked. "You spend all your time with the queen."

Lee sniffed and turned up her nose. "I am under no misconceptions about my position. The queen and I are not friends. I am here to serve her. No more, no less. Any future ruler of the kingdom must learn to accept such differences in the roles of royalty versus everyone else. It is the way the world should—and must—be."

HOMEWORK IS A ROYAL PAIN

Despite getting yelled at by the queen for taking Gen to the Brillat-Savarin Dairy Farms, Duke Charlemagne still showed up the next day to help Gen with her homework, and she was really relieved that he did.

"I can't even make sense of this definition," Gen said to the duke as they bent over her desk together. She jabbed at her homework about global sourcing. "'The economic efficiencies achieved through tariffs and differential tax breaks, most notably in the cross-border exploitation of products and services . . .' Ugh!!!" Gen thought it might be preferable to poke out her eyes with her pencil than to continue reading about this.

"Now, now," Duke Charlemagne said. "I know it sounds awfully dull, but let me help you. I happen to have a lot of insight on this subject, since I'm one of the key regulation makers on such matters." He waved his PalmPad at her to remind her that he drafted entire laws on the old thing.

"Yeah, but do you have insight that makes it interesting?" Gen asked.

"I like to think so." The duke walked over to the sitting area and sat in what had become his favorite armchair for visiting Gen. "Why don't you sit on something more comfortable. And leave that weapon of a pencil at your desk," he said, as if he knew that, mere seconds earlier, she'd been contemplating stabbing the economics book with it.

She splayed herself on the lounger. If Gen had to learn about Raldonia's trade policies, she at least wanted to lie down. So much of the stuff she was learning made her want to flop in defeat. School in New York City was never this hard. Maybe she wasn't cut out to be a princess after all.

"Promise you won't fall asleep," Duke Charlemagne said.

"I was already asleep the second I read the words *global sourcing*," Gen quipped.

"Haha," the duke said. "All right, as long as you're going to pay attention while lying down, here's an explanation in a nutshell. Imagine you have two countries with different natural resources. Country A has endless forests, and Country B has orchards and orchards of apples."

"Okay," Gen said. "That's simple enough."

"Now, say that Country A really loves apple pie."

"I like Country A's attitude," Gen said.

"And Country B is obsessed with baseball," the duke said.

Gen smiled. She could tell the duke was trying to appeal to her "Americanness" by using baseball and apple pie as examples, and she appreciated his effort. Somehow, an example using giant Raldonian shrimp and the game of cricket just wouldn't have the same ring.

"But the problem is," Duke Charlemagne said, "Country A doesn't have enough apples to meet its people's demands for pie. And Country B doesn't have enough wood for baseball bats for all the kids."

"Oh!" Gen propped herself up on her elbow. "But they could trade, huh? Country B has all those apple orchards. And Country A has a lot of forest for lumber, which can be turned into things like baseball bats."

"Precisely!" Duke Charlemagne said, delighted by how quickly Gen caught on. "The two countries can cooperate, and everyone will be happy. That's where diplomats like me come in. If Queen Michelina declared that Raldonia needed better trade relations in order to have access to apples, then it's my job to negotiate a deal with another country to get what we need. That, in essence, is global sourcing."

Gen grinned as she sat up. "I totally get it now, thanks! I wish you were the one teaching all my subjects."

"Goodness, no," the duke said. "I would be terrible at dance class or even Raldonian literature. With me at the helm, you'd end up confusing Richard Balmorant for Richard Baknomore!" He laughed heartily.

Gen didn't get it, but it was probably a joke about Raldonian authors with similar names? Or maybe it was just the kind of thing that adults found hilarious. In any case, she tried to smile politely and go along with it, which was something she'd just learned in etiquette class this morning: Always laugh at your guests' jokes to make them feel witty and welcome.

Suddenly, Gen missed the rules she used to live by. She hadn't had much use for her Good Detective Traits since she moved to Raldonia. It was as if the new lessons were meant to replace her old way of thinking. Was she still a detective? Or a hacker? There hadn't been a chance to use any of her old skills.

"Do you need any further help on your global sourcing homework?" the duke asked, bringing Gen out of her drifting thoughts.

"Um, not right now, thanks. I should probably finish reading this chapter, though. I'm supposed to do a whole report on it tomorrow." She groaned.

"I'll be right here if you have other questions," Duke Charlemagne said, smiling. "In the meantime, I've got work of my own." He pulled out his PalmPad and began tapping at the screen.

"Ooh, what is it?" Gen asked, happy to procrastinate doing her homework for a little longer.

"I'm drafting a new law to protect the majestic history, traditions, and culture of Raldonia. It's called the Charlemagne Heritage Law."

"Named after you?"

The duke chortled. "Oh no, I'm not that vain. It's in

honor of the great Charlemagne, our ancestor, remember? He was the legendary king of the Franks, king of the Lombards, and emperor of the Romans, and yes, that is where I proudly take my name from."

"Sounds interesting. Can I see?"

"Ah, it's all just boring legalese right now, nothing you'd find interesting." The duke hesitated, but then he said, "Don't worry, you'll learn all about the Charlemagne Heritage Law once I get it passed."

Gen slouched back over her textbook. So much for an excuse from reading.

"Knock, knock!" It was Trisha from IT at the door to the suite.

"I have that computer for you," Trisha said.

Whoa! Talk about good timing!

Gen also realized that if a computer was here, that meant the queen had come through for her. *Maybe she doesn't hate me!*

Okay, it was kind of sad that the bar was set that low—that Gen would be happy about the possibility of her grandmother not hating her—but hey, you have to start somewhere, and this was an improvement from the ice queen behavior where she treated Gen like something the RIA had picked up from the street on trash day.

Trisha wheeled in a cart that held a monitor and bulky desktop unit. They weren't the newest technology available, but they looked at least as good as the computers at the public library in New York. "Shall I set it up on the desk for you?" Trisha asked.

"Yes, please!" Gen's mood brightened immediately, and she rubbed her hands together. Now she'd finally be able to access all her files from the US. "Tell me everything: How many cores are in the CPU? How much RAM does it have, and is it DDR3 or DDR4?"

Behind her, Duke Charlemagne chuckled. "Well, if it's time to talk tech, then I am out of my depth." He waved his PalmPad in the air for emphasis. "I'll leave you two to it. Gen, if you have any more questions on global sourcing, imports and exports, or trade tariffs, I'll stop by again tomorrow afternoon."

Gen thanked him and eagerly turned back to Trisha.

Once the computer was set up and Trisha left, Gen threw herself into everything the computer had to offer. Despite the duke's reluctance to update his own technology, the palace's system wasn't actually bad. Sure, it was deficient in cybersecurity features, but Gen could help the IT team with that once she got more settled in. Even thinking about that made her feel a little more like herself, like the girl who knew how to program things and hack into any gadget you threw at her.

For now, though, it felt *really* good to be back on the internet again. The first thing Gen did was log in to her cloud account back in New York and download a copy of all her programming files, including the most important one of all, Hopper. Gen started working on her AI immediately, losing track of time and everything around her. Gosh, she'd missed coding!

The real Grace Hopper was Gen's role model, not only

because she was one of the first female computer scientists, but also because she never let anyone convince her that no was the final answer. Born in 1906, Grace Hopper grew up during a time when girls were expected to just be quiet, with no ambition other than becoming good, obedient wives. In fact, many people thought it was disgraceful for girls to have intellectual dreams or to want to have jobs after they were married.

But Grace Hopper did what she pleased, and she got a college degree and then a PhD in math. Then she tried to join the navy, but they said no. So she ignored them and went around their decision and joined the US Naval Reserve instead. And then she plowed ahead into the world of computers, which was supposed to be for men only, and she ended up leading teams of those very men in creating the world's first machine-independent programming language.

This is why Gen loved Grace Hopper. Because Gen never listened when someone told her something was impossible.

Gen was so wrapped up in the computer stuff that she didn't even notice the housekeeping team had come in to tidy up the Princess Suite. Had they stood at the door, frozen in a bow, until they realized Gen might as well be in another universe and wasn't going to acknowledge them? Maybe there was, like, a default amount of time when staff could resume their duties if the royal didn't directly command them to. They vacuumed around Gen's desk and under her feet, dusted the shelves, and remade her bed (apparently her technique wasn't quite up to standards yet), all without Gen looking up from her computer.

Then one of the maids said to another, "This should have been thrown out with all of her ratty American clothes, shouldn't it?" and Gen finally paid attention.

The woman was holding her nose with one hand and Gen's baby blanket between two fingers in the other, as if she couldn't stand the stench wafting off it.

"No!" Gen leaped from her desk chair and snatched the blanket away. "This is an imperial family heirloom, and it can never be thrown away!"

The maids glanced at each other, unconvinced that a faded scrap of fabric that smelled like milk could be worth preserving. But Lee was right about one thing, at least: The palace staff was trained to serve the royal family, without question. The two women dipped their heads in deference. "We understand, Your Highness. Please accept our apologies."

Gen instantly felt bad for being so harsh. But this blanket was the only thing she had from her parents, other than the pendant, and Gen hugged both tightly against herself. They were also the only real constants in her life. Even now, being in Raldonia, it didn't feel permanent. Gen was aware that one too many screw-ups might mean no coronation, no living in her mom's old suite, no chance to win over her grandma.

So maybe Gen was overreacting, and maybe a twelve-year-old shouldn't be this attached to a baby blanket . . . but it was *hers*, and she wouldn't let anyone take it away from her.

Thankfully, Hill chose this instant to pop in and break the awkward tension in the room.

"Hey, Gen! Are you done with your homework? I've got a brilliant idea!"

YOU'VE GOT TO BE SQUIDDING ME

I t turned out that the adults were *not* amused at Gen's and Hill's creativity. Apparently, using medieval suits of armor as target practice for racquetball was not only "undignified," but also "irresponsibly alarming." Because of the very noisy banging each time the ball hit a bronze breastplate or iron helmet, the Imperial Guard thought the palace was "under attack" and came charging into the armory storage room with their rifles drawn.

The queen grounded Gen for all of eternity and forbade her from associating with Hill ever again.

Gen accepted the punishment with a meek bowing of her head and no protest whatsoever. The grown-ups were pleased with her obedience and took it as a symbol that their princess-in-training had properly learned her lesson.

They didn't see the smug twinkle in Gen's eye as she retreated to the Princess Suite.

It didn't occur to them that their royal-in-training used

to be a savvy foster kid, well practiced in deceiving social workers, teachers, and pretty much anyone over the age of eighteen.

They 100 percent didn't remember that she had a door to a secret passageway linked directly to her room.

Good Detective Trait Number Two:

Never draw attention to yourself.

Holy mackerel, it felt good to be using her old sleuthing credo again!

As Lee deposited Gen at the door of the Princess Suite, Lee's headset started making noise.

"A meeting? It's not on the schedule," Lee said into her microphone. She paused to let whoever was on the other side talk. Then she said, "Understood. I'm dropping off Baby Fox and will head over to the throne room now."

Gen tamped down the instinct to ask what had happened to require an unplanned meeting (the palace schedule was infamous for being planned down to the minute, because Lee was in charge of it). But Gen also knew Lee wouldn't tell her what was going on.

What if it was a meeting about her? Or even better, a meeting about the curse?

Besides, if Lee was involved, Gen needed to be there. And that meant her plan to sneak into the kitchens would have to wait.

The moment Lee left, Gen skipped to her bookcase and

twisted Bronze Leopold (that was the nickname she'd given the bust of Leopold Schumfeld).

The bookshelf hinged open silently, and Gen slipped into the tunnel. After a week living in the palace, she had a mental map of the passageways, and she hardly even needed the faint trail of lights on the ground to make her way wherever she wanted to go.

Five minutes later, she arrived at the secret door she wanted. It was located right behind the raised platform that held the two thrones, hidden by a tapestry. Gen could hear voices yelling, but they were a bit muted by the wall. Given how loudly everyone was arguing, she took the calculated risk of opening the door a crack to better hear the meeting. As long as nobody went behind the tapestry, they wouldn't even know she was there.

Queen Michelina rapped her scepter on the dais, and the throne room instantly silenced.

A second later, Lee careened into the room, panting. "My apologies for being tardy, Your Majesty."

Huh, Gen thought. *I knew the tunnels were a shortcut, but they're really impressive if I could beat speedwalker Lee here.*

Queen Michelina only grunted at Lee's apology. "Let's bring this emergency meeting to order," the queen said. "Duke Charlemagne, please fill everyone in on what you know of the situation so far."

Gen held her breath as she pressed her ear to the crack at the door.

"The state of affairs is dire, Your Majesty," the duke said. "I have received confirmation that all of this week's seafood catches are rotten and unusable. Not simply the haul from one boat or a handful of vessels. But every single Raldonian shrimp, fish, crab, mussel, lobster, etc. is spoiled."

"Specific numbers, please?" the queen asked.

"Twenty-one thousand seven hundred thirty-four metric tons," Duke Charlemagne said. "In other words, nearly forty-eight million pounds of seafood have gone bad."

Gen gasped and had to slap her hand over her mouth. Luckily, they didn't hear her because the ministers' shock eclipsed hers.

"Forty-eight million pounds!" one of them cried.

"A travesty!" another moaned.

That is way too much rotten fish to have been an accident, Gen thought. *Someone made this happen.*

"It shall have devastating effects on our economy . . ." Gen recognized Minister Tallyho's voice from their lessons.

"How did it happen?" Lee asked in her ever businesslike tone. "Was there a power outage at the docks that affected the refrigerated warehouses?"

Gen frowned. Lee's calm was suspicious. She should have been freaking out like everyone else. Instead, she was too poised, as if she'd already known about the seafood problem.

Could she have had something to do with it?

"The power grids have been fully operational," Duke Charlemagne said.

"Pollution?" one of the ministers asked.

"No signs of that," the duke said. "Unfortunately, the public is blaming our soon-to-be princess."

What? Gen almost burst through the door and tapestry, because that was ludicrous. How in the world could she be responsible for ruined fish? It was only due to all her previous investigative experience that she managed to stay put in the secret passageway. Good Detective Traits Numbers Six and Seven:

Gather as much information as possible, and Be as invisible as a ghost.

"That wretched curse," Queen Michelina said.

A hush descended upon the throne room.

"Y-your Majesty," Minister Tallyho said. "You believe—"

The queen scoffed. "No, Minister, of course not."

Whew. Gen exhaled.

"I am saying that the people of Raldonia are latching on to that silly superstition, and this will only make matters worse," Queen Michelina continued. "We need to put a stop to it. The princess's coronation is only three weeks away. We need them to have faith in her. Let's spin the message about the seafood to calm the panic. Lee, do you have any suggestions?"

Gen leaned in to hear better. Her lessons so far hadn't included "How to Lie to Your Kingdom in Order to Prevent Mass Hysteria."

"I don't know, Your Majesty," one of the ministers said. "There's no obvious solution to this. Perhaps the curse is real."

"Indeed," Lee added. "About the curse—"

But she was cut off by another minister who'd chimed in.

Of course it's not real! Gen wanted to shout as the grown-ups talked about her. *I'm just an ordinary girl; I don't have some kind of evil magic!*

But then Gen chewed on her lip, thinking. Why was Lee egging on the minister about the curse? It was clear from Gen's conversation with her that she didn't actually believe in hexes.

Maybe Lee *wanted* people to believe in it. If someone didn't want Gen in power—because she wasn't 100 percent pure-blooded royal or for whatever other reason—that person could orchestrate a major disaster in Raldonia and blame it on the curse. It would take a whole lot of coordination, but as chief of staff, Lee's entire job was about coordination of complex logistics.

Hmm . . .

Duke Charlemagne spoke up. "Your Majesty, I actually disagree with Lee. We *can* spin this. I'd recommend we tell the public something they won't be scared of, and which would not have long-term implications for our fishing industry. How about a wayward bloom of algae that washed in because of a recent low-pressure weather system?"

"I vote against it!" a man said. "As minister of the interior, I am offended that you would blame Mother Nature for—"

"Enough," Queen Michelina said. "This is no time for

internal bickering. Duke Charlemagne, I like your idea. Work with the team from Hotshots PR to get a press release out immediately. I want as much damage control as possible."

Thank goodness for the duke, Gen thought. Hopefully, his plan would stop the curse rumors from getting any bigger than they already were. She was glad *someone* in this palace was on her side (besides Hill, of course).

The queen continued speaking. "I'm appointing Duke Charlemagne as imperial chancellor to navigate our kingdom through this crisis. There will be repercussions not only economically, but also in our trade pacts and international reputation."

"But, Your Majesty," Minister Tallyho said, "there's no need to appoint an imperial chancellor. We ministers can work together as usual to deal with this."

"No," the queen said. "I want leadership concentrated in one person right now. It will be more effective."

Duke Charlemagne cleared his throat. "You can count on me, Your Majesty."

Some footsteps sounded, a little too close to the tapestry for comfort. Gen hurriedly pulled the door to the tunnel closed and pressed her ear to it, at the same time trying to calm her racing pulse. She needed to be more careful; she'd almost been caught.

A moment later, Gen heard Lee grumbling right on the other side of the door. The queen and others wouldn't be able to hear her through the tapestry, but Gen could.

"Can't believe the queen is doing this," Lee muttered. "Her Majesty will rue the day she trusted Duke Charlemagne."

Gen's eyes widened. What the heck was that supposed to mean???

The thing Gen *did* know, though, was this: The curse wasn't just a harmless rumor. It was turning into something serious, with real consequences not only to Raldonia, but also to Gen, if more people started believing in it. She wouldn't be crowned princess if the country revolted against her.

And then what?

Queen Michelina would probably put her on the next plane back to New York. Goodbye family, goodbye to any chance Gen had of learning more about her mom and dad, goodbye to the hope of having a permanent home.

I will not *let that happen.*

There was a mystery to solve—maybe the biggest case Gen had ever had, with a heck of a lot riding on it. She gulped, thinking about what could happen if she didn't clear her name.

Luckily, Gen was also the perfect person for the job. She focused, thinking about her next step. Well, she should definitely come up with a name for the case, because all good mysteries needed a name. Not just about the spoiled seafood, but about the superstition itself: that if the throne were taken by someone without pure royal lineage, it would destroy everything and everyone in Raldonia.

She thought for a moment. And then it came to her:

The Curse of the Tainted Throne.

A chill ran up and down Gen's spine. She loathed the idea that she wasn't good enough. She hated the idea that *anyone's* ancestry could be used to decide their future.

Not on my watch, she promised herself.

SMELLS LIKE SABOTAGE

Gen sprinted through the secret tunnels. She had to find Hill to tell him what she'd overheard, and when she got to the kitchen door, she practically hurled herself through.

The kitchen was in absolute chaos. Cooks shouted for new recipes and flung open refrigerator doors, then slammed them shut again. Smoke billowed from an oven. Someone tripped and dropped a twenty-pound bag of flour, sending a cloud of white everywhere. Chef Brillat-Savarin stood on top of a counter shouting instructions to the different cooking teams, waving his arms like a deranged orchestra conductor.

Gen wove through the madness, narrowly missing a collision a couple times, until she found Hill. He sat next to a stack of egg crates taller than he was, cracking the eggs into a stainless steel bowl the size of a kiddie pool.

"What's going on in here?" Gen asked, still breathless from her run from the throne room.

"There's no seafood," Hill said, "so the entire eight-course dinner plan has to be changed. No shrimp cocktail tonight, no smoked salmon involtini or scallop crudo or bouillabaisse. Everyone's scrambling to make adjustments, and I'm in charge of cracking all the eggs they're going to need for the new menu." In the time it took for him to tell Gen that, he'd already gone through a dozen.

"Of course you already know about the seafood!" Gen smacked her forehead. How dumb of her to think she'd be the one to break the news to the kitchen staff.

"Yeah, the delivery didn't arrive today like it was supposed to, and all the phone lines at the fish companies were busy. So my dad went down to the port himself to see what was up."

Gen's ears perked. Good Detective Trait Number Six:

Gather as much information as possible.

"What did your dad find out?" She pulled up a stool and started helping Hill crack eggs. She wasn't as fast as he was, but she figured it would still go quicker with two people rather than one.

"Not much," Hill said. "Probably a mass power outage or something."

Gen was about to tell him that that was definitely not

the case, when he tilted his head closer to hers and lowered his voice.

"Actually," Hill said, "I know more, but I can't say it too loudly. I heard my dad talking to his sous-chef . . ."

"And?"

Hill glanced around to make sure no one was eavesdropping. "Dad says someone purposefully messed with the seafood haul. He saw it being tossed onto trash barges at the dock, and the fish definitely looked unnatural."

"What do you mean, *unnatural?*" Gen accidentally broke an eggshell in her excitement. She tossed it and grabbed a new egg, trying to look busy.

"He said the fish didn't seem like they'd just gone bad, or even like they were damaged from pollution. If that were the case, they might smell, but they would still be shiny and silver, you know?"

Gen didn't, but she nodded anyway.

Hill continued. "But the fish looked like they'd been burned by acid or something. They had all these random, melted-looking sections in them. Dad said it was really odd."

"Odd is a massive understatement," Gen said, forgetting all about the eggs she was supposed to be cracking. Instead, she thought back to the meeting in the throne room, and how weirdly calm—and then angry—Lee had been. *What game are you playing, Lee?*

But Gen couldn't just run to the queen and accuse her right-hand woman of a dastardly plot when Gen wasn't even sure yet what the plot was.

"We'll get to the bottom of this," Gen said, jumping up from her stool.

Surprised, Hill dropped a whole egg into the vat of cracked ones. "We will?"

Gen nodded vigorously. She might not be good at wearing pretty dresses, but she did have street smarts. "As princess," Gen said, "I have to protect Raldonia, and if someone's messing with my kingdom's shrimp and claiming it's because of some bogus old superstition, I'm going to investigate. We're going to solve the Curse of the Tainted Throne."

"Oooh, I like that name, even if it gives me the creeps at the same time."

"It's good, right?"

"*Really* good. But how do we investigate? I've never done anything like this before."

"I'll teach you." Gen rolled up her sleeves. "Besides, you already know a lot about strategy and planning and how to outsmart a wily foe from *Escape from Octopus Isle*, right?"

Hill's eyes twinkled. "Yeah, I do! First step is we gather information."

"Exactly! We'll go straight to the source and start with interviewing the fishermen and seafood sellers down at the docks."

Hill scrunched up his face skeptically. "Um . . . did you forget that the queen grounded you for all eternity?"

"Nope. Haven't forgotten. And also not worried about it." Gen turned back toward the secret passage door.

Then she grinned. "Be ready at dawn."

DRESSED TO KRILL

When the sun was barely over the horizon and the rest of the palace was still asleep, Hill knocked from inside the secret passageway. "Come in," Gen whispered. She'd already twisted Bronze Leopold so the bookshelf panel was unlatched, and the door was open a crack.

Hill tiptoed inside and did a double take when he saw her. "Whoa. Where'd you get that uniform? You look like one of us."

Gen smiled. A few days ago, she'd discovered the location of the staff closet and pilfered a white tunic and loose purple pants, because you never knew when a disguise might come in handy. Good Detective Trait Number Three:

If you're going undercover,
the best disguise is one that they will never suspect.

Besides, it would be easier to sneak out if she looked like a member of the staff. Genevieve Illona Caliste Aurelie of the House of Claremont, Princess of the Realm, Defender of Faith, Sincerity, and Justice was not supposed to leave her rooms. But Detective Gen Sun, undercover, could hopefully slip past the Imperial Guard.

She unrolled blueprints of the palace grounds (Gen had requested the maps from the minister of historical preservation, under the guise that she was very interested in all the different phases of castle architecture through the course of Raldonian history). She picked up a pencil and began explaining the route she'd devised to get out of the palace unseen.

"As you know, the secret tunnels run throughout the palace and lead to several different entrance and exit points," Gen said, pointing at the various X's she'd marked where there were doors. "There's one in my suite, obviously, as well as the throne room, the kitchen, the study, the queen's rooms. Most of these will be patrolled by guards, but—"

"Gen—" Hill tried to interrupt.

"Hold on," she said.

"Yes, but—"

"Don't worry, I've thought it all through," Gen said. "Look." She pointed at the queen's rooms. "This is technically part of a duo of chambers, originally known as the Monarch Suites. In olden times, the king and queen had their own separate set of rooms, connected by a sitting area. But since Queen Michelina didn't remarry after my grandpa died, everyone just refers to this as the queen's rooms now."

"Okay . . ." Hill said, shifting from foot to foot. Gen figured he was probably nervous about sneaking out, so she went into more detail to assure him.

"What most people don't know, though, is that the queen doesn't use the king's half of the Monarch Suites," Gen said, circling that part of the map. "The sitting room connection is closed, and the Imperial Guard only patrol outside *her* side of the chambers. But *both* parts of the Monarch Suite have hidden panels into the secret tunnels. So my plan is for us to take the passageways to the king's chambers, go through the hidden panel there, and exit out the main door of *his* side of the Monarch Suite."

"It's a good plan, Gen, but then what? We'd be inside the normal part of the palace, not the tunnels, and there are guards everywhere inside."

Gen nodded to acknowledge his astute observation. At the same time, she grabbed a notebook from her desk drawer. "These are the timetables for the patrols. I've matched them up to the map." She turned to the next page, where there was a detailed, minute-by-minute schedule. "As long as we follow this, we have a really good chance of not running into anyone while we make our escape."

Hill studied her schedule quietly. When he was done, he looked up but didn't say anything.

She had expected him to be impressed, but Hill just stood there.

"Uh . . . do you have questions?" Gen asked awkwardly.

Hill shook his head. "But I do have a tiny bit of feedback, if that's okay."

"Of course." Gen wasn't so cocky that she couldn't take some constructive criticism. "What is it?"

"Well, I think your plan could work. But I kind of already thought of an easier way out."

Gen blinked at him. "What?"

"There's this one guard, Monka, who I'm friends with. He really likes the chile-spiced pecans my dad makes, so whenever Dad whips up a batch, I swipe a bag for him. Anyway, Monka's on duty tonight at the kitchen staff entrance, and I'm ninety-nine percent certain he'll let us through without question. Especially since you're dressed in uniform."

"Oh," Gen said, glancing down at her elaborate timetables and map. "Well, I guess that *is* a lot more straightforward."

"Sorry," Hill said, shrugging. "I didn't mean to upend all your hard work."

"Nah, it's all right." Gen smiled at him. "Simpler is always better."

A few minutes later, they had gone through the tunnels, hurried past the early shift of bakers in the kitchen, and made it to the staff door at the back of the castle. As soon as they opened it and stepped outside, a very tall, broad-shouldered white man in an Imperial Guard uniform swiveled in their direction.

"Morning, Monka!" Hill said with excessive cheer to distract him. "We're just heading down early to the farmer's market. My dad heard there's a crop of moon drops coming in today, and they go fast! Hoping if we get to the market before they officially open, we can buy them off the farmer's truck bed before she even puts the grapes out on her stall."

"What are moon drops?" Monka asked.

"Deep purple–skinned grapes that're shaped like giant raindrops but taste like grape jelly," Hill said, waxing rhapsodically like a true chef's son. "I've been playing around with a new cake recipe any time we can get our hands on moon drops. I'm still working on it, but Dad said the flavor profile is *almost* right...."

Monka laughed at how passionate Hill was over grapes. "All right, well, good luck." He was about to go back to his post when Gen accidentally turned toward the sunrise and illuminated her face.

"Wait a second," Monka said. "You look an awful lot like—"

"This is, um, Sunny, a new girl on the kitchen staff," Hill said. He was shaking his hand toward her so hard, it was in danger of falling off.

Monka narrowed his eyes as he kept scrutinizing Gen. She tried to turn her face into the shadow of the palace walls again, and she stared down at her feet. "Hi," she squeaked, trying her best to sound shy and unsure of herself, like how a new member of the kitchen team might feel under the gaze of the intimidating Imperial Guard.

"We'll be back before anyone, uh, significant is awake," Hill said. "Seven a.m. at the latest."

(That was when Gen's lesson with Professor Règles was, so they *definitely* had to be back by then. Otherwise her absence would get reported to Lee and then straight to the queen. Luckily, Hill's contact would be up early.)

Monka hesitated, then relaxed his stance and pivoted so that he was no longer looking in Gen's direction. "Seven o'clock, Hill. For every minute after that, you owe me a bag of chile-spiced pecans."

Hill laughed. "I'd get you pecans anyway. But we won't be late, I promise."

"All right. You have a nice time at the market. And it was nice to meet you, Sunny."

"You too," Gen said. Her voice came out squeaky again, but this time it was because she felt relieved Monka was letting them go. She wasn't convinced he believed Hill's lie about who she was, but regardless, Gen was grateful for Monka's discretion.

Lee was wrong. It was a really good thing to be friends with the palace staff.

ORANGE YOU GLAD I'M HERE?

Hill and Gen stood on the porch of a small stone house near the sea, with fishing poles and nets and other equipment neatly piled in a lean-to next to salt-crusted life vests, hanging up to dry. Hill was about to knock on the cottage door when Gen said, "Wait."

"What?"

"Before we do this, we have to come up with a few signals, in case we get stuck in a situation where we can't communicate out loud. Like, if you're fine, tap your leg once. If you're in trouble, tap twice. And if you don't want me to panic because you've got a plan, tap three times." Good Detective Trait Number Eight:

**Always establish clear, nonverbal signals with your squad in case you can't talk to each other during an operation.**

Hill laughed and shrugged. "We won't need those here. Jonah's cool. I've known him forever."

"Okay, but still. I want us to have signals. Maybe not for now, but just in case it comes up in the future."

"Sure, that makes sense," Hill said. "So one tap means *Everything's fine*, two means *Help*, and three means *Things are bad but don't freak out, because I have something up my sleeve?*"

Gen smiled and nodded. Then she gestured at Hill to go ahead and knock on the door now.

An olive-skinned, bearded man wearing an old sweatshirt and worn jeans answered.

"What can I do for . . . As I live and breathe, is that you, Hill? Gadzooks, you've grown so much since I saw you last!"

"Hi, Jonah," he replied. "It's good to see you, too."

"You still gettin' underfoot in your dad's kitchen?"

"Sometimes. But I try to be more helpful than not nowadays." Hill smiled.

"I bet," Jonah said. "But I also bet you're not here just to pay a friendly visit to your dad's favorite fishmonger, are you?"

"Afraid not," Hill said. "Jonah, I'd like to introduce you to my friend, Sunny. We're a little suspicious about what happened with this week's seafood catch and were wondering if we could ask you some questions."

Jonah's expression darkened. "You accusing me of wrongdoing?"

Gen stepped forward. "Not at all, sir. We're here because we suspect that fishermen and fishmongers like you are victims of sabotage, and we want to get to the bottom of it. Hill said you might know something that could help us in our investigation, since you own the biggest seafood distributor in Raldonia and were the first one to discover the ruined haul."

He tilted his head and furrowed his brow. "Has anyone ever told you that you look an awful lot like—"

"Princess Genevieve?" she finished for him. She paused, then made a split-second decision. "That's because I am. You can call me Gen, actually."

Hill's eyes bugged out in panic. But Gen tapped her leg once, and he took a deep breath, seeming to trust she knew what she was doing.

Jonah, on the other hand, gawked at her, taking several steps backward. "Really?"

Hill nodded to confirm. "Yup, it's really her."

"Wow." Jonah scratched his beard as he processed the revelation, then bent into a deep bow. When Gen told him to rise, he said, "Well, Your Highness, I'm honored. I suppose I better invite you two inside."

(Gen's decision to reveal who she was was in direct opposition to Good Detective Trait Number Seven:

Be as invisible as a ghost.

But sometimes, blunt honesty got you more points than trying to be evasive.)

Gosh, it was nice to be out of the palace and working on a mystery! Gen was already starting to feel more like her old self again, not just a foreign girl trying to understand how a new country and all its formalwear worked.

Jonah ushered them into a cramped living room. Watercolors of boats hung on the walls, and spare fishing equipment filled every corner. The coffee table was actually an aquarium, the lamps were constructed from driftwood, and even the throw pillows on the small sofa were nautical-themed: one was shaped like an anchor and two were fish.

"Please, sit," Jonah said as he rushed into his kitchen and returned a minute later with a tin of cookies and two sodas. "I can't believe I've got royalty in my living room. I just want you to know, Your Highness, that I don't believe in that ridiculous old curse everyone's gossiping about. And you showing up on my doorstep, taking the initiative to try to solve this kingdom's problems on your own? That's proof of your genuine character right there, Your Highness."

Gen blushed. She wasn't used to being noticed by adults, let alone praised, especially when it involved sneaking around official channels. "Thanks, Jonah. I really appreciate that."

"Whatever I can do to help you out, count me in." He looked over at Hill, who was stuffing his face with cookies. He gave Jonah a thumbs-up.

Gen pulled out a pocket-sized notebook and pen. (At this moment, she could understand why Duke Charlemagne liked having his PalmPad with him at all times. She'd have to ask IT if she could get a phone or a tablet. Maybe she could load her artificial intelligence hacking program onto it, too!)

"Okay," she said to Jonah, "tell me how you knew something was off about yesterday's catch."

He leaned forward in his chair. "Well, the day started out normally. All the boats went out and came back with their nets full. There was nothing strange about the fishing itself, and everything that was caught seemed fine—shiny scales, only the smell of saltwater, not rot.

"But once back on land, when I started to unload all the seafood to pack it in ice for the warehouse, I noticed an odd grittiness to the shells of the shrimp. I checked the lobsters and other shellfish, and they were also covered in something like sand but chalkier.

"Soon after, a smell started to take over the wharf, almost like I was at a landfill instead of standing in the fresh air by the ocean. Then I noticed the halibut, cod, and other fish I'd hauled in had started glistening with unnatural orange specks. The chalky grains of sand I'd felt earlier had changed color, from gray to neon orange. And wherever those bright orange spots were, the flesh of the fish started disintegrating. It was like some kind of powerful chemical had been sprinkled all over everything."

"Weird!" Hill said, his mouth still half full of cookies.

Meanwhile, Gen studied her notes. "You said the smell began soon after . . . not right away. Was it possible that anyone else could have had access to the seafood between you hauling it in and packing it up into the crates of ice?"

Jonah ran his calloused fingers through his beard as he thought it over. "There was a short window of time when I went back into my office to take care of the paperwork that's always filed between accepting the haul from the boats and actually prepping the catch for storage. And one of the guards from the palace—you might know him, name's Monka—was working that morning. When he's not on duty with the Imperial Guard, he helps me with loading everything into the warehouse, you know, to make some extra cash. He's a big, strapping young man. But it couldn't have been him who tainted the seafood . . . Monka's a good fellow."

"Totally agree!" Hill nodded vigorously. "Monka can't be the culprit."

Gen, however, wasn't so sure. Monka was in the right place at the right time. And just because he seemed nice on the surface didn't mean he was nice underneath. Still, Gen wasn't going to say anything about it yet, not until she had more facts. Good Detective Trait Number Six:

Gather as much information as possible.

Hill turned to Gen. "Do you really think someone tampered with the catch while Jonah was in his office?"

"Maybe," Gen said. "But I also don't want to jump to false conclusions and cause panic in the fishing community. Jonah, can I have your word that you'll keep this quiet for now?"

"Fisherman's honor, Your Highness." Jonah solemnly held up two fingers in a fishhook–shaped oath. "For Raldonia's sake, though, I hope you find the villains soon."

NOT-SO-SLY FOX

Gen had a lot to think about as they left Jonah's cottage, so she didn't say much as she followed Hill to the town square, where the open-air produce market took place every morning. Hill really did have to get a crate of moon drop grapes for the palace kitchen. It's just that he'd bent the truth a teeny tiny bit when he told Monka about it. There wouldn't be a rush to buy the moon drops before anyone else did, because Hill's dad had already reserved them and paid in full. Hill just had to swing by the farmer's stall to pick them up.

When they arrived in the town square, the hustle and bustle prodded Gen out of her thoughts. She'd been so wrapped up in the mystery of the spoiled seafood that she hadn't really gotten a chance yet to purely enjoy being out of the palace for only her second time since she arrived in Raldonia.

And wow! Gen felt like she was walking in a brochure for a European vacation. The town square was paved entirely in cobblestones that still shone from the early morning dew, and dignified buildings made of brick lined the perimeter. All around Gen, farmers were setting up tables overflowing with colorful fruits and vegetables—purple plums and bright-red cherries, piles of yellow corn and mounds of deep-green spinach and broccoli. At the edge of the market, two bakers unloaded trays of pastries into a display case. Gen's nose steered her toward the muffins, but Hill breezed past and headed toward a weathered pickup truck instead. With a sigh, Gen went with him. After all, they had to be back at the palace in an hour if they didn't want anyone to notice they were missing.

"Good morning, Anita!" Hill waved at the redheaded woman wearing denim overalls who was climbing out of the truck bed. There were several crates of grapes stacked on the cobblestones nearby, as well as an entire truck full of fresh lavender flowers in industrial-sized buckets. "Do you have the moon drops I—I mean, my dad—ordered?"

Gen gawked at the grapes. They were like nothing she'd ever seen before. First of all, they were enormous and shaped like a giant's teardrops. Secondly, they were so dark purple, they were almost black. There were so many other grapes, too—some blue, others were green with red speckles, and another kind was ombre, starting out pink and shading into orange and then yellow.

She was so surprised that she didn't see the empty box in front of her, and Gen tripped. With a yelp, she flew forward and would have slammed to the ground if one of the bakers from the next stall hadn't leaped forward and caught her. Gen's face was literally two inches from the cobblestones.

"Whoa, there," the baker said, helping Gen to her feet. "You okay, kiddo?" He was a rotund white man with kind eyes and a short white beard. Actually, he looked a little bit like the Kentucky Fried Chicken colonel.

The other baker, a snowy-haired East Asian woman, hurried over, and Hill and Anita the grape-and-lavender farmer did, too.

Gen smiled sheepishly as she wiped some gravel off her pants. "Yeah, I'm fine. Thanks for catching me."

"It's his grandpa superpower," the woman said, beaming at the man fondly. "Sam just seems to know when a kid is in trouble, especially when they're about the age of our own grandchildren. It's like he's tuned to your frequency. Anyway, I'm glad you're okay, dear. I'm Ethel."

"Nice to meet you." Gen basked in Sam and Ethel's kind grandparent-ly glow. *Maybe if I solve the Curse of the Tainted Throne, my grandma will look at me this way, too,* Gen thought.

Anita, however, scowled. "You almost squashed all my grapes, missy. That would've cost you a month's worth of kitchen wages to repay me. I have half a mind to report your disregard to Chef Brillat-Savarin and—"

Something glinted on the ground, and Anita froze, mid-rant. All eyes went to the shiny thing on the cobblestones.

Anita's mouth hung open as if she'd suddenly forgotten what she was lecturing about. "I-is that . . ." She looked up and pointed at Gen. "A-are you . . ."

Gen's hand flew to her throat, where her necklace chain dangled open. *Oh no, the faulty clasp!* It must've come undone when she tripped. And now the Imperial Fox was lying on the paving stones, making it obvious to everyone that Gen was *not* actually one of the kitchen staff . . .

She snatched the fox pendant and stuffed it into her pocket.

Ethel and Sam gasped and bowed.

But Anita glowered. "I cannot believe you have the gall to return to the kingdom and curse all of Raldonia," she hissed. Then her voice got louder. "As if your mother wasn't bad enough—"

"Not here," Ethel cut in. "Inside the bakery van . . ."

"I have work to do," Anita said, crossing her arms and refusing to budge.

"We can't leave you to spread ridiculous rumors about a ridiculous curse," Ethel replied.

"I will *not* get in the van with *her.*" Anita scowled at Gen. "Your mother and father nearly put me out of business! Just being near you is probably enough to curse me."

Sam was also trying to get them all into his van for some privacy, but Gen felt rooted to the spot. Here was another tidbit about her mom and dad, and she wouldn't leave without it. "What do you mean, my mom and dad almost put you out of business?"

Anita snorted. "Princess Adrienne tapped me to be the

sole provider of grapes and lavender for her wedding. I was incredibly honored! A royal contract! But that was before the rats. The week before the wedding, hundreds of thousands of rats appeared out of nowhere and ate through every stem and leaf and root of my vineyards! That's what I got for trying to support the marriage of a Raldonian princess to a non-royal. The curse destroyed everything. The only reason I'm still here today is your parents left the kingdom and took the hex with them. And I will *not* let the curse come back to Raldonia again!" She glared daggers at Gen.

Gen staggered backward at the force of Anita's anger. Ethel caught her. "Come, Your Highness. Don't listen to Anita. None of it is true."

"That's where you're wrong," Anita said. The sunlight cast a glint in her eyes. "The curse is already back. It's going to get worse, too." She lowered her voice and stared straight at Gen. "And it's All. Your. Fault."

Goose bumps rose all over Gen's skin.

Hill tugged on her arm. "Let's get out of here."

Gen practically dove into Ethel and Sam's bakery van. Only there, surrounded by racks of warm pastries, did Gen stop shuddering.

"You'll be okay in here," Hill said gently. "Ethel and Sam are my friends' grandparents."

"We're sorry Anita said those things." Ethel passed muffins to Gen and Hill. The chocolate was still a little melty. "Not everyone in Raldonia is like that."

"It-it's all right," Gen said, trying to hide how it had shaken her up. "My teachers at the palace keep telling me that life as a princess is no picnic. Not only because of nosy reporters, but also because the citizens don't always agree with what the queen does. Which is fair. People should get to have opinions. It's just . . . well, a little over a week ago, I was a normal kid. I'm not used to people thinking that I'm a bad omen."

Sam waved his hand in the air dismissively. "People like Anita will change their minds once they see what a great princess you are. The curse is ludicrous. Ethel and I hate that the old rumors have been spreading again. We—and many others—will support you no matter what. In fact, you should meet our grandkids, Cara, Lilah, and Callan. Then you'll see that there are plenty of Raldonians who are on your side."

Gen perked up a little. She remembered that Hill had mentioned his friends Cara, Lilah, and Callan a while back. They were the gamers who played *Escape from Octopus Isle*. She hoped she could find time to meet them at some point. But her schedule ever since she arrived in Raldonia had been packed.

"And we assure you," Ethel added, "that we were huge fans of your mother. She was spunky and interesting. Don't ever listen to curmudgeons like Anita. The rats were a bizarre situation. What Anita is really mad about is your mother and father choosing to leave Raldonia. The truth is, your mother chose true love over politics; she listened to her heart, and that's the most important thing any monarch can do."

Gen smiled. She still didn't know much about her

parents, but it was pretty great to hear that Ethel and Sam and others in the kingdom had admired her mom.

And yet, a sense of foreboding hung over Gen. The fact that Anita—a real, live person—believed in the curse made it feel more like a threat than an abstract superstition. And even if the curse wasn't real, how far would Anita and other Raldonians go to force Gen out of the kingdom?

Maybe this is what happened to Gen's mom and dad— maybe people had been so scared of a potential curse, it had felt impossible for them to stay in Raldonia.

The clock tower outside chimed.

"Oh no!" Gen cried. "Is it already six forty-five?"

Hill dropped the remains of his muffin into his lap. "We'll never make it back to the palace in time for Gen to sneak back before her lessons start!"

"Oh yes you will," Sam said, going into grandpa-superhero mode. "Ethel, you run the stall. I'm going to grab Chef Brillat-Savarin's crate of moon drop grapes from Anita's truck.

"Then I'm driving the princess and Hill back to the palace as fast as this van can go."

TALK LIKE A PRINCESS

en tumbled in through the secret passageway door in her bedroom with just enough time to quickly change out of the staff uniform. She was finishing the knot on the fussy silk bow of her blouse right as Professor Règles knocked on the Princess Suite's front door.

"Good morning, Your—" Professor Règles did a double take. "Your *hair*..."

Oops. Gen darted a look at the mirror on the wall. Her ponytail must've gotten messed up when she threw off the uniform, and there were some muffin crumbs in the hair that framed her face. She swiped them off and watched as Professor Règles's disapproving gaze followed the crumbs onto the plush carpet.

Double oops.

Professor Règles let out a long, woe-is-me sigh. "Your

Highness, the coronation is in *three* weeks. Can't you at least *try?*"

Unfortunately, Gen's New York City philosophy of "if you act like you belong somewhere, people won't question you" didn't seem to be working here in Raldonia, and certainly not in the palace. Or maybe the problem was that Gen *didn't* feel like she belonged here, which made it a lot harder to act like she did.

"I *am* trying," Gen insisted as she tugged her hair tie loose and redid her ponytail low on the nape of her neck.

Professor Règles sighed again, but her job was to get Gen into tip-top shape no matter what, so she rubbed her temples just once, smoothing away the stress on her face, then stood straight as a steel rod again.

"We shall pick up where we left off yesterday. Royal elocution." She elongated all the vowels to emphasize them, as if Gen couldn't hear them otherwise.

Gen closed her eyes, trying to remember the sentences Professor Règles had made her memorize yesterday. But all she could think about were the questions that had popped up from her excursion out of the palace: How did Jonah the fishmonger's comments and Anita the farmer's accusations fit into the case? Who was behind the fish incident? Had the fish really been messed with to make it look like the Curse of the Tainted Throne was real? And if so, what was the motive?

"Welcome to, uh, Raldonia. I'm glad—I'm *pleased*— to, er, that you could come to . . ."

"Where is your mind today, Your Highness?" the professor asked.

Gen's eyes popped back open. "Sorry, I just got a little distracted." The understatement of the year. If only Gen could work on Hopper so the AI could help her investigate. But there had been so little time to tinker on her program, especially since Gen didn't have a mobile device and had to code while sitting at an actual computer.

Professor Règles clucked her tongue. "You must focus! There is *nothing* more important than your upcoming coronation."

I know! Gen wanted to shout. That's why she needed to solve this mystery, because if the curse rumors got too out of hand and more citizens like Anita blamed Gen, then there wouldn't be a coronation.

But one look at the stern, bespectacled professor, and Gen knew she wouldn't be a sympathetic ear. All Gen could do was get through these lessons and *then* she could turn back to the case at hand.

"Here," Professor Règles said, thrusting a notecard at Gen with the sentences she was supposed to recite. "Now, again, from the beginning." Professor Règles pushed her glasses all the way up her nose, which Gen had come to recognize as the professor's tell for when she really meant business.

Gen took a deep breath. "Welcome to Raldonia. It is an honor to meet you. We are so pleased you could travel all this way to attend my coronation."

"Tongue more relaxed, lips softer, please," Professor

Règles said. "You do not want to look like a snarling raccoon to the visiting dignitaries."

A snarling raccoon? Oh great.

Gen tried to manipulate her mouth and tongue shape, but *attempting* to relax only made it harder.

Meanwhile, Professor Règles kept spouting out more instructions. "Speak with confidence. Chin up, shoulders back. Future queens do not look around like they're lost. Future queens know exactly where they are going and what they are saying. Repeat after me: Welcome to Raldonia. It is an honor to meet you. We are so pleased you could travel all this way to attend my coronation."

"Welcome to Raldonia. It is an honor to meet you. We are so pleased you could travel all this way to attend my coronation," Gen said, trying her best not to slaughter the Raldonian vowels.

"Less crisp on the consonants," Professor Règles said. "Pronounce them softly, like ballet dancers dancing on feather beds."

Gen snorted. She'd been jumping on her big, fluffy bed yesterday when Professor Règles came in, and the professor had immediately scolded her that princesses did *not* jump on beds. However, it was apparently fine for ballet dancers to *dance* on beds. At least where pronunciation was concerned.

"Is something funny?" Professor Règles said. "Because if you take your oath on Coronation Day sounding like you're from Brooklyn, the media will devour you like a pit of hungry tigers."

(Actually, Gen's accent was from the Bronx. But she thought it better not to correct the professor right now.)

Then she registered the last part of Professor Règles's statement. Duke Charlemagne had smuggled a few copies of recent European tabloids for Gen to read, and the papers were all dying to catch even a glimpse of her. Since they had no real news yet, the so-called articles were full of speculation, mostly interviews of Raldonian citizens and random diplomats from other countries. But imagine if the press had photos—no, *video*—of Queen Michelina on Coronation Day, wincing at Gen's accent, or worse, video of the crowds throwing tomatoes at Gen and booing her for not being Raldonian enough to be their princess.

That, plus people like Anita who believed in the curse and *wanted* Gen gone . . .

To be clear, Gen wasn't ashamed of her American past or her American accent. But she *was* terrified of not being accepted by the people and the place that was supposed to be her forever home, and of not belonging in the family— and the country—that was supposed to be hers. Or getting booted out of it.

She took another deep breath and repeated Professor Règles's sentence, with rounder vowels and softer consonants. Not quite ballerinas on feather beds, but not tap-dancers on cement, either.

Without even a hint of a compliment, Professor Règles moved on to her posture. "Pretend there's a string running up your spine, through the top of your head, holding you upright. That will open up your diaphragm and allow you to project your voice." She reached above Gen's head and acted like she was tugging upward on a string.

Okay . . . Gen thought. *Now I'm a round-mouthed, ballet dancing marionette.* It was a feat to keep all of Professor Règles's similes straight.

"And don't forget to keep your arms slightly away from your body," Professor Règles continued. "It projects the sense that you're important. Insignificant people huddle. Consequential people, on the other hand, take up a lot of space."

"I disagree with that," Gen said.

"I beg your pardon?"

"Nobody is more important than anyone else. No matter how they stand."

Professor Règles frowned. "*You* are more important. You are about to be crowned a princess. That is the point of our elocution lessons."

"I get that. I just meant that as a human being, I'm not actually more valuable than anyone else." Of course Gen understood that some formality was required by the monarchy, because it helped inspire the citizens' reverence. Raldonia sure did love tradition, especially pomp and circumstance.

But Gen also believed it was possible to inspire admiration by treating people as equals. More and more, she wanted to be the kind of princess who everyone *chose* to look up to, not the kind they were forced to follow.

Professor Règles stared at her blankly. "I don't understand. Are you saying that you don't want to hold your arms slightly away from your body when you speak?"

Now it was Gen's turn to sigh. Maybe everyone in the imperial palace had gotten so used to Queen Michelina's frostiness that they'd forgotten it was possible for a monarch to both lead *and* show mutual respect.

When I'm in charge, Gen thought, *I'll change that.*

She was about to recite Professor Règles's sentences again—tongue relaxed, mouth rounded, string threaded through her spine and head, arms akimbo yet somehow still elegant—when the lights flickered.

They flashed ominously four times, then the entire room went dark except for the morning sun coming in through the gauzy curtains.

"What the—"

Professor Règles shot Gen a sharp look.

She defended herself. "I wasn't going to say a bad word!"

"Nevertheless, a princess must use more sophisticated expressions of surprise."

Gen pressed both hands delicately to her cheeks and said, with fake daintiness, "Goodness gracious, I do so wonder what has transpired with the electricity?"

But Professor Règles didn't have a chance to respond, because a squadron of the Imperial Guard burst into Gen's rooms.

"Your Highness," the captain said. "There has been a kingdom-wide blackout, and we are assigned to protect you until the Ministry of National Defense confirms that you are not the target."

Gen laughed.

No one else did.

"Wait, are you serious?" she asked.

"Yes, Your Highness," the captain said.

Gen glanced at the soldiers, who had brought in dozens of battery-operated LED "candles" and set them all around her room. Then they stationed themselves in the suite as guards. Gen spotted Monka among them. He gave her a friendly wave, and she waved back. But after Jonah the fish-monger's comment about Monka being at the docks on the day the seafood went bad, it seemed like he had a knack for being in the right place at the right time. Gen couldn't help wondering if he was somehow involved with the outage.

"The Imperial Palace is currently secure," the captain said to Gen, "so there is no need for evacuation protocols. You may continue what you were doing."

"Um, with you here?"

"Yes, Your Highness. Please don't let our presence interrupt your work."

Professor Règles shrugged and mimicked pulling a string in the air.

With a groan, Gen stood taller in the dim suite. And she spent the next hour pretending that everything was fine, practicing her soft O's, U's, and not-too-crisp consonants, with six fancily dressed members of the Imperial Guard as her audience.

One of whom might be sabotaging Gen and the kingdom.

LOST IN TIME

Three days later, the power was still out across all of Raldonia. At first it was fun, because the freezers couldn't run without electricity, and the palace kitchen needed help eating all the ice cream before it melted. So she and Hill were assigned the noble task of consuming as much Chocolate Brownie Chunk and Raldonian Lavender Honey Surprise as they could stomach. But after seventy-two hours, there was nothing left to eat other than shelf-stable crackers and canned beans.

All of Raldonia suffered. Work came to a screeching halt because no one could function without power. According to Hill, Sam and Ethel couldn't bake, all the fish and shrimp in Jonah's freezers had defrosted, and office workers had no offices to go to, because there was no power in the buildings, nor in the traffic lights and trolleys along the way.

The queen and the ministers were beside themselves, and Lee scurried around the palace like an ant who'd lost her trail, running this way and that as a relentless stream of orders flooded through her headset. If the spoiled seafood haul was a kick in Raldonia's gut, the massive power outage was an uppercut to the face.

On the morning of the fourth day, Duke Charlemagne appeared at Gen's door. "Psst," he said. "I'm skipping out on the interminable ministry meetings today to do something more interesting, which to be honest, is just about anything. Would you like to join me?"

She'd been alternating between reading a worn Raldonian-language textbook she'd found on the bookshelf (it had her mom's name written on the inside of the beat-up cover—so far the only evidence her mom had lived in this room) and tinkering with an old digital picture frame that Trisha from IT had given her to play with. Gen wanted a portable device to load Hopper onto, but the queen had nixed Gen's request for a phone or tablet. So Trish had scavenged up this broken digital frame, and Gen had happily accepted it, since she liked a good tech challenge (the frame had a very basic but functional operating system that she might be able to modify).

But the frame's auxiliary battery was running low, and there was only so much Gen could do to it without electricity, so she jumped at the duke's invitation. "You're ditching? I didn't know grown-ups did that."

"Only when an emergency requires it," Duke Charlemagne said, "and I deem our collective levels of boredom a state of emergency. I also extracted your friend from the kitchen, seeing as there is little for him to do there at the moment. We are, apparently, eating raldonberry jam sandwiches for our meals today."

Hill popped his head around the door frame. "Good morning, Gen!"

"You're both just in time," Gen said. "I was about to go cross-eyed, trying to work with only the light from my window."

"What would you like to do today?" the duke asked.

Gen chewed on her lip. There were a number of things she wanted to do, like delve deeper into the curse and figure out what—or who—was behind the seafood debacle and now this power outage. But it seemed unlikely that she'd get very far in her investigation without electricity (and internet access). So Gen turned to a smaller mystery she hadn't solved yet.

"There's a place I'd like to get into," Gen said. "When I was studying the Imperial Guard patrol schedules for . . ." She drifted off as she realized that Duke Charlemagne didn't know she and Hill had snuck out of the palace a few days ago to talk to Jonah, Sam, Ethel, and Anita. Gen needed to make up a reason. "For, uh, information about how palace security is keeping the royal family safe," she finished, hoping it was a good enough cover.

The duke tilted his head a little, but he didn't say anything.

Gen plowed onward. "Anyway, I noticed that there are extra patrols in a concentrated area on the palace grounds. At first I was confused because it looked like the guards were just marching around a random patch of the garden.

But then I realized that the area they were clustered in was the hedge maze. And *then* I remembered that the queen didn't want me walking through there."

"You think there's something hidden inside?" Hill asked, eyes widening.

"Maybe," Gen said.

Duke Charlemagne cleared his throat.

Gen raised her brows. "Does that mean I'm right?"

"I shall neither confirm nor deny," the duke said.

She grinned. That was enough corroboration for her. "Come on, then. Let's go do some sleuthing!"

The sunlight outside was shockingly bright compared to the dimness of the palace corridors. Gen had to shield her eyes for the first few minutes as they made their way through the Imperial Gardens, toward the maze.

"How are you going to get around the patrols?" Hill asked.

"Monka was stationed outside my door a few days ago, and I eavesdropped on his conversation with the captain," Gen said. She didn't mention *why* she was snooping on Monka, because for all Hill knew, Monka was his friend. But Gen wasn't ruling any suspects out. "I heard the captain telling Monka and the others that the Imperial Guard would be shifting their patrols to prioritize the palace during the power outage, which I hope means the hedge maze will be empty."

"Excellent deduction," Duke Charlemagne said.

Gen smiled. "Thanks!" She liked how generous he was with his compliments to her, and how game he was to go with them to check things out.

Sure enough, when they arrived at the maze, there were no guards in sight. Hill was about to let out a cheer, but Gen put her finger to her lips. Ironically, the complete lack of any security suddenly made Gen put up her guard. Sometimes, things that were too easy were too easy for a reason. This could be a trap.

"One of us should probably stay here at the entrance to the maze as a lookout," Gen said quietly.

"I can do bird calls," Hill whispered.

She shook her head. "I think it might be better if the duke is our lookout." What she was really thinking was that bird calls were way too obvious, but she didn't want to hurt Hill's feelings. Right now, he reminded Gen of when her foster brother Kenneth held his Frying Nemo menu in front of him like he was playacting what he thought a spy should do. A pang of missing her old life quivered through her.

But Gen shook it off. She had a mystery to work on, and this was going to be her best opportunity at whatever was inside the hedges.

"I suspect the duke knows exactly what's inside the hedge maze, but he can't tell us," Gen continued. "So if we get caught, it's better if he's not with us. He can say he was just out for some fresh air and totally deny knowing anything about what we're up to."

"A grand plan," Duke Charlemagne said. "As a signal,

I can set off an alarm on my PalmPad." He pulled his beloved device out of his suit jacket. "If I turn the volume to maximum, you ought to be able to hear it, even inside the maze. And no guard would suspect anything of me. I always have this with me."

Gen squinted at the blinking green power light. "How is it still charged? This is the fourth day without electricity."

The duke sheepishly pulled something else out of his suit jacket. "Portable chargers. I simply cannot live without my PalmPad, so I always have a dozen backup batteries charged up in case of something like this. I carry a spare battery with me at all times."

"Whoa," Gen said. "Now, that's what I call disaster preparedness." She turned back to the maze. "Okay, so the duke will stay out here and set off his alarm if anyone approaches. Meanwhile, Hill and I will navigate our way inside and see what we can find."

"Good luck," the duke said. Then he lowered his voice and said to her, "You might want to aim for the center of the maze. But I'm not the one who told you that."

She nodded conspiratorially. "Understood. Thank you."

Duke Charlemagne took his post while Gen and Hill darted into the hedge maze.

"What are we looking for?" Hill whispered, looking up at the brambles overhead.

"I'm not sure," Gen said, "but I hope we'll know it when we see it. Stay close. We're going to have to try every nook and cranny to find the center, and I have a feeling it's about to get really twisty."

She followed the path as it curved to the right, then veered in a U-turn, then curled into itself. "Shoot. Dead end." Gen retraced their steps until they reached the first fork in the maze, and this time, she followed that one. Left turn, left turn, right swoop, then sharp right. That spit them out at a three-way split in the hedges.

"Now what?" Hill asked.

"We're going to keep following paths for a while."

"Are we going down every single one? No offense, Gen, but that'll take forever. What if the guards come back?"

Gen shook her head and smiled. "We don't need to chase down every possible path in the maze. I'm making a 3D map in my head as we try different routes. Once we go down a few, I'll be able to rule out some of the paths by process of elimination. Since our goal is to get to the middle, we can safely ignore any parts of the maze that are cut off from the center, or that circle in on themselves into dead ends, that kind of thing."

Hill gawked at her. "I'm sorry, I'm still stuck on the part where you said you're making a 3D map of the maze in your head. How???"

She shrugged. Mapping the hedges was as easy to her as memorizing the secret tunnels in the palace. It was simply a matter of remembering little landmarks. Often, silly mnemonics worked best, because they stuck in your head. Like the three-way split they were at: It had three curls of vine that sprung out of the top of the hedge, so Gen dubbed it Three Spaghettis. That name would help her distinguish it from other three-way splits in the maze, which wouldn't have the same pasta-like curls.

Besides, knowing your surroundings was crucial for a sleuth, because you never knew when trouble might be coming for you. Good Detective Trait Number One:

Know exactly who and what is around you. At all times.

Fifteen minutes later, she had a pretty good idea of how to get to the middle, where Duke Charlemagne had hinted she'd find what she was looking for. It was a simple matter of a right turn, a left turn, a 180-degree rotation at the hedge with a slight divot in its trunk, then two more rights, three lefts, and then a hairpin turn.

"This should be it," Gen said, just as she and Hill spilled out into a narrow clearing with . . . a rectangular hedge in the middle.

"Um, yay?" Hill said. "We found another hedge?"

Gen scrunched up her face as she studied it. "Yes and no. This isn't the same kind of plant. It seems to be some kind of vine—like ivy—that's grown over something solid, I think. But it *does* look a lot like the other hedges. Probably on purpose." She walked all the way around. "Aha! Hill, I think there's a door behind this."

He hurried over to join her on the other side of the hedge.

All he saw was a thick layer of leaves and branches. "I don't see a door."

"Me neither, but I *do* see that the branches here are a lot younger and thinner than the branches on the rest of the plant. Look." She pointed up, across, and down as if tracing a door frame. And sure enough, Gen was right. Whereas the branches on most of the hedges were an inch thick, the ones here were only an eighth of that. "That means someone has broken these branches more recently, and they had to grow back."

Gen wedged her hand into the vines and felt around. Her fingers grazed over what felt like metal. "I think I just found the door handle. Help me clear the leaves around it!"

They shoved aside handfuls of vine, trying to rip off as little as they could. They didn't want to leave too much evidence that someone had opened the door. Gen figured they'd be able to burrow their way in through some of the branches, since the vines were still young and pliable.

Soon enough, they uncovered a handle.

The door was locked.

Hill slouched. "Now what?"

Gen smiled and pulled her lock-picking kit out of her pocket. Duke Charlemagne wasn't the only one who had a beloved tool he always carried with him.

Hill stood up straight again. "Is that . . ."

"Yep." She took a moment to examine the lock in the handle, then chose the right picks.

Gen had just inserted them into the lock, though, when they heard footsteps a short distance away. Hill looked around frantically. "A guard? But the duke didn't signal us!"

"Shoot," Gen said. "I didn't think about the fact that the patrols could be *inside* the maze, too. " She started jiggling her lock picks faster. She and Hill would have to either run back into a different part of the labyrinth or get inside this door. Whichever one it was going to be, Gen probably only had about ten seconds.

A few leaves fell where she'd pushed them away to access the lock.

Hill started nervously tapping his foot.

Gen shot him a look, and he stopped.

The marching of the guard's boots were getting closer. Gen wondered if it was Monka.

But there was no time to find out. The guard would be rounding the corner any second, and—

Click!

Gen turned the handle and eased the door open a crack. She waved Hill through, then slipped in and closed the door behind them.

She and Hill held their breaths. Oh no! In her haste, she'd forgotten to pick up the leaves that had fallen when she was working on the lock! *Please don't see the leaves please don't see the leaves please don't see the leaves,* Gen thought silently.

The guard's marching got closer.

And then Gen thought she caught the sound of an electronic alarm going off in the distance. "The duke!" she whispered to Hill. "He must've realized what was happening; he's making himself a decoy!"

The guard's marching turned into a run, in the opposite direction of where Gen and Hill were hiding.

"Thank goodness." They both let out huge sighs of relief.

Now they could turn their attention to the room they'd broken into. The light switch didn't work without power, of course, but it didn't matter because the ceiling was entirely glass, and sunlight came beaming through. It looked like someone had taken great care to make sure the vines didn't grow over the top of this place.

"Where are we? A storage bunker?" Hill asked, spinning around to take in the narrow room. There were two file cabinets along one wall, and half the space was full of plastic bins stacked one on top of another.

"Not just any storage bunker," Gen said, walking as if in a trance to one of the corners. She reached out and touched a mannequin that was standing on a long platform. The mannequin wore a white wedding gown covered in delicate lace and beading. At the center of the bodice was an embroidered fox. *The* Raldonian Fox. And around the mannequin's neck was a gold necklace with two charms—one of the letter *A*, and the other shaped like a sun.

Adrienne + Lucas Sun.

Gen swallowed the lump in her throat. "I think this room is storage for all my mom's stuff."

BUGAPALOOZA

N o wonder the queen hadn't wanted to come into the hedge maze the other day. This was where she'd buried her past—everything about the daughter she wanted to erase from the palace and from the kingdom's memory.

And everything Gen had been dying to know.

Unfortunately, she heard shouts in the distance, guards yelling about checking the hedge maze again more carefully. So as much as Gen wanted to spend days going through the plastic bins that probably held her mom's books and memorabilia and other personal things missing from the Princess Suite, Gen didn't have that luxury. She needed to focus on the crucial information she hadn't been able to get anywhere else—what the heck was The Incident, and why was it such a big deal that no one was allowed to talk about it?

"File cabinets," Hill said. "This is just like an underwater room we broke into in *Escape from Octopus Isle*. There was a timer, and if we didn't get the information we needed by the time it expired, the ceiling would collapse and the ocean water would rush in and drown us."

Gen blinked at Hill. "That sounds . . . unpleasant."

"Yeah, my team died about ten times before we figured out how to solve the room. You have to be targeted in what you look for. You can't waste time reading every scrap of paper you get your hands on."

A smile tugged at Gen's mouth. Hill might be new to sleuthing, but he was a really fast learner. His experience as a commander of his gaming crew was helpfully relevant.

"Agreed," she said. "So let's pull anything you can find about what happened to my mom and dad, and why they left Raldonia."

"On it!" Hill flung open the closest set of drawers.

Gen dove into the other file cabinet, her fingers flicking through the folders as fast as she could. They were labeled by year, so for now, she ignored anything from her mom's childhood. Gen would have to find a time and a way to come back later to read through all that.

"All the stuff in here is old," Hill said. "Birth certificates, newspaper clippings about the king and queen coming home from the hospital with your mom."

"Same here," Gen said with dismay as she flipped through folders of her mom's math homework, school art projects of oil pastels and watercolors showing lavender field landscapes and the fishing boats at sea. It was sort of interesting, but not in the way Gen needed it to be.

"We have to go soon," Hill said, anxiously eyeing the door. The guards' voices seemed to be getting closer.

She knew Hill was right. But Gen needed to look in one more place. She yanked open the bottom drawer, expecting to find folders of her mom's later schoolwork, essays about Raldonian economics and trade, that kind of thing.

But instead, Gen found a box full of old USB drives, with stickers on them indicating specific years, starting a couple years before Gen was born and ending a year after.

Were the labels about the information each USB drive contained? They had to be.

"Jackpot!" Gen said.

She and Hill stuffed their pockets with the USB drives as fast as they could. Then they made sure the room looked like it had when they'd entered.

After poking her head out of the door and checking that the coast was clear, Gen climbed out of the bunker, and Hill followed. Gen locked it, and Hill rearranged the vines to hide that they'd been disturbed. Gen swiped the leaves that had previously been torn off and stuffed them in her pockets.

Several pairs of footsteps marched in the labyrinth around them.

Quick! Gen jerked her head to the left to indicate to Hill which way to go.

With her in the lead, they snuck back through the maze. Thank goodness for Gen's earlier mapping. Gen and Hill tiptoed around a block of hedges with a guard on the other side, matching their steps with the guard's and inching away from him as silently as possible. As soon as they were clear of him, they started power-walking. Then Hill began to sprint, but Gen shook her head vigorously. Running would be too loud.

They turned left around a sharp bend in the labyrinth.

Gah. There was a guard only a couple yards away. His back was to them, but Gen had almost run smack into him.

With her heart practically leaping out of her throat, she frantically signaled to Hill to pivot into a dead end. She darted in after him at the last second, just as the guard was turning around.

Did he see us? Hill's panicked look said.

I don't know, Gen mouthed.

They huddled there, pressing themselves against the hedges and holding their breaths.

The guard muttered to himself and clomped around the area for what seemed like forever.

Eventually, though, the sound of his boots retreated farther away.

Gen and Hill exhaled. "That was close," Hill said.

Too close, she thought.

Finally, Gen and Hill slipped out of the exit of the hedge maze. Duke Charlemagne was on the other side of the nearby fountain, hiding behind a set of tall Italian cypresses. He waved subtly at them, and they ran over.

"The power came back on while you two were in there," he explained, "so all Imperial Guard patrols reverted to their usual schedule."

"Ah," Gen said. "That explains why there were so many of them."

The duke nodded. "But did you find what you were looking for?"

"I don't know," Gen said, reaching into her pockets and showing him a couple of the USB drives. "I guess I'll find out when I get back to my computer. But thanks for being our lookout today. Hill and I couldn't have done it without you."

Duke Charlemagne shook his head and smiled. "No need to thank me. I am always happy to assist."

They began to head back to the palace, taking a circuitous route around the Imperial Gardens to make it look like they'd been on a casual stroll, not infiltrating the queen's secret bunker in the middle of the hedge maze. They had just stepped onto the broad driveway leading up to the front of the castle when one of the royal messengers ran up behind them, dripping with sweat.

"Is the queen here?" he panted. His purple uniform was rumpled, and his eyes were wild and panicky. He wasn't addressing anyone in particular. Gen wasn't sure he even knew who he was talking to, since he hadn't bowed or anything.

Duke Charlemagne stepped forward and took charge. "Her Majesty is busy, dealing with the ministers on important matters now that power has been restored to the country. But I can receive your message. What is it?"

The man nodded, sweat dripping down his brow. "A massive infestation has swept through all of the kingdom's lavender. Not just one kind of pest—there are spittle bugs, white flies, aphids, leafhoppers, woolly bear caterpillars, and more. It's like . . ." The messenger shuddered. "It's like the pests coordinated somehow and invaded all at once."

Duke Charlemagne gasped. "The lavender?"

Gen and Hill gasped, too. She remembered how pretty it was, seeing Raldonia from the sky, a purple island in the middle of the sea. And from her lessons with Minister Tallyho, Gen also knew that lavender was the second-biggest Raldonian export, behind seafood. It was an incredibly important source of money for the kingdom.

"A-are you sure?" Duke Charlemagne asked the messenger.

"Yes, sir. All of Raldonia's lavender fields have been destroyed."

Early the next day, Lee arranged for the queen to visit some of the ruined lavender farmers, and Queen Michelina insisted that Gen go with her. Gen was surprised that the queen was lifting her grounding for an outing, but Lee explained this was grave business, and any future leader of Raldonia needed to see not only the kingdom's successes, but its failures and disasters as well.

The queen's limousine pulled up to the first lavender fields, and Gen, Lee, and Queen Michelina stepped out into the dirt.

Seconds later, a woman in overalls stomped through the fields toward the limo. "No! No! No! I will not have that child cursing what is left of my poor farm! Didn't your daughter already do enough?!"

Oh no . . . This wasn't just *any* lavender farm. These fields and vineyards belonged to none other than I-believe-in-the-curse Anita, the one who'd ranted at Gen in the town square.

And Anita was so upset now, she even dared to yell at the queen.

Gen staggered backward, pressing herself against the limo.

Lee's face went fluorescent pink like her blouse, and she simultaneously looked like she was about to faint. She'd probably never witnessed anyone who didn't bow to the queen, let alone shout at her.

Queen Michelina, however, was unfazed. "Gen, why don't you wait in the limo?" she said quietly. Gen gratefully threw herself back inside and pulled the door almost—but not quite—shut behind her. (That way, she'd still be able to hear everything outside clearly.)

The queen turned to Anita. "You have every reason to be upset, my dear." Her voice was as soothing as a warm bubble bath. "I cannot begin to express how sorry I am over what's happened to your flowers, and to all the lavender farmers in the kingdom. My ministers are working on financial relief for you and all who were affected. But I came personally today to see if there was anything else we could do for you."

Gen frowned. The queen had never used that tone of understanding or kindness with her. Why not? She was her own granddaughter. Didn't Gen deserve the same gentle-ness as Anita?

Hearing the queen's genuine concern, the furious red in Anita's face drained away. "I— I apologize, Your Majesty. You're right. I'm mad—*beyond* mad—but you coming in person to visit gives me hope. Would you, er, like to see the damage the pests caused?"

"Yes, please," the queen said, gesturing Gen to come out of the limo.

"No," Anita said. "I know I'm being rude, but I don't want *her* to come." She pointed an accusatory finger at Gen through the window.

"I assure you, the princess is not the cause of—"

"With all due respect, Your Majesty... no." Anita crossed her arms.

As before, Queen Michelina took it all in stride. She didn't even hesitate before she said, "Very well. Gen, stay in the limo. Lee and I will be back soon." And with that, Lee hurried after the queen and Anita into the lavender fields, leaving Gen in the car with the chauffeur.

What was the point of my even coming today? Gen thought, fuming. She'd much rather be back in her room, because she hadn't had time yet to go through the USB drives from the secret bunker. Instead, she was stuck here on political goodwill visits, which so far had turned out to mean getting yelled at for a curse that wasn't her fault (or even plausible!), then being left behind as if she were an old coat the queen decided she didn't need.

"Um . . ." The chauffeur wasn't sure what to do with his

sudden new babysitting duties. "There's some chocolate back there in the pullout table if you want it."

Gen started to reach for the compartment he was talking about. But she also eyed the still-open limo door, and an idea came to her.

"Actually," she said to the chauffeur, "I'm pretty zonked from all the hubbub over the lavender. Do you mind if I put up the partition and take a nap?"

"Not at all, Your Highness," he said, voice steadier and clearly relieved that there was an easy solution to their time together. "I'll raise the privacy divider right now." He pushed a button up front, and the opaque, soundproof partition slid up.

He wouldn't be able to see or hear a thing in the backseat of the limo.

Perfect, Gen thought.

She gave the driver a minute to settle in. Then Gen slipped out of the door (thankful she hadn't shut it all the way, because it didn't make any noise as she opened it now) and slunk around the edge of the limo, keeping low just in case the chauffeur happened to be looking at the rearview mirror or something.

When she was out of his line of sight, Gen hurried toward the nearby lavender fields, but in the opposite direction that Queen Michelina, Lee, and Anita had gone. If the queen was going to drag Gen out to see the devastation caused by all the bugs, then Gen was going to make sure she actually saw it.

The scent of lavender filled the air, and for a moment,

Gen felt relaxed. Lavender was a huge part of Raldonia's trade because the flowers were prized not only for their beauty, but also for their calming properties. Dried lavender blossoms were used as remedies for everything from anxiety to headaches, and lavender oil could relieve tired muscles and even help with insomnia. Or so people claimed. Gen didn't know if any of it was true, but that didn't change the fact that the world wanted lots of lavender, and they were willing to enter into favorable trade agreements with Raldonia in order to get it.

As Gen actually stepped foot into the lavender fields, though, she came to a screeching halt.

What the—

Instead of rows of beautiful purple blooms, an endless expanse of dead flowers drooped on limp stems. Bugs had gnawed through almost all the petals and leaves, and the ground was littered with them, like wilted, compost confetti. For as far as Gen could see, it was more of the same: slumped, lifeless flowers shedding their hole-ridden petals onto the dirt.

No wonder Anita thought it was the curse. How could anything natural destroy an entire kingdom's lavender fields in a single day?

Could *it be me?* Gen thought.

But she dismissed the idea as quickly as it'd come, because that was, quite frankly, preposterous. Something else was going on here—something *huge*—and Gen was more determined than ever to get to the bottom of it.

Not only to save her own future, but also to save Raldonia's.

HURRICANE GEN

First, Raldonian fishermen lost forty-eight million pounds of seafood.

Then the power went out across the kingdom for almost four days.

After that, pests gnawed through all the lavender grown in Raldonia.

Gen was pretty certain it couldn't get worse.

Until a day later, when a freak hurricane manifested out of nowhere and slammed into the island. The wind knocked down phone lines and tore trees out by their roots, and the waves sent boats careening into piers. Streets flooded, and by the time the hurricane subsided, the beaches and harbors were a disaster, and all the homes and shops near the coasts were soggy shambles.

Gen worried about Jonah and his small cottage by the shore. Had he been able to evacuate to higher ground? Had he lost his home and everything else?

Another urgent meeting convened in the throne room, attended by Queen Michelina, Duke Charlemagne, Lee, all the ministers, and the team from Hotshots PR.

Several guards provided security for the high-level meeting, including Monka, who had seemed to, once again, manage to be in the right place at the right time.

Hmm.

Gen eavesdropped again from behind the tapestry.

"The citizenry are devastated, Your Majesty," Duke Charlemagne said.

"And Raldonia has nothing left to trade," Minister Tallyho moaned. "It's absolute calamity. It will almost bankrupt the imperial treasury to help pay for hurricane repairs, in addition to supporting the lavender farmers who've been harmed by the beetle infestation and the fishermen affected by the seafood disaster."

"Something must be done," Duke Charlemagne said.

A moment of silence settled in the throne room. Gen leaned in a little farther, worried she might miss what was said next.

Queen Michelina made a tiny sniffing noise, which Gen had learned meant she disapproved of whatever had been said last. "You are the imperial chancellor, Duke Charlemagne. What more can we do?"

But it was Lee who jumped in. "Talk of the curse is spreading like a forest fire, Your Majesty. You witnessed it yourself with many of the farmers you visited yesterday. And it's gone beyond the lavender community. What was once viewed as an outdated old legend has gained credibility.

In other words, more and more of Raldonia believes that Princess Genevieve's arrival caused all these misfortunes."

Behind the tapestry, Gen clenched her fists. *It's not really my fault. I'm just the scapegoat.*

There had to be a logical explanation for everything that had happened. The acid-like orange spots on the seafood were obviously not caused by a freak algae bloom, no matter what Lee and Hotshots PR wanted the public to think. The timing was way too suspicious.

And what about the power outage? In Gen's lessons with the minister of public works, she'd learned that the kingdom's electricity grid was state of the art, one of the best in the world. So it seemed impossible to Gen that the Raldonian Gas and Electric Company had zero clues as to how the whole kingdom lost power, and no rationale for why it had taken almost four days to get things back up and running. That just stank of dishonesty. What were they hiding, and why?

As for the bugs, they weren't intelligent enough to plan a coordinated attack on the lavender, yet it was too perfectly synchronized to be a fluke of nature.

Could Anita have been involved? She'd made it very clear in the town square that she didn't like Gen. And Gen remembered something Anita had said: *The curse is already back. It's going to get worse, too.* That sounded awfully like a threat now that she thought about it.

Gen peered out from the tapestry. *How can the adults running this kingdom not see the suspicious patterns here?*

But Gen also knew from experience that she couldn't

burst into the throne room and tell this to the queen and her advisors. Grown-ups didn't listen when kids presented hypotheses without evidence; they always dismissed it as "childish, overactive imagination." Besides, Gen didn't want to reveal her suspicions in front of everyone yet. Especially with Lee and Monka around.

Gen needed to gather more intel in order to assemble her case. And the most recent disaster—the hurricane— was at the top of her to-investigate list.

She'd do what she could within the castle walls, but she also needed to get back out to see what was really going on in the kingdom. (Gen had decided on a flexible inter- pretation of being grounded for life. It was for the good of Raldonia, really.)

First stop: the offices of the Royal Weather Service.

TODAY'S FORECAST: FOGGY WITH A CHANCE OF COINCIDENCE

The Royal Weather Service offices were in a triangular building, and the way the streetlamps reflected off the pointy top at night cast an eerie glow. It looked like that creepy pyramid on the back of American dollar bills, the one with the floating all-seeing eye above it. The Royal Weather Service logo glowed in that halo, as if it were tracking Gen's every movement since she'd arrived five minutes ago.

A chill tremored through her spine, and Gen wished Hill was with her, like he often was when she snuck out of the palace. In fact, she wondered whether it had been wise to sneak out tonight at all.

She could still go back. She'd moved through the secret tunnels and to the king's half of the Monarch Suites. It was easy enough, since she'd researched the patrol schedules earlier, before she and Hill had snuck out the first time. The Imperial Guard didn't patrol the king's side, and Gen had slipped through the empty, dusty rooms where all the furniture was covered in sheets, then out of the palace. It was a twenty-minute jog from there to the Royal Weather Service and its creepy, all-seeing eye.

It's not really watching me, Gen tried to convince herself.

Still, she wanted to get inside as fast as she could.

As usual, Gen had her lockpicking kit with her in her backpack, along with a few other tools. But before she could choose a door, she heard whistling and the jingling of keys from the parking lot, coming nearer to her. She plastered herself to a shadowed part of the wall.

A woman in a janitor's uniform came into view under a streetlamp. *Oooh, maybe I can follow her in.*

She waited until the janitor had unlocked the front door and gone inside. Right before the door shut, Gen caught the handle. She held it so that it looked closed, just in case the woman turned back, but in reality, the latch hadn't caught.

Once the janitor's whistling had grown faint, Gen slipped inside the Royal Weather Service.

Now what?

Gen needed to look at the recent logs of storms and wind patterns. If she could have done this from the comfort of the Princess Suite, she would have, but unfortunately, this level of information wasn't available online. Probably because most ordinary people didn't care about detailed meteorological data. (Or possibly also because the RWS's IT systems needed to be updated, just like the palace's did. Maybe that was a project Gen could tackle when she was officially a princess: Raldonian technology upgrade.)

For now, though, it meant Gen needed to find a computer to hack into. She listened again for the janitor. Thankfully, the woman was a dedicated whistler, and Gen could tell she was starting her cleaning on the far end of the first floor.

To be safe, Gen would work on the second floor.

She tiptoed up the stairs. Here, there was a long corridor of private offices with locked doors. She started to reach for her picks, but then stopped. The bosses wouldn't be the ones with the kinds of records that she wanted to look at. Later, if Gen uncovered anything questionable in the weather logs, she'd break into these offices to see if there was some grand plan to cause a hurricane.

But I seriously doubt that's possible, Gen thought. Her hunch was that the hurricane was a really, really bad coincidence that just so happened to hit Raldonia right after the seafood disaster, power outage, and pest infestation.

At the end of the dark hall, Gen found what she was looking for: a big room with several computers, and maps of Raldonia, Europe, and the entire world pinned up to the wall. She sat down at a computer that was hidden from view from the door. Gen didn't want to take any chances if the janitor's keys suddenly stopped jingling or if she decided to stop whistling.

Gen rubbed her hands together in excitement as she booted up the computer. A login screen appeared, asking for a username and password.

She had a password-breaking program she'd written back in New York, which, when plugged into the port of any computer, granted her full network access in thirty seconds or less. (Usually less.) But oftentimes, people were a lot worse at cybersecurity than they ought to be. They'd leave sticky notes on their keyboards with their login information. (Not the case here, oh well.) Or they'd use their own birthday, which was easy enough for even the most amateur of hackers to figure out with a quick internet search. Worst of all (or best, if you're looking from the hacker's point of view), they'd do something they thought was clever but was actually super common: They'd use the word *password* as their password.

"Let's give it a try," Gen said, wiggling her fingers over the keyboard as if warming them up.

She typed *admin* into the username field. This was short for *administrator*, which was the name for the master account on any computer. If Gen could get access to the computer as an admin, it would grant her a lot more permissions than if she were logged on just as the user assigned to the machine.

Then she entered in *password* in the password field.

Password is incorrect.

"Darn." But at the same time, Gen was glad that the computer was better secured than something a simple hack could thwart. She didn't want the Royal Weather Service to be subjected to dangerous cyber attacks. She just wanted to be able to look at their storm logs.

She retrieved her password breaker from her backpack—

one of the few possessions she'd taken from New York—and plugged it into one of the computer's open ports. Numbers flashed by on the screen, tallying the possible passwords it was plugging into the login screen.

In 22.17 seconds, the login screen disappeared, and the main Royal Weather Service dashboard appeared on the monitor.

Gen unplugged her password breaker and kissed it. "You are a work of art." (She was well aware that she was complimenting her own genius, since she was the one who wrote the program. But come on, it was pretty awesome!)

The janitor was vacuuming downstairs. Gen started clicking through different files on the screen. The user interface was clunky. Seriously, the font was green and blocky on a plain black background that looked like it dated back to whenever Duke Charlemagne's PalmPad was invented.

With tech like this, there's no way the RWS could have some secret invention that would grow a storm out of nowhere.

Seriously, if they did, Raldonia wouldn't be worrying about spoiled seafood and wilted lavender. Instead they'd be selling their weather device all over the world and making humongo bucks. If they could create rain at will, it would solve so many crises—droughts, wildfires, world hunger.

Eventually, Gen found what she was looking for: detailed, minute-by-minute records of recent weather patterns.

But it had data not only for Raldonia, but the entire world. There were too many numbers to sort through just by reading them, and the whirring of the janitor's vacuum was getting closer.

"Time to write a script to make this go faster," Gen said. And because she had admin access, she could pull up a command script or open up the computer IDE (Integrated Drive Electronics) and code a quick program that would process all this data for her, sorting it into something more coherent.

Her fingers flew over the keyboard, and after double-checking her code, Gen hit RUN.

Like her password program, this data-sorting script worked at supersonic speeds. Soon, Gen had a spreadsheet with all the weather patterns organized by region, by temperature, by potential causality, by wind currents, etc. and cross-referenced with other events like crop harvesting, mammal or insect migration, and more.

If Gen only looked at what had been happening in Europe, then she'd get to the same conclusion that others had: The hurricane had materialized out of the blue.

But if the meteorologists had had the benefit of Gen's data-sorting program, they might have seen what she did: The seed of the storm had started off the Eastern coast of Africa last week, then traveled a circuitous (and non-intuitive) route down to Antarctica, then dovetailed with an abnormally large migration of whales that caused a wind pattern that whipped the small storm into a hurricane that went careening into Raldonia.

This was all the evidence she needed to show that the hurricane was caused by natural forces.

"Thank you, science," Gen said to herself as she downloaded the information onto a thumb drive.

Now she just had to get proof that the curse wasn't the cause of everything else.

SHIVERRR ME TIMBERRRS

Gen snuck out every single day for the next week. Often, Hill went with her if it was before dawn and his kitchen duties. It was on one of those early mornings that they found out Jonah was safe; his house, sadly, had been destroyed by the hurricane, but Sam and Ethel had taken him into theirs.

Sometimes, though, Gen would slip out of the palace at night, making sure to get back while everyone was still asleep.

One night, as she tiptoed back into the Imperial Gardens, a man cleared his throat.

Gen froze.

"Good evening, Your Highness," Monka said as he stepped out from behind the topiary of a dragon. "I had a feeling I'd meet you here."

Not good, not good, not good.

Her face must've betrayed her, because he laughed.

"Don't worry, I won't tell the queen you've been breaking her rules. As far as she's concerned, you're abiding by your grounding and staying put in your suite."

Gen exhaled. Not fully, because she still didn't know what Monka wanted, but at least Queen Michelina and her icy glare wouldn't be involved.

"Uh, thanks," Gen said, trying her best to keep her voice casual, like it wasn't a big deal he'd just caught her in the gardens at midnight. "It's a lovely evening for a stroll, isn't it?"

Monka laughed again. "I'm not as oblivious as the rest of the adults here, Your Highness. But I *am* curious what a twelve-year-old girl might be doing in the city at so late an hour."

Gen couldn't decide whether there was menace laced through his tone, or if it was just that he hadn't used his voice in a while. He probably didn't talk to many people during night patrol.

Still, she needed to be careful what she told Monka. If he was out here waiting for her, that meant he was at least a little suspicious of her, which in turn meant that Gen had to give him enough information that he felt like he'd succeeded in catching her at something. (But she wouldn't actually tell him the truth.)

"I'll tell you if you promise not to roll your eyes at me," she said.

"I would never," Monka said.

"Okay, but let's go into the hedge maze." Even though it was late and nobody was around, she wanted to be extra sure they had privacy. Being a master eavesdropper also meant Gen was aware that others could be listening in on her at any time, too.

Monka let her go first.

Is this a test? Gen thought. Maybe he wanted to see if she knew where she was going. Did he suspect—or know—that she'd been in the maze before? And the secret bunker?

Gen walked with the kind of confidence Monka probably expected from a kid who was about to be crowned princess, but she made sure that she led them straight into a dead end.

"Shoot," she said. "Well, let's try this way instead."

Gen proceeded to lead them into another dead end. "Seems like I have a knack for going the wrong direction."

She retraced their steps, then marched off on a different path, which ended at a wall of hedges. "Another dead end!" Gen threw up her arms in fake exasperation.

"Actually, Your Highness, this is the same dead end as last time," Monka said with a hint of superiority.

"It is?"

"Yes. We went in a circle."

"We did?" Gen pretended to pout. (But in reality, she knew perfectly well that they'd gone in a circle. She'd planned it that way to convince Monka she had no idea what she was doing in the maze.)

"Would Your Highness like me to show her to a bench where she can rest and then tell me what she's doing out here in the middle of the night?"

"That would be amazing," Gen said. "I have a headache

just trying to remember where the entrance to this thing was."

Once at the bench, Gen confessed to Monka. "I've been trying to get to the bottom of the problems going on in the kingdom. I know more and more people are blaming the curse, but I'm not buying it."

Why did she come right out and tell this to one of her prime suspects? Because Gen wanted to see if he'd do anything to reveal himself.

But Monka didn't flinch. He was an Imperial Guard, the best of the best of Raldonia's soldiers, trained to perform under stress and duress.

Still, it seemed he was already wary of her; isn't that why he was lurking out here in the gardens, to run into her? So Gen was going to throw Monka a bone and make him think that was all there was to it. Good Detective Trait Number Three:

**If you're going undercover,
the best disguise is one that the crooks will never suspect.**

In this case, that meant 'fessing up to her investigation, but looking incompetent about it. Gen wanted Monka to think she was as lousy at sleuthing as she was at finding her way through a maze.

"No offense, Your Highness," Monka asked. "But Raldonia has a lot of great minds working on this."

"Sometimes kids connect dots that grown-ups don't see. Like, for example, the letter *R*."

Monka raised a brow under the moonlight. "The letter *R*?"

"Yeah. Have you noticed that the letter *R* is involved in all the disasters so far?

"Spoiled seafood: *R*aldonian sh*r*imp.

"Powe*r* outages: *R*aldonian Gas and Elect*r*ic Company.

"Lavende*r* infestation: leafhoppe*r*s and woolly bea*r* caterpilla*r*s.

"And the hu*r*ricane: *R*oyal Weathe*r* Se*r*vice."

"Er . . ." Monka stammered.

"Exactly! *Er!* The sound that *R* makes!"

Monka stared at her with his mouth open. It was exactly the reaction Gen had been hoping for. An OMG-the-princess-is-a-clueless-child reaction. (This was a lesson Gen had learned from being a foster kid back in New York: Adults often expected so much less of kids than they were capable of. And Gen knew how to play that to her advantage.)

"O-kaaay," Monka said. "But what does this have to do with your sneaking out of the palace?"

"I wanted to see for myself that my theory was right. So I visited the docks, the utilities company, and the weather service. Sure enough, all their names had *R*'s in them."

"Wow," Monka said.

Gen was pretty sure that was an I-can't-believe-this-girl-is-that-dense kind of wow. But she pretended to take it as a compliment. "I know! This could be a huge breakthrough. Now we just need to find out *why* the letter *R* is involved, and *who* has a motive to use it. Like, is there someone who particularly loves *R*'s and would use it as their calling card for their crimes? That's what villains in movies always do— they leave some kind of symbol or other sign to claim the crime, to rub it in the good guys' faces. So I want to ask the queen if we can do a search for citizens with multiple *R*'s in their names."

"Well, Your Highness, I'm impressed with your initiative." Monka said it with the placating tone of someone who didn't want to burst a kid's bubble and therefore would let the kid continue imagining up whatever she wanted to. "I was concerned you were getting into mischief, but you've proved me wrong. I'm glad."

"You are?" Gen asked. "And you're not going to tell me to stop investigating?"

"Of course not," Monka said. "I understand that sometimes, you can rely on no one but yourself to get an important job done. However, please be careful."

"Careful?"

"Occasionally, when you dig too much, people get nervous. And nervous people can make bad things happen."

Gen shivered, and she wasn't sure if it was because the night had suddenly gotten colder, or if Monka's warning reminded her that she wasn't rescuing action figures from teenaged skateboarders anymore. Gen was in the big leagues now, unofficially involved in government espionage.

She swallowed hard. "Thanks for looking out for me," Gen said.

Monka bowed slightly. "Of course, Your Highness. I'd do anything if I thought it was good for Raldonia. *Anything.*"

RAPUNZEL'S TOWER, WITHOUT ALL THE HAIR

Gen's coronation was only one week away, but during her regular eavesdropping in the tunnels and whenever she and Hill snuck out of the palace, Gen heard more and more reports that the kingdom was in an awful state of panicky despondence. Everyone was on edge from the bug infestation and hurricane, and the national mood was *not* celebratory.

At one of the latest meetings she'd listened in on, Lee and Hotshots PR suggested that Queen Michelina find a way to cheer up the kingdom. So the queen declared a National Raldonian Cake Day. Gen begrudgingly admitted that it was a good idea, even if it *did* come from Lee and her publicity minions.

The queen commissioned Hill's dad to come up with a new recipe for the occasion, and his cinnamon-roll pound cake with toffee crunch topping was an instant hit. The kicker was a thin layer of moon drop grape jam running through the center, which Hill had come up with. Bakeries around the kingdom could barely keep up with the orders, and those who couldn't buy a cake baked their own at home. The secret to making it all taste so good was rich Raldonian butter, which came from the Brillat-Savarin farm.

On the morning of National Raldonian Cake Day, every single citizen ate a slice (or two or three) for breakfast. And every single citizen was filled with pride at the simple yet extraordinary delights their country could create.

Duke Charlemagne brought an entire pound cake to Gen's room, just for her. She barely had time for a couple bites before her first lessons of the day began. She decided she'd save it for a snack between lectures—and perhaps sneak into the kitchens to add some ice cream.

Unfortunately, Gen's plans and Raldonia's sweet celebration were short-lived, because that afternoon, the same royal messenger who'd delivered the bad news about the lavender fields returned to the palace. His skin was grayish-green and lumpy, more suited to a toad than a man. He stumbled into the entryway and fell to his knees on the marble floor.

"Mysterious malady," he gasped. "Curse . . . Everyone's skin . . . All over Raldonia . . ." Then he made a deep ribbiting sound (again, very toad-like) and passed out cold.

The Imperial Guard sounded an alarm. "Emergency protocol, red level! Repeat, emergency protocol, red level!"

Gen had fallen asleep at her desk, drooling on her homework, when Monka charged into her rooms. "Your

Highness! There's been another disaster. You need to come with me, now!"

Suspicion spiked in Gen's veins, even as she rubbed the sleep from her eyes. What was happening? Was this a trick? What was Monka up to?

The captain of the guard rushed into the Princess Suite. "Your Highness, something's happening across the kingdom that's turning people into toads," he said. "Not literally, but close enough. We don't know what it is yet, only that many have already been struck by this cur—" He stopped himself before he finished, but Gen knew he'd meant to say *curse*.

Still, she could now believe that something bad really was happening. If it had just been Monka, Gen would've been dubious. But she had no reason to suspect his boss.

"You need to come with us so we can protect you," Monka said. "Under Imperial Protocol section 7.553 subsection (b), in the case of imminent threat, the monarch and all direct descendants of the throne must be immediately separated from one another and securely isolated from the rest of the population."

"Why?" Gen said. "You didn't do that when there was a power outage."

The captain and Monka looked at each other as if neither wanted to spell it out. Finally, the captain said, with lowered voice, "Last time, we had confirmation that the palace was secure. But this time . . . we don't understand the threat. So we have to make sure that at least you or the queen survive whatever this malady is. *Someone* has to be able to rule Raldonia."

Holy mackerel.

Now Gen was wide-awake. She grabbed her backpack, stuffed a few things into it, and hurried out the door after Monka and the captain.

Monka led Gen to one of the Cinderella-looking towers. Actually, it was probably more like Rapunzel's tower.

As Gen moved through the dusty corridors, she realized it was more complicated than Rapunzel's though. The tower wasn't just a single spiraling staircase to a solitary room at the top. It was much wider, full of its own labyrinthine hallways. Gen tried to make a mental map, but Monka kept rushing her, passing by broom closets with rusty doorknobs, then turning into another meandering hallway, then up more winding stairs through crumbling archways and cracked wooden doors. It was clear no one ever came up here.

When they finally arrived at the room at the top of the tower, Gen peeked out the solitary window. She saw that she was many, many stories above the ground. Probably like seventy plus feet high. No evil, toad skin–causing curse was getting in; not even a person could scale those smooth, straight walls.

Then it occurred to her: What if the Imperial Guard wasn't protecting her from the rest of Raldonia? What if it was the opposite—Gen was being isolated to protect *Raldonia* from *her*? From the Curse of the Tainted Throne?

"Sit tight, Your Highness. Someone will be up in a little while to bring provisions," Monka said. Then he locked the door from outside.

Gen's heart sank.

She really was cordoned off in nowhere land. She walked through, inspecting the living quarters. The room itself was decorated for a royal, with hardwood floors and heavy drapes, a canopy bed and a big marble fireplace. But the air smelled simultaneously damp and stale, and it was clear the tower had been hastily cleaned—there were still spiderwebs in the ceiling corners and dust bunnies behind the big rocking chair.

Then there was the matter of the steel box on the bed.

Gen lifted the lid, finding a vial labeled POISON TESTER, a dagger, and several flares to shoot from the window. She felt sick just looking at the self-defense box; this tower really was outfitted as a worst-case-scenario room. It was beginning to sink in that being royalty didn't only mean wearing silk gowns and speaking with a soft Raldonian accent. It also meant people might try to kill you.

Gen gulped, hard.

When dinner arrived, it was pushed through a small panel at the base of the door, presumably so assassins couldn't burst in to attack her. There was a fancy-looking plate covered by a silver dome, but inside was just an MRE— Meal, Ready to Eat—a hermetically sealed, military pouch of food. In this case, it was BBQ pork in a can and just-add-water octopus casserole.

A notecard reminded her to add a drop of the poison testing fluid into her meal before eating. If it turned purple, the food was safe. Orange, and it wasn't.

Orange ... Gen knit her brows as the color reminded her of something. Oh, of course. Jonah had mentioned strange orange spots on his spoiled fish and shrimp. And Lee had decided to tell the public there was an orange algae bloom that damaged the seafood.

It didn't make Gen feel safer about eating her dinner.

Still, this just-add-water, MRE octopus would have been dehydrated and packed away long before the recent disaster. Gen added water to rehydrate the meal, then dutifully tested it.

The droplet sizzled on the octopus.

After a few seconds, it turned purple. Gen's pulse slowed. Just a little.

The food was . . . one step above awful. But she was so hungry, she ate it anyway. She hoped the poison testing kit was right, because Gen would hate for her last meal to be reconstituted octopus.

After dinner, she unpacked the meager set of things she'd brought in her backpack. Her lock picks, her baby blanket (as a foster kid used to being shuttled from home to home on short notice, Gen automatically scooped up that blanket to take with her whenever anyone informed her of another move), her mom's Raldonian-language textbook (Gen liked going through the lessons and imagining a young Princess

Adrienne doing the same thing), the digital picture frame Trish had given her to tinker with, and the USB drives that she and Hill had swiped from the secret bunker.

In the past week, Gen had had her hands so full with investigating the disasters that were supposedly caused by the curse, she hadn't had a chance yet to look at the contents of the USB drives. But the one silver lining of being locked up here in the tower was uninterrupted time for herself.

She picked up the digital picture frame. Gen had originally intended it for Hopper, but she'd realized that the operating system and memory capacity of the picture frame was too slow for the AI program, and had to stick to her desktop. That didn't mean the frame couldn't help her read whatever was on these USB sticks though.

Gen picked the USB drive labeled with the year of her birth and plugged it into the digital frame.

After a minute, a directory appeared on the screen. But even though there were a ton of files on this USB drive, there were only two folders: Granddaughter Photos and News Clippings.

If she wanted information about her parents, Gen probably ought to open the News Clippings file first. But she was too curious about herself—presumably, she was the "granddaughter"—so she opened that folder first.

There were thousands of photos, organized by Gen's age: Week 1, Week 2, Two Months Old, Three Months Old, etc.

She clicked open the Week 1 folder. Inside were photos of herself as a baby, but even more importantly, her mom and dad, looking so carefree and happy, cooing over their daughter. Her mom had lush, wavy chestnut-colored hair; a round, rosy face; and the kind of bright personality that shone even from a photograph. Her dad was raven-haired, with deep brown eyes that smiled at the edges and broad, muscled shoulders that made him look like a warrior prince from an ancient legend. Gen had her mom's hair and her dad's eyes and maybe, she wanted to believe, their bold and brave spirits. She reached out and touched the screen as if that could bring them closer to her.

"Hi, Mommy, hi, Daddy," Gen whispered, not even caring that it sounded juvenile. Besides the picture that Agents 34 and 43 had shown her, these were the only images she'd ever seen of her parents. A knot formed in Gen's chest, and she couldn't tell if it was sadness or happiness or a little of both.

If Mom and Dad knew me today, would they be proud of who I've become?

There were so many more photos, too. Dad pretending to feed Baby Gen a hot dog at a Yankees game. Mom showing Baby Gen all the light-up gadgets at the Hall of Science. All three of them smiling with Santa Claus at Christmas. The pictures made Gen smile now, too.

It wasn't until she was well into her Five-Months-Old pictures before it occurred to her—where did all these pictures come from? None of them looked like her mom or dad knew they were being taken.

Had Queen Michelina hired someone to snap photos of them?

That was . . . a little creepy. But also surprisingly tender that the queen—who Gen had come to think of as the Ice Monarch—would care enough to want pictures of her grandchild.

What had happened to the queen and Gen's mom that put a rift between them? What was the Incident that no one was allowed to talk about?

Gen glanced out the tower window. The sun had set quite a while ago, and it was starting to get chilly. She made a fire using the log rack and a book of matches near the hearth, and then she dove into the News Clippings folder on the drive.

They were articles about the car crash that killed her parents.

And there were only four of them.

Gen had half expected big *New York Times* headlines like, "Princess and Family Killed in Devastating Wreck." But when she saw only small, two-sentence reports in local newspapers' police blotter sections, Gen remembered that no one in the United States had known who her parents were. The sum total of the news clippings amounted to: "1:36 a.m. Car crashed into tree on I-95. No survivors."

Tears trickled down Gen's cheeks at the family she'd had, and lost. A vibrant, clever mom and a strong, funny dad.

She let herself feel the sadness for a while. But then eventually, the other USB drives called to her, as well as the mystery of the Incident that broke her family apart.

Get yourself together, Detective, Gen thought.

Wiping away the last of her tears, she plugged in a USB

drive from the year before her birth. There wasn't much on it, other than photos of her mom, pregnant, and her dad. Walking around their neighborhood in New York, eating at sidewalk cafés, and enjoying, from the looks of it, being totally unknown in America.

But the next USB drive—from two years before Gen was born—contained *only* news clippings, and no photos. All the articles were from Raldonian and European papers, tabloids, and magazines. And there were a ton of them.

"Wedding Disaster! Is the Curse of Raldonia Real?"

"What Was Princess Adrienne Thinking? Marriage to Commoner Breaks Centuries-Old Royal Lineage"

"Imperial Bloodline Muddled— The Future of Raldonia Is at Stake!"

"Princess Adrienne and Baseborn Hubby Whine: 'The Media Is Killing Us. We Can't Take the Heat!'"

"Is the Scrutiny on Princess Adrienne and Her Husband Unfair?"

"Queen Michelina Ashamed of Princess; Duke Charlemagne Attempts to Reconcile Them"

"Breaking News: Princess Adrienne Will Reportedly Renounce Claim to Raldonian Crown"

"Scandal Alert! Where Have the Princess
and Her Husband Gone?"

"Once-Warm Queen Michelina Turns Frosty—Is
Her Daughter's Disappearance to Blame?"

Gen read every single article. Many were over-the-top, sensationalized to sell more copies or get more clicks. But now she finally understood what the Incident was: After a string of disasters that seemed to amount to some very bad luck (like the rat infestation at Anita's farm), the wedding of Gen's mom and dad was drastically downsized to a private, family-only affair, rather than the grand, kingdom-wide celebration it was intended to be. But the damage had already been done, and belief in an old curse—*the* curse Gen was dealing with now—had been resurrected.

According to the articles, the Curse of the Tainted Throne had begun back in 1343 when King Herbert married Leonida Crow, a non-royal rumored to be a witch because "only a deal with the devil could have made a woman so beautiful." Shortly after their wedding, King Herbert—who had been fit as a fiddle until then—suddenly keeled over and died. Raldonians went berserk, stormed the castle, seized the queen, and burned her at the stake. Leonida Crow cackled as the flames grew around her, and the last thing she said was, "You will pay for this! Raldonia shall never escape this curse!" Gen's eyebrows shot up. What a story.

She kept reading. Legend had it, the kingdom suffered

for the next twenty years—bees abandoned Raldonia and no crops could grow; tidal waves pummeled the shore, making it impossible for ships to bring trade to harbor; and King Herbert's brother, Fergus, who'd inherited the crown, merely huddled in fear in the palace, afraid to do anything in case the curse killed him, too.

Of course, historians had since proven that those "curse-related events" were mere coincidence. There was a documented, continent-wide bee shortage during the mid-1300s, and a couple years of bad winter storms that seemed to have become exaggerated into tidal waves. As for the failing economy of Raldonia during that time, that was the fault of weak King Fergus not doing anything to lead the country.

And yet, the curse persisted through the centuries. Only two other Raldonian royals dared to marry a "commoner," and every time, fear-mongers whipped up a frenzy, linking unrelated misfortunes to the weddings.

It was no different when Gen's parents got married. After the ceremony, the press wouldn't leave them alone. They drummed up panic and paranoia about the curse, and although they did get a lot more clicks on their "news" websites, they also drove an irredeemable wedge between the royal family and the Raldonian public.

It seemed like Queen Michelina blamed her daughter—Gen's mom—for the kingdom's strife. If Princess Adrienne had cared enough about Raldonia, the story went, then she would have married someone from one of the many royal families in Asia, Africa, or Europe. Instead, she selfishly chose to fall in love with Lucas Sun, whose father was the ambassador from South Mallanthra.

There was nothing wrong at all with South Mallanthra, of course. They were a small but mighty economic powerhouse in Asia with an imperial family. But Princess Adrienne didn't choose one of the South Mallanthran princes when they came to Raldonia for trade talks and attended political summits. She fell for Lucas, who was smart and handsome and . . . common-born. And in so choosing, Princess Adrienne recklessly, unforgivably picked love over duty to her country and its age-old traditions.

At the end of all the articles, there was a single, different file. It was close to three in the morning now and Gen's eyes were drooping, but still, she opened the document.

Raldonian Intelligence Agency, Confidential Report

Per Her Majesty the Queen's request, all news outlets have been financially persuaded to take offline any and all articles regarding the Incident.

Thereafter, the RIA performed a thorough survey of internet archives, search engine results, and other databases and can confirm that no mentions of the Incident remain publicly accessible.

```
We can also confirm that the princess and
her husband have successfully integrated
into New York City anonymously.


No further action required.


End Report.
```

So that was that, huh? But something niggled at Gen, a missing puzzle piece that didn't make sense. If Queen Michelina was so relieved to see her daughter and son-in-law renounce and leave Raldonia, then why, years later, did she send the RIA to bring Gen back to become heir to the throne?

Gen yawned. She didn't mean to, but it was really late, and her eyes were crossing from staring at the little screen for too long. She'd have to deal with the question about the queen's motives later, when she wasn't exhausted.

After shutting down the digital frame, Gen crawled into bed. She had just started to doze off when she heard strange voices, light and ethereal and echoey at the same time. Like fairies trying to communicate from another realm.

Oh boy, I'm starting to lose it, Gen thought groggily. Or maybe she was coming down with the toad-skin malady—did toads dream of fairies?

The echoey talking sounded again. Although exhausted, Gen wasn't the type to leave an enigma alone, so she climbed out of bed, unlocked the heavy wooden door with her picks, and tiptoed out to follow the voices.

Gen was good with mazes when she was fully awake, but right now, the tower was disorienting. Still, she was surprised when she got lost. Her internal compass spun around in her head uselessly, and the odd voices disappeared before she could find their source. Also, Gen had ended up inside a broom closet full of dried up, musty mops.

Major fail.

She sighed, tried to retrace her steps, and got lost again. It was another hour before she found the correct staircase and climbed up to return to her room.

By the time Gen reached the top of the stairs, she was so tired, all she wanted to do was tumble facefirst into bed. But when she pushed open the oak door, smoke billowed out of her fireplace.

"My blankie!"

She lunged for the fireplace tongs and snatched the keepsake off the still-burning log, hurling it onto the tiles and stomping on the flames.

Finally, when the fire was out, Gen gathered up the little yellow blanket to survey the damage. The edges were burnt, and there were multiple holes scorched through the center. The embroidery of her name and the sun was black with soot.

For the second time tonight, tears ran down her cheeks. But these were angry ones. She knew she'd left the blanket on the far side of the room. Which meant someone had broken into the private tower meant to keep her safe. And that someone had tried to send her a message.

But what kind of awful person would throw a baby blanket in the fire?

Then Gen realized that the blanket had only been the beginning. The entire room could have caught fire.

Gen's heart raced. She didn't sleep a wink that night. Because whoever was behind the fire, the curse, and everything else had just made it very clear that they would do whatever it took to terrify her—and the entire kingdom.

They wanted to make sure Gen never became princess of Raldonia. By any means necessary.

PANNING FOR BRASS

As the sun rose, the flames in the fireplace snuffed out completely. Gen picked up one of the iron fireplace tools and poked around in the ashes, looking for any possible clue to who'd snuck in last night.

It was just a dusty gray mess, though, like trying to use a pencil to dig through a mountain of eraser shavings, and she didn't even know what she was looking for.

"There's gotta be a better way to do this," Gen said. There was no one to hear her in the tower, but regardless, she felt more sure of herself saying it out loud.

She glanced around the room. Other than the bed and chair and rack of fireplace tools, it was really bare.

Oh! But maybe her dinner tray was still on the ground outside her door, waiting to be picked up? Gen hoped the kitchen staff hadn't come up the tower staircase yet to grab it. She bounded to the door and opened it.

Aha! There it was, a silver tray with a porcelain plate, decorated in elegant gold-and-purple curlicues (as well as a few crumbs of the octopus à la parmesana from last night). But what she really wanted was the silver dome that had covered the plate, the kind you see in movies when the characters stay at fancy hotels and get room service. (Professor Règles had told her the silver covers were called cloches, which was French for "bell.") Gen snatched it and darted back into her room.

She sat cross-legged in front of the fireplace and scooped some ash into the cloche. There was a small hole in the top of the dome, and Gen used it to slowly funnel out the ash. Basically, she was panning for gold, like the forty-niners did during the Gold Rush in California, except that now Gen was panning not for gold, but for clues.

She shook the cloche gently from side to side, letting the ash sift out through the hole in the dome. The idea was that if there was anything other than ash, it would be left inside the cloche.

It took a lot of patience. And it was also super messy. But this work was very, very important. Good Detective Traits Numbers Four and Six:

Remember—everything _is a piece of the puzzle,_
and Gather as much information as possible.

An hour in, the floor in front of the fireplace looked like a volcano had erupted nearby. Fine gray ash covered every inch of the ground and Gen's pants and hands.

But she'd only found bits of wood that had broken off from the main log.

"This was a dumb idea," Gen muttered to herself.

She decided to finish the last cloche-ful, though, since she was already holding it. With a sigh, Gen swirled the ash around and around the silver dome, watching it slowly funnel out the hole.

Suddenly, though, the sunlight streaming in through the window caught a glint inside the last bits of ash. Gen nearly dropped the cloche in her excitement.

She fumbled inside the ashes and plucked the shiny thing out.

"A button!" Gen rubbed off the gray dust on its surface. It was brass, with an eagle imprinted on it. She squinted as she studied it, because the button seemed vaguely familiar.

Where had Gen seen it before?

She ran through a list of the people in Raldonia she knew and cross-referenced them with people who would wear something with such ostentatious buttons.

Gen gasped when she realized who it was. "Lee," she whispered. The queen's righthand woman always wore bright blouses with elaborate cufflinks, or loud blazers with polished metal buttons.

It made so much sense. Lee was the one who first brought up the curse in that meeting in the throne room when Gen arrived in the palace. Lee was the one with access to the castle and to other areas of the kingdom, who had powerful connections because she was the queen's most trusted employee. Lee could also control the narrative of the press: If she wanted the people of Raldonia to believe that Gen had unleashed the curse on the kingdom, Lee could make it happen simply by telling Hotshots PR what to say to the newspapers.

I've gotta tell Hill!

Gen jumped up. Forget about separation of lines of succession, or whatever it was called. This alleged toad-skin malady wasn't real. It was just part of a human-caused ruse that was supposed to seem like the curse. Gen leaving the tower wasn't going to turn her into a human toad. She grabbed her backpack and baby blanket (no way was she leaving it out of her sight while Lee was prowling around the palace) and rushed out of the isolated tower room.

As Gen got closer to the kitchen, though, the castle corridors grew noisier. What was going on?

Yelling broke out in the kitchen. Gen arrived to find a crowd inside, pots and pans abandoned on the stove, and mixing bowls overturned with their goopy contents dripping onto the floor. This chaos explained why her dinner tray had still been outside her door; usually the staff were quick to clean up after every meal.

Gen pushed through the cooks and servers, toward the yelling.

She emerged to find the Imperial Guard flanking Chef Brillat-Savarin, who stood with his arms limp at his sides, bewildered and still holding a spatula that dripped with sauce. Monka had his hand on Hill's shoulder, watching him closely. Monka wouldn't meet Gen's eyes.

She sucked in a breath. Was the guard also in on this abominable plot? Were Monka and Lee in cahoots together?

"What the heck is going on?" Gen asked.

No one heard her as Hill's dad continued to struggle and shout.

So Gen climbed up onto the counter, stuck two fingers into her mouth, and let out an ear-piercing whistle.

The kitchen froze and went absolutely silent.

Gen put on the most imperious, royal expression that Professor Règles had taught her. "That's better," Gen said, hands on her hips. "Now, I demand to know what is going on here. What possible reason could you have for arresting Hill and his dad?"

The guards bowed in deference to Gen, although Monka's looked a little curt. When they rose again, Monka answered. "I'm afraid Hill and Chef Brillat-Savarin have been charged with conspiracy and treason, Your Highness."

Gen could feel the color draining from her face. "No . . . that's impossible. On what grounds?"

Monka shrugged, looking guilty again. "We're just following orders from the queen. There were traces of toxins found in the butter used for National Cake Day. They've been accused of poisoning the kingdom."

FRAMED FAMILY PORTRAIT

"I swear, Your Highness, we're innocent!" Chef Brillat-Savarin cried.

Hill's eyes were wide with fear. "We didn't do it." His voice trembled and came out like barely a whisper.

"I believe you," Gen said. Her fingers drummed against her leg three times in quick succession, using the sign they'd established when they'd first visited Jonah's seaside cottage. Good Detective Trait Number Eight:

> **_Always establish clear, nonverbal signals with your squad_**
> **_in case you can't talk to each other during an operation._**

Gen wanted Hill to know she had a plan.

Well, she didn't have a plan *yet*, but she was going to make one.

Hill bit his lip as he noticed what she was doing and nodded once.

At that moment, a man in a trench coat arrived in the kitchen. He flipped out his badge and said, "I'm Chief Inspector Fedorov with the Raldonian Capital Police. Thank you, guards, for apprehending our suspects. Load those two into my car. I'll take it from here."

"Now, wait a minute," Gen said. "You can't haul them away just like that."

"I sure can, missy," Inspector Fedorov said, shoving his badge in her face to make sure she knew he was important. "And you better hold your tongue unless you want a one-way ticket to prison with them."

Gen rolled her eyes. "And maybe you should think before you speak." She pulled the Imperial Fox pendant out from under her collar and held it up to *his* face. Let's see what Inspector I'm-So-Official-and-Powerful thought of *her* authority.

His face turned the color of putrid olives. "Oh good gracious! Your Highness, forgive me!" The inspector fell to his knees and bowed until he was laid out flat on the kitchen floor.

Gen sighed. She hadn't meant to make him worship her. She'd actually just been offended that he would be so rude to someone he thought was ranked below him (a mere kitchen girl), and Gen had gone a little overboard in making her point.

"Rise, please, Inspector," she said.

Inspector Fedorov stayed in his bow for a few more seconds before climbing back to his feet. Bits of eggshell and spatters of hollandaise sauce clung to his trench coat, and he definitely did not look as intimidating as he did when he first barreled into the kitchen.

"What I was trying to say earlier," Gen began, "was that you can't come in here and start labeling people as criminals before they've been to trial. What happened to the whole innocent-until-proven-guilty philosophy?"

"That's a very American concept." Inspector Fedorov chuckled but then stopped, realizing that he probably sounded condescending. "I apologize, Your Highness. But the judicial process here in Raldonia runs a little . . . differently, seeing as we're a monarchy and all. It is true that, at this point in time, Chef Brillat-Savarin, his son, and the rest of their family, are merely suspects. However . . ." Inspector Fedorov stood straighter and pulled his shoulders back. "We have a significant amount of evidence against them that I strongly believe will prove to the queen that they are, indeed, the culprits behind the vicious reaction that has overtaken the kingdom!"

Gen, who was still standing on the counter, looked down her nose at him. "What evidence, exactly?"

"W-well . . ." The inspector suddenly got more nervous again. (Professor Règles would be so proud of Gen's "princess glare.")

"Well what?"

Inspector Fedorov frowned. "Well, the details are confidential." He gestured at the kitchen, overflowing with cooks and other staff.

But Gen wasn't going to let the inspector get off that easily. Not with a weak excuse like that.

"Okay, then, come with me." She hopped off the counter and led Inspector Fedorov into the walk-in pantry where all the snacks were. When they were both inside and sure no one else was hiding in the aisles, she shut the door firmly.

Gen cleared her throat. "By the power vested in me through my royal, uh, presence, I hereby lift all restrictions of confidentiality. In other words, you're allowed to tell me anything."

(She didn't really have any powers like that. Not that Gen knew of. She'd made it up and hoped it sounded official.)

But Inspector Fedorov's face got very serious—his eyebrows furrowed like he was concentrating, and he tilted up his chin as if he were a soldier reporting to his superior officer. "I understand, Your Highness. What would you like to know?"

"The accusations against Hill and his family are ridiculous," Gen said. "I want you to tell me about the supposed evidence you have on them."

With a serious nod, Inspector Fedorov began. "It started with a tip that the toad-skin malady wasn't contagious, but rather that it was coming from the kingdom's food. We started interviewing farmers at the produce market, thinking that maybe we had an outbreak of E. coli or other bacteria on our hands. However, quick field tests showed no contamination on the fruits and vegetables."

"But what does that have to do with Hill and his dad?" Gen asked.

"There were a lot of reports of Hill loitering around the fish and farmers' markets recently, acting suspicious," Inspector Fedorov said.

Shoot, Gen thought. That was probably her fault. She and Hill had been splitting up whenever they snuck into town, and since he knew the markets better than she did, Gen had assigned him that area to investigate. She'd given him some pointers for sleuthing, but she hadn't had time to observe Hill to see if he was being too conspicuous.

"Okay," Gen said, leaning against a shelf of cereal. "But if there was nothing wrong with the produce, why does it matter that Hill was at the market? Besides the point that he's *supposed* to go to the markets. It's part of his job in the kitchen."

"Of course," Inspector Fedorov said. "Our true suspicions arose, though, when we questioned the bakers in town."

Not Sam and Ethel! Gen thought. They wouldn't falsely accuse Hill, would they? Sam and Ethel had claimed to be such big supporters of Gen. It didn't make sense that they'd be stoking rumors of the curse behind her back.

Right?

"The bakers with a stand at the farmer's market?" Gen asked, reaching for an open box of Super Choco Puffs and eating a handful to pretend she was 100 percent calm and collected.

"No, no," the inspector said. "Those bakers were useless. They didn't give me a single iota of information!"

Gen exhaled in relief. Sam and Ethel *were* on her side.

"I mean Katarina, Mbaye, and Hiroto, the bakers at the shops around the edge of town square," Inspector Fedorov said. "One of the farmers, Anita Bloom, suggested we interview them."

Anita! Like Monka, she kept appearing at suspicious, curse-related moments.

"The bakers," Inspector Fedorov said, "informed us that big boxes of butter from the Brillat-Savarin Dairy Farm arrived the morning of National Raldonian Cake Day. And since the recipe specifically called for butter with eighty-six percent butterfat—much higher than normal butter, which only contains eighty percent—every baker in the nation used the Brillat-Savarin Farm butter for their cinnamon-roll pound cakes that day."

"And that's the day everyone got sick. Or, more accurately, had horrible allergic reactions." Gen suddenly couldn't stomach the Super Choco Puffs, and she let them clatter to the pantry floor. She understood why Hill and his family were suspects. Gen didn't believe they were guilty, but she could see why Inspector Fedorov and the police force did.

Inspector Fedorov nodded gravely. "Correct, Your Highness. With that tip, our labs conducted analyses on cinnamon-roll pound cakes throughout Raldonia, and we confirmed that the milky-white sap from the very allergenic oleasteros plant had been incorporated into the butter. Including the butter used in the cakes fed to both you and Her Majesty, the Queen. In fact, in higher concentrations, oleasteros sap can be fatal."

Gen stared at the inspector, but it definitely was not her imperious princess glare, just a bewildered one.

He reached out and took her hand. "I know this is difficult to process, Your Highness. But the evidence is clear that your friend and his family tried to poison you and Queen Michelina. Thankfully, physicians are distributing antidotes to everyone who needs them. But attempting to murder the royal family is high treason, and the guilty shall pay."

Because Gen was too stunned to reply, Inspector Fedorov kept talking. "We are also collecting evidence that they were behind a vast conspiracy to convince people that your return to Raldonia has revived the curse. It was the Brillat-Savarins who caused the seafood spoilage, the power outage, the lavender flower infestation, and the hurricane."

The sheer ridiculousness of that final claim jolted Gen out of her shock. "You think they caused a *hurricane?* How???" She couldn't help it; she burst out laughing.

"W-we . . . we're working on figuring that out!" Inspector Fedorov tried very hard to look authoritative by puffing up his chest. But he didn't realize that the eggshells and hollandaise sauce on his trench coat had dripped farther down his front, and he looked more like a man who'd spilled his breakfast all over himself than a serious detective.

"With all due respect," Gen said, "*no one* has the ability to create hurricanes. Tell the Royal Weather Service to check the ocean off the eastern coast of Africa one week before our hurricane. I think they'll find a seed of a storm and a bizarre but real wind current and migration of whales that brought that storm here."

"How—"

But Gen didn't let him finish. "Look, I'm glad that I'm not the only one who finds all this curse business suspicious, but I also know that Hill and his dad are good people. They love me and the queen, and they love Raldonia. They'd never do anything to hurt us."

"Your naivete is endearing," Inspector Fedorov said.

Gen scrunched up her nose. Why did she even bother? She hated when adults like Inspector Fedorov condescended and acted like her ideas were silly just because she was young. She resisted the urge to pick up the box of Super Choco Puffs and toss some of them at the inspector's smug face.

He didn't seem to notice her reaction, though. Instead, he continued lecturing her. (*Sighhh.* Gen was so tired of being lectured.)

"When you're older," Inspector Fedorov was saying, "you'll realize that even the friendliest-seeming people have hidden agendas."

"Yeah, but even then, they have motives," Gen said. "What could possibly be Hill and his dad's motive for trying to poison me, the queen, and the entire freaking kingdom?"

If she thought she'd stump the inspector, though, Gen was wrong. He simply shrugged. "Disgruntled employees can get very creative," he said.

With that, he bowed and asked if he could be excused. "I must drive the suspects to jail, then return to the police station to carry on with my investigation."

"Yeah, sure, you can go," Gen said, not wanting to be

around Inspector Fedorov anymore. He bowed again and scurried out of the pantry, leaving Gen alone.

She slid down to the floor and leaned against the shelves to think. Gen knew Hill and his dad—and their whole family—were innocent. They'd clearly been framed.

Gen decided to review the facts she knew.

Whoever set this up had covered their bases, and they also had friends in influential places. How else could Gen explain a coordinated sabotage of the entire seafood haul, followed by a kingdom-wide blackout, then an infestation that just so happened to include every kind of bug that kills lavender, and finally, a mass food poisoning? (The hurricane was an unfortunate coincidence. It was what detectives called a red herring—something that seems like a clue but is actually misleading.)

The person behind all the Curse of the Tainted Throne catastrophes would have to be cold-hearted, too. No one but a calculating, callous human being could have unleashed all these problems on the people of Raldonia.

Gen reached into her pocket for the button she'd found in the fireplace, rolled it in her palm, then curled her fingers tightly around it.

Lee fit that description to a T.

Maybe Monka was working for her. And even people not on the palace payroll, like Anita, could be under her employ, too. Gen wasn't quite sure yet how they all fit together, but she did know one thing: It was time to pay Lee a visit.

KNOCK, KNOCK ... WHO'S THERE?

Gen needed an address. She ran through the secret tunnels and burst through the hidden panel in her bookshelf, skidding to a stop at her computer. Without even sitting down, she furiously typed commands to hack into the imperial database. For anyone else, this would have taken days—or might even have been impossible—but Gen had learned from her very first meeting with Trisha and Miguel from palace IT that the royal intranet's cybersecurity measures left a lot to be desired, especially for a seasoned hacker.

Still, she glanced wistfully at the other file she had open on her computer. When Hopper was finished, Gen would be able to direct the AI to do all this code-writing for her (ethically!), and Hopper would be able to find what Gen needed even faster than she could. Hopper's program was close-but-not-quite finished, and Gen had only been able to work on it in small scraps of time here and there. So for now, she had to rely on her own brain and fingers to sneak into the imperial database.

A couple minutes later, a new box popped up on her computer screen. *Please enter login credentials,* it said.

"Bingo!" Gen pumped her fist. Then she ran her never-fail password-breaking program, and she was in.

What she needed was the staff directory. Gen found it quickly and typed in the name of her suspect: *Lee Jiménez.*

An address for an apartment in the capital flashed onto the screen.

"Excellent," Gen said.

With the palace in an uproar over Hill and his dad's arrest, no one noticed when Gen slipped away. She wasn't even disguised as a member of the staff this time, because she didn't want Lee to see the uniform and figure out that that was how Gen was evading detection in the first place. Instead, Gen just threw on the simplest outfit she could find in her closet and covered the still-too-fancy silk blouse with a giant coat. (Seriously, why did the royal tailor think a twelve year old needed to wear silk?)

Half an hour later, Gen stood outside Lee's apartment door. The building was bland and nondescript, all beige paint and beige doors, nothing garish like Gen would have expected given how bright Lee's clothes always were. Talk about hiding in plain sight.

Gen *could* knock politely and wait for Lee to let her in.

But then Lee might have a chance to cover up incriminating evidence in her apartment, or even destroy it. Better for Gen to be sneaky.

She pressed her ear to the door to listen for noise inside. The TV was on, but not very loudly. That would make what Gen was about to do a little trickier, but that was okay. She liked a challenge.

Gen checked her surroundings to make sure no one was watching. The apartment complex hallways were clear, so she pulled a lock-picking kit out of her coat pocket.

The lock on the door was as uncomplicated as the paint on the building, and it only took a few seconds for Gen to solve it. The door unlatched almost silently.

Determined to clear Hill's name, though, Gen did not *enter* silently. She flung herself into Lee's apartment and yelled, "Stop what you're doing and freeze!" Good Detective Trait Number Nine:

Utilize the element of surprise.

Instead of finding Lee hunched over a stack of nefarious plans, though, Gen found Lee huddled under a blanket on the couch. Her skin had that awful, grayish-green toad pallor, and she looked . . . feeble. She wore limp, colorless pajamas, and a bucket sat on the worn carpet next to her, and the air smelled distinctly of sour vomit. Gen stifled the urge to gag.

Lee squinted at the light coming in through the front door. "Y-Your Highness? Is that you?" Then she moaned and clutched her stomach.

Gen stared at Lee for a moment, trying to understand the scene in front of her.

1. The queen's austere assistant was a victim of the same food poisoning that had racked all the other citizens.

2. Lee was most definitely *not* masterminding an evil plot against the kingdom at the moment.

Which meant . . .

3. Lee was not the culprit Gen had suspected.

"Did you come all this way to check on me?" Lee asked weakly from the couch. "Oh, Your Highness, you are much too kind."

Gen's cheeks flushed. *Kind* was *not* the word to describe how she'd been thinking. Gen had jumped to conclusions too early, based on unproven, circumstantial evidence, which was something an amateur sleuth would do.

It's exactly what Inspector Fedorov had done with Hill and his family.

Ugh.

The difference between her and the inspector, though, was that Gen knew how to backtrack and to open her mind to alternative possibilities. And she also knew how to swallow her pride and apologize when she'd made a mistake.

"I'm sorry, Lee," she said.

Lee blinked up at her from the couch. "Why should you be sorry, Your Highness?"

Gen took a few steps closer. "I, well . . . I actually came to your apartment to confront you. I'd been trying to figure out what was causing the so-called curse disasters." Lee's eyes widened, but Gen kept going. "And since you're so involved with the queen and seem to have contacts everywhere, well ... I thought you might be the evil brains behind it all. But I was wrong, I see that now, and I'm really sorry."

Lee whimpered a small shaky laugh, pulling a quilt over her. "I would never do anything like that ..." She seemed to want to say more, but instead she just folded into herself, a sad, sick lump on the couch.

Gen shifted in place guiltily. "Can I get you something? Water? Crackers? Another pillow?"

"A drink would be nice, thank you." Lee's voice was so frail, Gen was worried the usually fierce woman might shatter right there on the sofa.

Gen went deeper into the apartment to find a small but tidy kitchen. She pulled a glass out of a cabinet and filled it with water and three ice cubes from the freezer and a lemon slice from the fridge (her go-to when she was feeling sick), then brought it back to the couch. Lee gulped it down. "I've been too weak to get up," she said, smiling up at Gen like she was the sun itself. It made Gen feel even worse for thinking Lee was the villain in this whole thing.

"I really am sorry that I thought you were involved with the curse," Gen said.

Lee turned the empty water glass in her hand and shook her head. "It's all right. I understand. I *am* everywhere and I do know everybody, so I get why you'd suspect me. But I love the queen, and that means I love you."

"I don't know why you'd love *me*," Gen said. "I just got here."

Lee patted the empty space next to her. When Gen sat,

Lee said, "Both my parents worked for the government, and I grew up watching Queen Michelina, King Randolph, and Princess Adrienne in elegant parades, giving brilliant speeches, and being brave when things were hard. I just . . . All I've ever wanted was to be a part of that magic, a part of Raldonia. To serve the imperial family is a fantasy come true. That's why I wanted to assist you the moment the agents dropped you off in the driveway. That's why I've tried to make sure you had everything you needed, that I set you up for success the best I could. Besides, even if you weren't royal, you're smart and energetic and kind, and that makes you easy to love. So please, Your Highness, tell me what I can do to help you solve the mystery of the curse. . . ."

"I appreciate your offer," Gen said. "But first, let *me* help *you*. We've gotta get you back to the palace to see the royal physician."

APOLOGIES COME IN PAIRS

L ee had no idea there was an allergen antidote for the oleasteros sap. When the sickness struck, it'd hit Lee so suddenly, she'd fallen to the floor in the palace greenhouse, breaking her headset. The royal medical team had whisked her away back to her apartment, and ever since then, Lee hadn't had a single communication from anyone.

She didn't even know about Hill and his dad's arrest.

Gen filled her in during the taxi ride on the way back to the palace. (Gen had offered to drive Lee's car, but Lee wasn't *that* sick to have lost her mind—there was no way she was going to let a twelve-year-old behind the wheel.)

When Gen was finished, Lee shook her head in disbelief. "I don't buy for a second that Chef Brillat-Savarin or any member of his family had anything to do with the curse."

"I'm glad *someone* believes me," Gen said. "But unfortunately, I'm also back at square one about who's actually behind it all. I mean, don't get me wrong, I'm glad it isn't you! But I have a lot of work to do if I'm going to solve this. Who else has the kinds of connections you do? Who set fire to my baby blanket, and who does the fancy button belong to?"

"I don't have any ready answers for you," Lee said, "but I'll help however I can."

When they arrived at the palace, Gen helped Lee hobble into the medical clinic located in the southern wing of the castle. As soon as the nurse saw Lee, she hurried them into an examination room. The doctor rushed in a minute later.

"Lee! Where have you been? Why haven't you gotten the antidote yet?"

"I was at home, Melissa," Lee said. Apparently, she was on a first-name basis with the doctor. "I didn't even know you had a cure. Her Highness is the one who kindly brought me in."

The doctor startled, only now noticing Gen in the seat in the corner. "Oh, Your Highness! Forgive me!" She bowed.

"It's okay, Dr. Bhatnagar," Gen said, reading her name off the fancy diploma on the wall. "Please rise. I'd rather you get that antidote into Lee than bow to me."

Dr. Bhatnagar smiled and nodded. The nurse brought in a golden vial, and the doctor had Lee drink the tonic.

"That will take effect almost immediately," Dr. Bhatnagar said, "and you ought to feel one hundred percent better within half an hour. However, you can stay here for a while if you'd like, and I can always give you more tonic if you need it."

"Sounds good, Melissa. Thanks."

Dr. Bhatnagar bowed to Gen once more, then left her and Lee alone.

"Thank you again for bringing me here, Your Highness," Lee said. "I realize that I also owe *you* an apology."

Gen frowned. "Why?"

"Because I gave you bad advice," Lee said. "If you had listened to me and held yourself up as better than the staff, then I wouldn't be here. I wouldn't have the oleasteros antidote."

"Yeah, but—" Gen was about to point out that she'd actually gone to Lee's apartment to accuse her of a villainous plot, not out of goodwill.

Lee waved her hand in the air, though. "I know what you're about to say. But the thing is, you realized your mistake, and instead of digging yourself in deeper, you admitted you'd been wrong and immediately shifted modes to taking care of me. Only a person with a truly good heart would do that."

Gen felt all warm and fuzzy inside. She liked to think she had a strong moral compass, but no one had ever complimented her on it before.

Lee settled against the back of the exam chair. "You know, now that I really think about it, the team from Hotshots PR might have antiquated notions about what it means to be a royal. In the olden days, the monarchy was always so separate from the people of the kingdom. The king or queen would rule from a golden pedestal, and the subjects of the land worshipped them like gods. But I have to admit . . . it seems outdated now."

"And short-sighted and pathetic," Gen added.

Laughter caught Lee off guard, and she accidentally snorted. "You know what, Your Highness? You're right. It *is* short-sighted and pathetic. Why shouldn't you be allowed to be friends with Hill? Why shouldn't you be permitted to get closer to the very subjects you're supposed to rule?"

Gen scooted to the edge of her seat. "Yeah, I agree. I mean, won't I be a better princess—and one day a better queen—if I actually know what the people in the kingdom want and how they're feeling?"

Lee nodded at her from the exam chair. "The fact that you realized this—and that you saw it before the rest of us— is proof you're going to be an excellent princess. Lead with your heart, Your Highness, and you will never fail."

Now *that* was a royal philosophy Gen could live by. (Everything else, she'd be happy to get rid of. Like all the bowing.)

"However . . ." Lee said.

Gen went still. She didn't like *howevers*.

"However what?" Gen asked, not really wanting to know the answer.

Lee shook her head fondly, in that way adults have when they're chastising a cute but misbehaving kid. "However, you were supposed to be grounded and limited to the palace. So I'm still going to have to tell the queen that you've been sneaking out."

Gen sighed. "Yeah. I kind of figured you might."

FROSTY THE GRANDMA

Gen had never seen Queen Michelina's half of the Monarch Suites before. That wouldn't have been strange for most people—after all, a bedroom is a very private and personal place—but the queen was Gen's grandmother. You'd think there would have been an invitation to look through old family trees or take afternoon tea in the month since Gen had been here.

Nope.

So when Queen Michelina invited Gen to her suite that evening, Gen was surprised. Actually, that's an understatement. Gen was stunned. Astounded. Scrape-your-jaw-off-the-floor stupefied.

She put on her best gown, a gold brocaded A-line dress with puffy cap sleeves. Gen normally wouldn't be caught dead in something as frilly as this, but she desperately wanted this chat to go well. True, Gen didn't do well with authority figures. But Queen Michelina was *family*, a concept that was still very new and fragile for Gen. And because of that, she let Lee (who had recovered thanks to Dr. Bhatnagar's excellent antidote) put her hair up into a fancy chignon and decorate her like a jewelry display, with shiny emerald earrings and a platinum-and-emerald bracelet to match.

Ten minutes later, she stood outside the queen's antechamber. Gen stepped inside, and her eyes went wide at the opulence. "Holy royal mackerel!" she exclaimed before realizing that was not at all the way a princess would behave.

The antechamber was like a giant, gilded entryway. Oil paintings of all of Raldonia's past queens stared at her as if studying whether Gen would one day be fit to join their ranks on the walls.

The captain of the Imperial Guard stood at the door that separated the antechamber from the rest of the queen's rooms. Like the king's side of the Monarch Suites (which Gen *had* seen before, when she snuck through it on her way to the Royal Weather Service), Queen Michelina's side was several interconnected rooms, more like a full apartment than a bedroom.

"Are you ready, Your Highness?" the captain asked.

Gen took a deep breath, then nodded.

He opened the door and announced her. "Genevieve Illona Caliste Aurelie of the House of Claremont, Princess of the Realm, Defender of Faith, Sincerity, and Justice!"

For once, the formality didn't make Gen feel awkward. She was already too full of nerves from being at the threshold of her grandma's private living room.

As Gen stepped through, she realized this was very different from the king's side of the Suites. The king's living room (which was officially called a receiving room) was all musty furniture covered up in sheets, devoid of any human presence. The queen's receiving room, however, looked like it came straight out of a brochure for Versailles, the ultra-fancy French palace of Louis XVI and Marie Antoinette. A chandelier dripping with crystals hung from the ceiling. Gold-framed chairs and settees and chaise longues with purple velvet cushions stood over plush silver carpet. And above the fireplace hung an enormous coat of arms featuring the imperial fox. The same one Gen wore on the pendant around her neck. In awe, she gawked at her surroundings and forgot to bow to the queen.

The captain of the guard behind her said gruffly, "Your Highness. You must pay your respects to Her Majesty."

Yikes! Queen Michelina sat primly on one of the gold-and-purple chairs, her mouth pinched like she'd just eaten an entire lemon. So much for Gen making a good impression today.

She curtseyed hastily. It wasn't pretty, but it was better than the weird bow-legged partial curtsey she'd done on her first day in the palace.

The queen dismissed the captain and motioned for Gen to sit in the most uncomfortable-looking seat in the room, the only one without a velvet cushion. It was pretty—carved of polished mahogany—but 100 percent hard surfaces. Gen suspected that the queen made people she didn't like sit in this particular chair. Or maybe it was like the foster homes that made sure the kids got the stain-proof spots.

Gen sat and tried to look as happy as possible, even though the bare seat was harsh on her bony butt. "Thank you, Your Majesty, for inviting me here," she said, pronouncing her consonants softly and her vowels roundly, just like Professor Règles had taught.

"It has been brought to my attention that you have flouted the rules and violated my punishment that you be grounded," Queen Michelina said.

Okaaaay. Guess she was going to skip over the pleasantries and just get right to it. Gen's stomach curdled. She'd been in this position of getting in trouble way too many times in her life, and she knew the angry shouting that was coming.

But Queen Michelina didn't yell or stomp her feet or get up and hiss in Gen's face like some past foster parents had done. Instead, she sat on her chair and didn't move a millimeter. Her brutally calm iciness was actually even worse than the spitting shouts Gen was used to, because at least the foster parents had felt enough emotion toward Gen to raise their voices. The queen seemed like she didn't have any feelings about Gen at all.

"The coronation is six days away, *if* it takes place at all," Queen Michelina said. "Rumors of the curse have caused many of our citizens to question whether you should be allowed to officially hold the title of princess."

Gen blinked at the queen, not knowing how to respond. In the back of her mind, Gen had known it was a possibility that she would be rejected—every foster kid knows this deep in their abandoned hearts—but hearing Queen Michelina herself say that there might not be a coronation made it horrifyingly more real.

What would happen to Gen if there was no ceremony? Would she still get to stay in the palace? Or would she be shipped back to New York, since she wouldn't be of any use to Queen Michelina?

The queen didn't notice Gen's discomfort, and instead kept talking in her all-business monotone. "Despite the arrests of the culprits behind the supposed curse events, many Raldonians are still worried about the curse. Therefore, you cannot give them *any* other reason to doubt you. Which means you *must* be on your best behavior."

Oh! Gen allowed herself to breathe. It sounded like there was still a possibility of salvaging her coronation.

"It is imperative," the queen was saying, "that you remain in the castle at all times until the ceremony to avoid any public interaction, which could easily grow into unfavorable rumors. I am assigning an Imperial Guard to stand outside the Princess Suite, as well as one inside the hidden panel in your bookshelf—yes, I know you've been using the interior tunnels as your personal playground, and I must remind you that they are for emergency evacuation purposes only, not for visiting your miscreant friend in the kitchen or for sneaking out of the palace."

Gen had been trying to remain composed and proper, but this was too much. She leaped out of her chair. "Hill is not a miscreant! Everyone's treating him and his dad like they're guilty, but they're being set up!"

"I will be the final arbiter of that," the queen said.

"They're innocent and shouldn't be labeled like criminals."

"If and when other evidence or suspects are identified, I will consider them as well. I assure you, I am a fair-minded monarch."

Gen worked overtime not to huff and fling her arms in the air. "Fair-minded? You have guards posted around me twenty-four/seven like I'm a prisoner, too. Do you even *want* me to succeed and become your heir?"

Seething anger simmered in the queen's eyes, and yet they somehow became even frostier. "Are you accusing me of deliberately subverting your path to the throne?"

"No, I—"

"Next, you'll be accusing *me* of being behind the rumors of the curse."

"I would never do that! I misspoke." Gen sat back into her chair obediently, terrified that if she angered the queen any more, there'd soon be a plane ticket to New York with Gen's name on it. "I— I apologize, Your Majesty. I was out of line. It's just that, the idea of having guards trail me everywhere . . . What about privacy?"

Queen Michelina huffed. "Privacy? You will learn soon enough that royalty have no privacy. The public will analyze every curl of your hair and every twitch of your little gloved hands. The reporters will dissect whether you put too much weight on your left foot when you walk or if you stand an inch closer to Duke Charlemagne than to me, looking for gossip and secret meanings in your every minuscule move.

Even within these palace walls, you are constantly being observed."

"That's unfair," Gen said softly. In truth, she was outraged, but she was trying to keep a lid on her temper. She didn't want to set off the queen again.

"It is better for you to realize quickly that there is the way the world *is*, and the way the world *should* be. Your mother lived in a fantasy where she wanted the latter, and she couldn't deal with the difficult facts of what it means to be a member of the monarchy. Will you be any better?"

Gen shrank under the queen's scrutinizing scowl. She had certainly mastered the whole imperious glare thing.

But even though Queen Michelina didn't seem to have a grandmotherly bone in her body, and even though she was ruthless in her assessment of Gen's mom (the queen's own daughter!), Gen wasn't ready to give up. She had changed Lee's mind about royalty being friends with staff. Maybe the queen—and Raldonia—just needed more time to change their minds about what a "proper princess" ought to be.

Gen sat up in the chair, pulling her shoulders back and holding her head high. "Your Majesty, I may be a little unorthodox and not what the kingdom is used to, but I *do* think I'm up to the task. And I want to be part of this family." She gestured toward the antechamber and the paintings of all the queens who'd come before her.

Queen Michelina was quiet for several minutes, which seemed to be her trademark move. But now that Gen was actually in front of the queen—rather than eavesdropping on her without seeing her face—Gen saw her pensive expression. Maybe Queen Michelina's quiet was less about freezing the other person out and more about the queen giving herself time to think. So Gen sat as still as she could instead of interrupting like she might have done in the past to break the silence.

Finally, Queen Michelina nodded curtly. "Very well. Over the next six days, you shall focus on your imperial obligations and rehearse for the coronation. It is extraordinarily important to the kingdom that this go well. Understood?"

"Yes, Your Majesty. I promise I won't let you down."

THE APPLE DOESN'T FALL
FAR FROM THE TREE

Okay, so technically, the promise not to let the queen down was about *general* expectations, right? And not *exactly* about following the rules? Gen leaned out of the window in her bedroom, estimating how far a climb down it would be. She could make a rope out of blankets, tie it to one of the canopy bedposts, and probably make it to the ledge below. From there, it was still a significant drop, but her fall would be broken by the phoenix topiary. . . .

Someone rapped loudly on her door, and Gen jumped back from her window so fast, she hit her head on the frame.

"Ow!"

"Your Highness?"

"Duke Charlemagne!"

"It's lovely to see you so . . . spirited. What, exactly, were you doing?"

"Um, I was just wondering how the palace window cleaners managed to wash everything," Gen lied.

The duke smirked. "Are you sure you weren't plotting a way to climb *out* the window? Say, with a rope made of blankets?"

"What? No, never! Why would you even suggest that?"

He turned and looked pointedly at the mound of blankets on Gen's bed, several of which she'd tied together as a sample. Oops.

"I was just practicing my nautical knots," Gen lied. "From the minister of fisheries' lesson."

Duke Charlemagne raised his thick eyebrows. They looked like caterpillars trying to crawl into his hair. Then he laughed. "When your mother was a teenager, she attempted to leave the palace via blanket rope. Back then, there was a big elephant topiary beneath the window, so the fall was shorter. Still, she ended up with a broken ankle and no escape, and the queen had the royal landscaper change the topiary into a phoenix. Skinnier and shorter, even harder to land on."

"Oh." Gen's first reaction was disappointment that her plan wasn't original and had already failed before. But then she smiled because she realized that the person who'd tried the plan was her mom. Great minds thought alike! Or at least, mischievous, rebellious ones did.

"I'm just like my mom," she said wistfully.

"Just like her," Duke Charlemagne echoed.

"So are you gonna tell the guard outside the door what I was up to?" Gen asked, suddenly chastened again.

"Your secret's safe with me, as long as you don't actually try it," the duke said. "I was coming in to alert you about something else."

Gen exhaled in relief. "What is it?"

"There are some visitors here to see you."

"Hill?" Gen jumped in place.

"Unfortunately not," Duke Charlemagne said. "I don't know who they are, but they claim to be your friends. We don't usually let anyone into the palace who hasn't been through a very thorough background check, but I sense you could use a pick-me-up after the devastating betrayal by Hill and his family."

Gen had plenty to say about how untrue that last part was, but she didn't want to lash out at Duke Charlemagne. He wasn't trying to make her upset by bringing it up. He was only saying what he'd been told about the Brillat-Savarins. What everyone in Raldonia had been told.

"Thanks," Gen said. "I would love to see these visitors, whoever they are."

Maybe they could help her, even just by telling her what was going on outside these palace walls. Honestly, that's why she'd been thinking about sneaking out of the palace again. Gen couldn't just sit inside for six days until the coronation while Hill and his family waited in jail. She needed to solve the mystery of who was behind all the curse disasters in order to set Hill's family free.

The duke asked the guard outside Gen's door to escort her to Nautilus, a small and simple receiving room that had a round table shaped like a nautilus shell, half a dozen chairs, and not much else. Gen was grateful that for once, the guard on duty wasn't Monka.

As soon as Gen stepped into Nautilus, her face broke into a grin. "Jonah! Sam! Ethel! And ... Anita?"

The fishmonger, bakers, and farmer bowed deeply.

Gen rushed at them and gave everyone a hug.

"Your Highness," Jonah said, "thank you for taking the time to see us."

"Of course!" Gen said. "I'd never turn down a visit from you. How are you all doing? Are you holding up after what's happened?"

All four of them had suffered under recent events. But from the way that Jonah, Sam, and Ethel beamed at Gen, you wouldn't be able to tell. Anita, though, looked nervously down at her weathered hands.

"I don't deserve your kindness," Anita said, "after the way I treated you at the market and later, at the lavender fields. But I realized I was very wrong, and I came to apologize. I am so sorry, Your Highness."

Gen blinked at her, confused for a second. But then she remembered what Lee had said about it being a great quality to be able to admit to your mistakes and move forward. "It's okay. Apology accepted." She squeezed Anita's hand.

"Would you like to sit down?" Gen asked everyone. She may not be the fastest learner when it came to court etiquette, but she knew to offer her guests a seat.

They settled into the chairs around the carved wooden table. What a funny-looking group they were, just normal people (Gen included), huddled around a priceless piece of centuries-old imperial furniture.

Anita smoothed down the front of her plaid shirt. "I'm sorry. I was wrong about the curse. It's clear now that the police have evidence that the so-called curse catastrophes are man-made, not some kind of evil magic. And that proves that the curse isn't real."

Ethel smiled gently. "That's what we were trying to tell you before, dearie."

"I know. I was too pig-headed to listen," Anita said. "But I've known Chef Brillat-Savarin and his family for a long, long time, and I'd bet my farm that they would never be involved in any of the things they've been accused of. I want to help clear them of wrongdoing. "

"That would be great," Gen said. "I'm supposed to stay in the palace until the coronation, so it would be really valuable if you could be my eyes and ears in town. Anything that looks or sounds off, or anyone acting weird—"

"Actually," Jonah said, "we already have something to share with you."

Gen leaned across the table. "Really?"

Anita nodded. "I think I might have a clue."

SUPERNATURAL

nita fidgeted with one of the straps of her overalls as if that would give her the courage to say whatever it was she was about to say. Then she took a deep breath, and began.

"A few nights ago, before National Raldonian Cake Day, I stopped by the Brillat-Savarin farm. But it was late, so the dairy was closed for the night. I happened to see Hill's older sister as she was about to lock the door to their shopfront.

"'Hey, Cleo,' I said. 'Might I trouble you for a quart of milk before you leave?'

"'Oh, hi, Anita,' Cleo said. 'Not a problem at all. Do you want whole, two percent, or non-fat?'

"'Whole, please. My cat, Barney, likes the rich stuff.'

"'You got it. Give me a sec and I'll grab it from the refrigerator.' She disappeared back inside the shop.

"I didn't need to follow her inside, because she'd only be a minute. Besides, Cleo had probably mopped the floors to a gleam—the whole family is careful about cleanliness because they never want any risk of their dairy products getting bacteria in them and spoiling—so I didn't want to tromp in there in my dirty work boots and muck up her pristine floors.

"While I was waiting, though, I noticed something odd and out of place. You might know that the Brillat-Savarin Dairy Farm is a very large property. The little store I stood in front of is the closest to the road, but behind it sprawl several barns—you need a lot of space to house all those cows, you know—as well as pastures.

"It ought've been completely dark out there. The Brillat-Savarin family cares so much about the well-being of their animals, they make sure there are no artificial lights anywhere near the barns at night so that their cows can get the rejuvenating rest they need.

"But instead of pitch-black, I saw an eerie green glow shining from one of the barns. Had one of the dairy-hands forgotten to turn something off before they left? That didn't seem right to me, though.

"Cleo reappeared then with the milk bottle.

"I looked away from the barn to get out my wallet. As I grabbed a few bills, I asked, 'Y'all working late in the barns these days, getting ready for Cake Day?'

"She smiled under the glow of the single lamp on the front of the shop. 'We're working doubly hard during the day, but it's still important to let our ladies sleep in the evenings. In fact, it's even *more* important now to shut everything down once the sun starts setting, because they're working extra hard. I think they're as excited as we are to make all the butter for the kingdom for my dad's cake.'

"I handed over the money for the milk. 'Well, you might want to swing by that barn over on the east side to turn off the—' I looked up in the direction of the green light, but it was gone.

"'Shut off what?' Cleo followed my gaze into the pure darkness.

"'I could've sworn I saw green light in that barn a minute ago.'

"Cleo shook her head. 'Impossible. I closed that one up myself half an hour ago. Triple-checked that everything was off, too.'

"'Huh. I must've imagined it. Eating too much spinach and seeing green everywhere, I guess. Anyhow, I best be on my way. Thanks again for holding the shop open for me so I could get my milk.'

"As I was heading back to my truck, another car pulled up to the Brillat-Savarin store. It was Katarina, Mbaye, and Hiroto, who run a bakery at the edge of the town square. Their car doors opened, and I overheard Mbaye telling Hiroto it was too late, that the dairy shop would be closed. But Katarina told him that she'd recently seen some bright green lights flashing at the farm, so that might mean that Cleo was still working.

"I jogged over to let them know that Cleo was, in fact, still in the shop if they hurried.

"After that, I drove home and forgot about that out-of-place green light. . . . Until the news spread that the entire

Brillat-Savarin family had been accused of poisoning their butter and arrested. I tell you, that dairy farm is more hygienic than a hospital operating room. And they are very respectable people, as are all the dairy-hands, whose own families have worked there for decades. They take a great deal of pride in making Raldonia's finest milk, butter, cream, and yogurt.

"So when the police inspector came around, I told him so, and also told him that there had been a strange green light at the barns right before Cake Day. Then I sent him to Katarina, Mbaye, and Hiroto because they'd seen it, too."

So Anita had only asked Inspector Fedorov to interview the bakers to corroborate her story, which she figured would help Hill's family, Gen thought. She'd really pegged Anita wrong all along.

Finally finished with her tale, Anita let out a long huff of a breath and slumped back into her seat as if that was more words than she was used to saying in an entire day and the effort had taken everything out of her. But it was fine, because then the others jumped in to continue the story for Gen.

Ethel leaned into the round table. "Of course, you have to understand that as bakers, Sam and I had bought the Brillat-Savarin butter and made plenty of our own cinnamon roll pound cakes to sell. We were mortified to find out our customers had gotten sick from food we made for them! We, ourselves, were also ill, because we'd taste-tested many of the batches of cake. But not for one second did we even suspect the Brillat-Savarin family! They are wonderful people, and the accusation against them is absurd!"

"Thanks to the quick rollout of the antidote," Sam said, "we soon recovered. But when Anita came up to our bakery stall the next day, I remembered that I'd had another conversation about a green light a little while ago."

Jonah piped up. "That would be where I come in. Remember when all the seafood went bad?"

Gen nodded. How could anyone forget?

"Well," Jonah said, stroking his beard, "after you and Hill left my cottage that day, I remembered something I'd forgotten to tell you. While I was packing up my fish, I saw a greenish hue farther down the docks. But I didn't bother to follow up with you, because sometimes the sea does glow green— it happens once a year when the bioluminescent Raldonian jellyfish come to the surface. However, when I heard that Anita had seen an unusual light at the dairy barn, I realized that this isn't the time of year for jellyfish bioluminescence in the sea. Not even close! So the green light Anita saw and the one I observed have got to be related, don't you think?"

Gen fiddled with her necklace chain as she thought it all over. "Yeah, I think you're right. Your green light coincided with the rotting seafood haul. And Anita's green light appeared just before the tampered batches of butter."

Ethel shuddered. "It's spooky, though. I don't believe in the silly curse . . . but what else could cause such a supernatural glow?"

At that moment, Gen's faulty necklace clasp unhooked— she really needed to get that fixed—and the imperial fox pendant fell with a clang onto the table.

Gen's mouth fell open as she stared at it.

"I've got it!" She leaped from her chair.

Sam, Ethel, Jonah, and Anita just looked really confused.

"Got what?" Jonah asked.

Gen reeled. "I know what the connection is."

Ethel beamed at her in awe. "We're lucky to have such a sharp mind as our princess."

And I'm lucky to have Hill as a friend, Gen thought. It was because he knew so many people—and because everyone loved him—that Sam, Ethel, Jonah, and Anita had shown up to help solve the case. And because of him that they knew Gen and had such faith in her. No wonder Hill was commander of his *Octopus Isle* squad. He was the kind of person people would do anything for.

But Gen still had plenty to do if she was going to convince everyone else in the kingdom about the true story behind the curse, and of Hill and his dad's innocence.

She snatched up her pendant from the table and addressed her friends. "I really appreciate you four coming here today to tell me about this. But if you'll excuse me now, I've got evidence to compile.

"I think I know who the real culprit is—and it's not going to be easy to prove."

COUNTDOWN TILL CROWN TIME

Over the next few days, Gen spent her time doing one of two things:

1. Preparing for her upcoming coronation (trial hairstyles with the stylist and dress fittings with the royal tailor, elocution drills with Professor Règles, and rehearsals of the ceremony); or

2. Hunching over her computer.

Right after Anita, Jonah, Ethel, and Sam came to visit her, Gen rushed back to her room to hack into the palace intranet. But the evidence she needed—if it existed at all—was well buried, and given the number of files that existed in the palace system, Gen wouldn't be able to sift through it herself. Not if she wanted results in less than ten years, anyway.

And she did, because Gen was constantly aware that the longer she took, the longer Hill, his dad, and the rest of their family remained trapped in a dank jail cell.

Plus, Gen needed to solve this case before the coronation ceremony. Otherwise, there was a good chance that the citizens of Raldonia would rebel and refuse to let her officially have the title of princess. The mass food poisoning made those who still believed in the Curse of the Tainted Throne believe more fervently. And even those who didn't believe in the curse were probably seriously wondering whether a new princess would be a good idea, seeing as everything had been fine before Gen showed up.

But if Gen could prove to everyone that none of the disasters were her fault—and also prove who was actually behind them—then she would ensure her own coronation ceremony while also rescuing Hill and the rest of the Brillat-Savarins.

I will *make that happen,* she thought. *With some help.*

Which is why Gen turned all her effort onto finishing Hopper.

She'd spend the past three days working through the wee hours of the night, and now she put the finishing touches on her AI program. Gen grinned sleepily at her desk as she looked at the code one last time. Then she stroked the computer fondly, like petting a prized puppy, and said, "You know what to do, Hopper. Go get 'em."

If the guards had peeked in on Gen, they might have thought she'd lost her marbles.

Gen finally hit start. And then she tumbled headfirst into bed and passed out into a deep, deep sleep.

The next morning, her alarm clock went off way too early. Gen groaned as she hit the snooze button and pulled the covers back over her. Then, a couple minutes later, she forced herself out of bed. She had a full day of rehearsals, and Gen needed to shower and get dressed and eat breakfast within half an hour.

But first, she wanted to check on how Hopper was doing. Gen leaned over her computer and wiggled the mouse. The screen flashed on (she'd set it on sleep mode for the night, but the computer had stayed on so the AI program could keep running).

"Oooh, nice work," Gen said, nodding appreciatively at a couple of the files that Hopper had found. Gen clicked on them and scrolled through the contents quickly. "I'm going to need more than this, but I think we're on the right path."

She keyed in a few more specific commands to Hopper, then left the computer to do its work while she showered.

If only Gen could bring Hopper with her during the day. It would be hard to concentrate on walking down carpeted stairs with elegant posture while knowing that more important—and more interesting—things were happening on her computer. Too bad palace IT hadn't been able to get her a tablet or phone.

As Gen shampooed her hair, she thought through what she'd need to do if Hopper found the rest of the evidence she was hoping for. The next step would be tricky to accomplish.

"Oh!" A solution suddenly popped into her head. Gen also got a mouthful of sudsy water in the process.

Coughing, she hurried the rest of her shower, then threw on her robe and ran to her old camouflage backpack in the closet. There, in the zippered front pouch, she found the receipt Agent 34 had given her on the day she'd arrived in Raldonia.

If you need anything, you can call me on my direct line, okay? he'd said.

"I hope you really meant it," Gen said to herself as she dialed his number.

A robotic voice answered on the first ring. "Hello. Thank you for calling the Raldonian Pop Culture survey. We thank you for your interest in helping us gather data on what our kingdom's citizens love best. Before we begin, please record your name at the chime."

What? Gen looked at the phone number on the receipt. She must have dialed wrong.

Gen hung up and tried again.

"Hello," the robot voice said again. "Thank you for calling the Raldonian Pop Culture survey. We thank you for your interest in helping us gather data on what our kingdom's citizens love best. Before we begin, please record your name at the chime."

A high-pitched *ding* sounded over the line.

O-kaaaay.

Gen didn't say anything. She was sure she'd dialed the right number this time.

But then it occurred to her that maybe this was a test? Agent 43 had said that it was a violation of RIA protocol for Agent 34 to give Gen his direct line. And surely the

Raldonian Intelligence Agency couldn't just trust anyone who called them. What if Gen had dropped this receipt on the ground and a random person—or a bad guy—picked it up?

The robotic voice repeated, "Please record your name at the chime. If you do not wish to continue with the survey, this call will automatically end in five seconds. *Ding!*"

"My name is—" Gen almost blurted out her real name, but then she remember that Agent 34 had given her a secret code name.

"Sunbeam!" Gen said. "My name is Sunbeam."

"Pass phrase?" the robot asked.

What was her password? Gen racked her brain. If she'd gotten more sleep recently, her memory would be working a lot faster.

"Um . . ."

"*Um* is not a valid pass phrase. Please try again or this call with automatically end in five seconds."

Water dripped from Gen's hair onto her face while she tried to remember. At the same time, she wondered why the RIA would let someone try so many times to get through on this phone line. The robot was awfully patient.

But then it occurred to Gen that the reason you'd let someone stay on the line this long was so you could trace their call.

Her eyes widened. What if the RIA thought she was an enemy of the state and was sending an assassination squad to her bedroom window right this very second?

As soon as Gen tried to actually imagine that happening, though, all she could think of was Agents 34 and 43 in their black suits, unsuccessfully trying to blend in at the Frying Nemo Diner. She laughed at the image of other RIA agents like them, rappelling down the palace roof and—

Your pass phrase will be the name of the diner where you first spotted us, Agent 34 had said.

Of course! Gen smacked her wet forehead.

"Frying Nemo," she said into the phone.

The voice at the other end of the line started laughing softly. "Took you a while, didn't it, Your Highness?" Agent 34 asked.

"Wait? You're not an automated robot?" Gen asked.

"No, I just use that voice to deter people who shouldn't actually have my number. But the caller ID said you were calling from the Raldonian Palace, so I had a feeling it might be you. What can I do for you, Your Highness?"

Gen laughed a little at herself for thinking that the RIA might've been sending a hit squad after her.

"I need your help with a couple things I can't do on my own," she said.

"Uh-oh," Agent 34 said. "You're not going to get me into trouble, are you?"

"I hope not. . . ."

ONE DAY TILL CROWN TIME

Gen lost track of time on the afternoon of the dress rehearsal. Instead of getting ready like she was supposed to be doing, Gen hunched over her computer, grinning wildly.

"You are a genius!" she said to Hopper. (But like with the password-breaking program, this compliment was really for herself.) Hopper had uncovered some huge breakthroughs for the case, and Gen thought it might just do the trick to prove to everyone what had really been happening with the "curse." She started saving and filing classified documents, her heart racing.

But because she was so engrossed with her computer screen, Gen didn't hear Lee's heels pounding through the palace hallways until Lee flung open the door to the Princess Suite and yelped.

"Your Highness, you aren't even dressed!"

Gen startled in her chair. "Dressed?"

"The final run-through for your coronation ceremony was supposed to begin fifteen minutes ago! You were supposed to be in your rehearsal outfit, in the queen's receiving room with the rest of the royal party at two o'clock!"

"And now it's . . . " Gen looked sheepishly at her computer. The time display read 2:30.

She swallowed hard. Queen Michelina was *not* going to be happy about this.

"I'm really sorry," Gen said. "I can be ready in ten minutes."

"Make it seven and I'll see if I can cool down the queen's temper."

"Deal. And thank you."

Lee nodded just once before she ran back out into the corridor, her heels clacking like an Olympic sprinter in stilettos.

Gen raced to her closet and threw on the rehearsal dress, which was a simpler version of the fancy gown she'd wear tomorrow at the real ceremony. This one was plain gray satin, though, so she'd be able to tell the difference between the practice dress and the lavender, official coronation dress. (The royal tailor had learned quickly that Gen didn't have an eye for fashion and could confuse a potato sack with a proper gown.)

She pulled on her practice gloves (also gray, not gold like the ones for tomorrow), and her imperial fox pendant on the new platinum chain that Lee had given her as a pre-coronation gift. She'd made sure the clasp was an extra secure one.

Gen was supposed to put on sheer pantyhose, but they were so tight and uncomfortable, and she usually managed to tear them before she even finished the "grand entry" part of the rehearsal. Besides, there were only three minutes left.

Gen decided to skip the tights.

She scooped up the practice ballet flats (again, gray, unlike the golden ones for tomorrow), because she'd be able to run faster barefoot than with expensive shoes on, even practice ones.

Two minutes.

There was just one more thing Gen needed to do. She rushed over to her computer and smiled one more time at it. "Okay, Hopper. Let's do this thing."

Then Gen hit SEND.

She careened into the queen's receiving room with four seconds to spare. Lee winced because Gen hadn't put on her shoes yet. Duke Charlemagne arched an amused brow at her. And the rest of the royal extended family—distant uncles and aunts whom Gen had only heard about but hadn't met until this moment—shifted nervously, not quite sure what to make of this awkward scene.

"Hey, everyone! Waiting for me?" Gen said, attempting humor to lighten the obvious fact that she'd held up the entire dress rehearsal.

Nobody laughed, although a few muttered under their breaths. Gen caught someone whispering, "Is that really her?" as if disbelieving that a princess could behave like, well, a kid who grew up on the streets of New York.

Queen Michelina didn't say anything, although she exhaled heavily, then gave Gen a cutting look. "Now that all members of the royal party are here, let's begin, shall we?"

She rose from her velvet armchair and started walking to the receiving room door, where she was supposed to lead the royal processional to the Monarch's Balcony, a grand stone terrace that opened up to the lush gardens and fountains at the front of the castle. Tomorrow, the gates to the usually private Raldonian Palace would be thrown open, and those very same gardens and the entire long, winding driveway would be full of the kingdom's citizens.

Assuming all went well and there *was* a coronation. Gen was still unsure what would happen next. But she knew she was ready for it.

Here goes nothing. Gen climbed up onto the hard-backed wooden chair that she'd sat in the last time she was here in the receiving room. "Actually, I have something important to say before we continue," she announced in a loud, clear voice.

Several royal relatives gasped at her boldness.

"How appallingly rude!"

"Is this what passes for manners with the youth these days?"

"She's not wearing any shoes!"

Queen Michelina turned her frostiest glare yet at Gen, like an icy laser pointer. "Genevieve, what is the meaning of this?"

"I apologize for the delay and interruption, Your Majesty," Gen said, executing a perfect curtsey (she'd been practicing all week). She was sure it even looked elegant while standing barefoot on top of a chair. "But what I'm about to tell you is about the future of Raldonia, and I think you'll want to hear it.

"You see, there's a traitor in our midst . . . in this very room."

HEAD IN THE CLOUD

The group tittered in alarm, muttering to one another in hushed tones.

"Cancel the coronation," the queen said to Lee. "I cannot have such an immature child in line for my crown."

"No!" Gen shouted. "You'll only be doing exactly what the traitor wants. Don't you see, Your Majesty? It's a trap!" She swiveled around to point her steady finger at the figure standing next to the door. "And Duke Charlemagne is behind it all."

Duke Charlemagne folded his hands calmly in front of him. "Genevieve, sweetheart, please. I don't know what you're going on about. You're embarrassing yourself, and you're embarrassing the entire royal family."

"*You're* the one who's an embarrassment. You caused all the 'curse' catastrophes, and you framed Hill and his dad."

The duke chuckled indulgently, like any adult does when they think a child has let their foolish imagination run away from them. "Don't be silly. I'm your ally, remember?"

"Genevieve—" Queen Michelina started.

"I'm *not* being silly." Gen turned to Queen Michelina. "Your Majesty, the duke masterminded a multi-pronged plot against Raldonia."

She took a deep breath, feeling everyone's eyes on her. It was time to lay it all out. "Step one was to make the kingdom distrust me by reviving talk about the curse. He was no stranger to making this happen; Duke Charlemagne had waged a similar smear campaign before, when my mom fell in love with a non-royal and, in the duke's opinion, 'besmirched the House of Claremont name.'

"Step two was to lay blame on my only friend—Hill— and therefore isolate me further than I've already been. Without friends, Duke Charlemagne thought no one would defend me.

"Step three was set for tonight—he would leak to the press that I was the one behind the curse, and that I'd faked the DNA test. Everyone in Raldonia has known the duke for ages, and they have no reason not to trust him. He would discredit me, and that would be the final nail in my proverbial coffin. No coronation."

The entire receiving room was tensely quiet.

Finally, though, the silence broke. Duke Charlemagne whooped and slapped his thigh, as if everything Gen had just said was hilarious. "Didn't I tell you?" he said to the queen between peals of laughter. "It was folly to think your wayward daughter's daughter—who grew up in a foreign country—could ever be worthy of your throne."

Gen crossed her arms. "And here you were pretending to be my ally. Also, you didn't actually deny anything I just said."

The duke stuttered. "W-well . . ."

"If you're innocent, prove it," Gen said. "It's treason to lie to the queen. So go ahead and tell her right now that what I said is false."

Surprisingly, Queen Michelina didn't jump in here. Instead, her gaze flitted between Gen and Duke Charlemagne, and back again.

The duke scoffed. "Of course it's false! It's made-up stories by a *child* who's watched too many detective shows on the internet. I've always said that new technology rots our brains, and look!" He jabbed his finger at Gen, who was still standing shoeless on the queen's furniture. "*This* is what our world has become."

Now the queen spoke up. "You've leveled some dire accusations, Genevieve, and I do not look lightly upon pranks, especially those with serious consequences."

But a smile cracked Gen's face. Because now that she'd gotten the duke to make a clear statement to Queen Michelina, Gen could finish what she started. Duke Charlemagne wasn't the only one in this room who knew how to lay a trap.

"I have incontrovertible evidence, Your Majesty," she

said. "The duke made it easy. He hates new technology so much, he insists on using an old PalmPad. But that Palm-Pad was also his downfall."

Duke Charlemagne whipped his beloved handheld out of his pocket and waved it in the air. "This simple machine? That's laughable!"

"On the contrary," Gen said. "Note the flashing green light at the top of the device. No modern-day phones have such an obnoxious battery indicator. But that electronic green light was spotted by eyewitnesses at multiple sites of the curse incidents, including right before the discovery that the seafood catch had been spoiled and the day before the Brillat-Savarin Dairy Farm's milk was churned into butter for National Raldonian Cake Day.

"Also, on my very first day in Raldonia, your PalmPad's battery ran low while we were in the kitchen. You had to leave to go plug it in. But later, during the kingdom's power outage, your PalmPad was suspiciously charged, even on the fourth day when we were out in the hedge maze. You claimed it was because you always have backup batteries on you. But that certainly hadn't been the case in the kitchen on my first day. Which leads me to the conclusion that you knew ahead of time that the power outage was coming, didn't you? You were specially prepared for it."

"Th-that's not incontrovertible evidence!" Duke Charlemagne exclaimed. "That's mere conjecture and coincidence!"

"I knew you'd say that," Gen continued. "Which is why

I went further in my investigation. I delved into the palace cloud."

"I don't know anything about the clouds!" the duke spluttered.

"Exactly," Gen said. "You see, I remembered that you mentioned writing all your correspondence and even new laws on your PalmPad. But because you don't understand how current technology works, you didn't realize that your PalmPad was also backed up on remote servers—also known as the cloud."

Duke Charlemagne looked dizzy.

"Let me put it simply," Gen said. "I have copies of everything you've ever written on your PalmPad: emails, forged documents, recipes for the powdered acid you sprinkled on the seafood catch and for the oleasteros formula that poisoned the butter. There's even a receipt for all the beetles and bugs you purchased to infect the lavender fields.

"Oh, and I almost forgot." Gen pulled her baby blanket from the pocket in her dress's skirt. The burnt blankie was folded into a neat little square.

Gen unwrapped it and held up a brass button. "I found this in my fireplace, the night someone tried to burn down the tower room, with me in it. The missing button belongs to you, doesn't it?"

"Why would you think—"

"Because the button has an eagle on it. . . . The symbol of the ancient King Charlemagne—your namesake and pride and joy."

SEWER SCUM AND ROYAL RATS

D uke Charlemagne scoffed. "Your Majesty, I stand by my previous declaration. It is Genevieve Sun who is a liar and a threat to Raldonia. Not I."

"Wait, shush." Lee pressed one hand to her headset, listening intently to something, and held her other hand up in the air.

The queen wasn't used to people shushing her. "What is it, Lee? Can't you see we're in the middle of an imperial crisis here?"

"Yes, sorry. . . . But that's what this is about." She tapped on her headset. "The Raldonian Intelligence Agency has just published a treasure trove of Duke Charlemagne's personal documents on the RIA website. Seems like everything Gen—I mean, Her Highness—said is true."

Gen said a silent *thank-you* to Agent 34 for coming through on her favor. She'd done the detective work herself, but she was also smart enough to know that she needed help on the credibility front. It was easy for adults to dismiss a kid and her crime theories. It was a lot, lot harder for them to deny the truth once it was vetted by their own national intelligence agency. Which is why Gen had sent all of Hopper's findings to Agent 34 and had *him* publish it all on the RIA's website. Maybe in the future, once the grownups here got to know Gen, things would be different. But for now, she was really glad to have Agent 34's help.

At that moment, reinforcements from the Imperial Guard arrived outside the receiving room door.

Lee pressed her fingers to her headset again. After a moment, she said, "The press is all over the documents and the news is already blasting out nonstop headlines about the duke's treason. The Raldonian police are on their way here to the palace with an arrest warrant. And Chef Brillat-Savarin and his family will be released from jail, with all charges dropped and dismissed, and a public apology made to them."

Duke Charlemagne's face turned ashen.

He turned to Gen. "You . . ." he sneered. "You are Just. Like. Your. Mother."

For a moment, Gen's heart sank. All the times before when the duke said she was just like her mother, it hadn't really been a compliment.

But then she shrugged. Who cares how he meant it! Gen was still proud to be like Princess Adrienne.

Queen Michelina hissed at Duke Charlemagne. "I have treated you extraordinarily well and given you a great deal of power in the day-to-day operations of Raldonia, even appointing you as imperial chancellor amid all the recent trouble. So I am at a loss ... What possible motivation could you have had to plot against our own family—our own kingdom—like this?"

The duke's expression turned snake-like. "What motivation??? Your Majesty, my motivation has been the preservation of Raldonian honor. Ever since your daughter decided to marry that *commoner*, I have made it my mission to save our kingdom from decline. For centuries, Raldonia has stuck by our traditions."

Gen crinkled her forehead. That line sounded familiar. ...

Ah yes. The duke had said something similar to her when she arrived at the palace. He'd pointed at her imperial fox pendant then. Gen thought he'd meant it as a show of support, but now it was clear what he really believed: Tradition wanted pure royal blood, which was *not* Gen, and the duke intended to take that imperial fox for himself.

Queen Michelina narrowed her eyes at him. "You were the one who pushed me into severing ties with my own daughter."

"For the good of Raldonia!" Duke Charlemagne said. "You were too focused on your love for your daughter to see that putting her *common-born* husband in line to one day become king would sully the monarchy's name and all the history that has come before."

One of the other members of the royal family snorted like an angry rhinoceros. "Well then, the princess's car crash must have been rather convenient for you, wasn't it, Duke?"

"I didn't *want* it to happen," Duke Charlemagne said. "But when it did, I realized I could steer the situation for the benefit of the kingdom. The queen was distraught over the news, so I took the matter into my own hands. I paid the American authorities to keep the baby's survival hush-hush. I made sure that Child Protective Services had no idea who she was. I made sure that *Gen* had no idea who she was."

"You horrible, soulless, selfish jerk!" Gen wanted to launch herself at him. She imagined clinging to him with her legs wrapped tightly around his middle and pulling on his hair. She was pretty sure it was a toupee, and without it, he'd lose some of his self-righteous dignity.

But the anger on Gen's face, and the queen turning on him, was apparently enough on its own to send the duke staggering backward. He bumped into the wall behind him, where a painting of King Randolph—Queen Michelina's husband—glared down as if ashamed they were related.

Gen felt that way about the duke, too. If only she'd seen through him sooner. But late was still better than never, and at least justice would now be served.

"You see," Gen addressed the group again, squeezing her palms, "Duke Charlemagne has been tricking everyone here for a very long time. He thought he'd succeeded, too, until that insurance agent stumbled upon evidence that I'd actually survived the accident. So then the duke had to do everything in his power to both discredit me and make sure that all his past subterfuge was never discovered.

"As soon as I arrived in the palace, he pretended to

be buddy-buddy with me to get intel. Everything's written down in the 'private' diary he kept on his PalmPad: Duke Charlemagne never wanted a brash American girl who was half non-royal to have a shot at the throne. Instead, he wanted the people of Raldonia to resent me. That way there'd never be a coronation, and I'd never officially be granted the title of princess. You've been plotting to become king of Raldonia for years, not just the weeks since I've been here."

"But that doesn't make sense," Queen Michelina said. "The duke has never been in the line of succession. Before I knew you were alive, the crown would have gone down a different branch of the family tree."

Gen shook her head. "I also discovered drafts of something called the Charlemagne Heritage Law in the cloud. It would have changed the rules around succession of the throne, and with the duke being so well connected with the ministers, he could have pushed through approval of the law.

"If I wasn't crowned princess, it would mean Your Majesty had no eligible direct heirs, and then guess who would be next in line for the throne? The imperial chancellor— which just so happens to be the title the duke had wrangled for himself by creating all the curse disasters in the first place. Isn't that right, Dukie?"

Shaking, the queen turned to the duke. "Is it true? Were you hovering like a vulture, waiting for me to retire or die so you could claim the throne?"

The duke gritted his teeth but said, "At least if I were the heir, the blood of the monarchy would remain pure and undiluted. A hundred percent royal."

Ugh. His way of thinking was so . . . disgusting.

Queen Michelina circled the duke like a shark studying her dinner. "So let me get this straight," she said to Duke Charlemagne. "You presided over the ousting of my daughter from the imperial family. You orchestrated the 'disappearance' of my only grandchild. You have been undermining my rule for more than a decade. And you were attempting to change Raldonian laws without my knowledge, to benefit yourself.

"All of that, in itself, is grounds for charges of treason, many times over. But to top it off, you attempted to cover everything up. You *lied* to me. You committed fresh acts of betrayal right before my eyes and in front of all these witnesses." Queen Michelina gestured at the rest of the royals in the room.

The duke began to tremble under the queen's frigid glare. "B-but, Your Majesty! It was for the greater good of our kingdom! Many men of Raldonian lore have had to undertake seemingly illegal actions in the past, only to emerge as heroes. I swear I only did it because you didn't know any better. Without a king by your side, you needed my guidance to help steer the monarchy—"

"Enough!" the queen screamed. "I do not need a king or anyone else to 'help' me run the kingdom. Duke Charlemagne, you are an all-around backward-thinking, stuck-up irrelevance. You are a disgrace to the monarchy and a disgrace to the kingdom of Raldonia."

Those last sentences were like a fatal wound. Duke Charlemagne's knees gave out, and he sank onto the carpet.

At that moment, the Raldonian police arrived, led by Inspector Fedorov.

"Duke Charlemagne," he said, "you are hereby under arrest for conspiracy and treason." One of the other officers handcuffed the duke and dragged him up to his feet.

And then they took him away to the gallows.

Just kidding. This wasn't the Middle Ages, for Pete's sake. According to Agent 34, the duke would get a trial in compliance with Raldonian laws and procedures, and when found guilty, he'd be stripped of his title and property and sent to prison.

For now, though, Inspector Fedorov and the police just led Duke Charlemagne out of the room, head hanging limply.

No one in the room seemed to know what to do after that. Awkward silence filled the space until Lee tapped on her clipboard and said, "Well, we're a little behind schedule, but we could still catch up if we—"

The queen tiredly waved her gloved hand in the air. Somehow, it was still free of wrinkles, unlike Gen's entire outfit, which looked like it'd been run over by a steamroller.

To be fair, Gen had had quite a morning, what with catching a traitorous villain and all . . .

"I'm canceling the dress rehearsal," Queen Michelina said, sinking into her favorite armchair. "I think we'll do fine at tomorrow's coronation without it."

Gen's heart skipped with glee. The coronation was still

on. And all because she'd solved the Curse of the Tainted Throne.

Queen Michelina dismissed everyone from her receiving room. But just as Gen was about to file out, the queen said, "Genevieve . . . please stay behind. I'd like to speak with you. Would you care to have a seat?"

She patted the chair next to her. Not the unforgiving wooden one Gen sat in last time, but a soft, velvety cushioned one with beautiful gold arms and a gilded crown molded into the back.

A chair fit for a princess.

Gen smiled. "Yes, Your Majesty. I'd like that."

GOOD DETECTIVE TRAIT
NUMBER ELEVEN

After everyone else had left, the queen said to Gen, "Please, call me Amma. It's the Raldonian equivalent for *grandma*. And nowhere near as stiff as *queen*."

"Amma?" Gen said.

A real grandma. This is what Gen had wanted since she arrived in Raldonia, but now the word *Amma* felt clumsy on her tongue.

The corners of Queen Michelina's mouth turned down sadly. "Well, only if you want to."

"I do!" Gen said, perhaps too emphatically, because the queen startled in her armchair. "I mean, I'd love to call you Amma."

There. The word flowed much easier the second time. Maybe Gen just needed some practice. She'd never had a grandmother—or any real family—before. (Duke Charlemagne certainly didn't count anymore.)

Queen Michelina smiled brightly. Gen didn't know that was possible. But in that moment, the room seemed to warm several degrees in temperature, and all the frost from the ice queen melted away.

"And may I call you Gen?" she asked with more timidity than the ruling monarch usually had in her voice.

Gen nodded. She was smiling so hard, she couldn't speak.

The queen reached over and clasped Gen's hand. "I owe you an apology, dear. Both for not noticing how Duke Charlemagne was playing with your future, and for my being so irresponsibly distant from you. You see, I've lost so much in the past, and I was afraid to lose more. When my beloved husband passed away, I couldn't bring myself to have his throne removed. And then when my daughter— your mother—left Raldonia, I felt even more alone.

"After Adrienne's death, I was overfull with regret over my rift with her. And when you arrived in Raldonia, you reminded me so much of her, I found it painful even to be around you. I know that sounds awful, and it's not an excuse for how I treated you. What I mean to say is, I am deeply sorry, Gen, and I hope someday you'll forgive me."

Gen opened her mouth to say something, but the queen squeezed her hand and kept talking.

"The truth is, Gen, you are the best thing that's ever happened to me. I was ridiculous for pushing you away. You have your mother's energetic, curious spirit, and your father's honor and courage. I loved them both before politics and old-fashioned ideas of duty tore us apart. And

I also love you, even though it's frightening to me to do so, because as I've learned, any time you love someone, you risk losing them, too.

"But I made that terrible mistake once before with my daughter, and I won't make it again with you. I may not be the kind of grandmother who bakes cakes and pies—to be honest, I don't even know how to turn on an oven. But I will love you with my entire soul and teach you everything I know. For now, you will sit in the throne beside me, one I thought would never be full again. And when you're old enough and ready, I will set the crown on *your* head to make you Queen Genevieve.

"All of which is a long way to say—Gen, I would be honored to have you as my granddaughter and to crown you tomorrow as the official princess of Raldonia, if you're willing." Queen Michelina opened up her arms, beckoning Gen for a hug.

However, Gen held back. She *wanted* the hug, but not yet. Because finally, she knew who she was meant to be. Gen was no longer a scrappy New York City foster kid, but she wasn't ever going to be a prim and proper royal either. Instead, she would combine the past version of herself with her new role in Raldonia, and become a new kind of princess, on her own terms.

She gave Queen Michelina a sly grin and said, "I'll accept your offer under a few conditions." Good Detective Trait Number Eleven—this was a new one!—

Always use leverage when you've got it.

The queen stared blankly at Gen for a second. Then she laughed. "I admit I'm not accustomed to people making demands of me, but I appreciate your candor. Tell me what you want." She dropped her arms and folded her hands politely in her lap.

"Okay, first, I want the palace employees to have better pay and benefits. They need to feel like they're appreciated and respected. And I don't want them bowing to me all the time. It's pretentious and stuffy and weird. Plus, I want to be able to be friends with the staff. I mean, seriously, we're a modern country! What does it say about our kingdom if we think allowing a princess to be friends with the people who spend all day working with her—as a team—is a bad thing?"

Queen Michelina went quiet as she thought it over.

"All right," she said. "I can agree to everything you said, except the bowing. There must be some preservation of custom. The formalities surrounding the monarchy have been put in place to create a sense of majestic awe, and it's not because we're arrogant. People like having a regal idea to look up to. There's a reason fairy tales are so often about kings and queens and princesses and princes. You and I are not merely leaders, Gen. We are also symbols of Raldonia. That's part of the rationale behind the bowing and all the other pomp and circumstance."

"Hmm." Now it was Gen's turn to wiggle her nose as she considered this. Queen Michelina's explanation actually made sense.

After a minute, she looked up. "How about a compromise?"

"A compromise?"

"Yeah. Maybe instead of a full bow, the staff can just do a quick bow of their heads? At least on ordinary days. And on fancy days, then we all ratchet it up several notches. You and I put on elaborate gowns and tiaras, and the staff wear their dress uniforms and also do the full, bend-at-the-waist bows."

The queen nodded. "That could work. All right, consider it done."

"Awesome! But there's more."

"Of course there is." Queen Michelina smirked playfully. Maybe she was already getting the hang of who Gen was. Or maybe this was also what Gen's mom was like. Either way, it made Gen happy.

"After the coronation," Gen said, "I think we should get out of the palace more often and mingle with the people. I'm new to Raldonia, and I want to learn about our kingdom from our subjects, not from ministers reciting from textbooks. I also think that getting to know people—no matter what their job or status is—will help me serve them better as their princess. Like, what are their greatest wishes and desires? What can be done to help business owners? What do families need most—and what about orphans like me? Basically, I want to know: How can we make Raldonia a kingdom not just for the few of us living in the palace, but for everyone?"

Queen Michelina couldn't help beaming now. "I have a feeling that you're not only the best thing that's happened to *me*, but also the best thing that's happened to Raldonia."

Gen's smile was as bright as the sun, too.

Which reminded her . . .

"Can my official title not just say that I'm part of the House of Claremont? Can it include my dad's last name, too?"

"You mean, House of Claremont-Sun?" the queen asked.

Gen nodded.

"I'll have Lee amend the script for the coronation to make sure of it. Is that all? May I have my hug now?" Queen Michelina tentatively opened her arms.

"Just one more request. Can we ask the palace kitchen to make fries once in a while?"

The queen laughed so hard, her crown fell off her head. When she finally caught her breath and picked up the crown from the carpet, she said, "You drive a hard bargain, but I expected no less. You really are so much like your mom. I didn't realize until now how much I missed that. So . . . how about we make every Friday, *Fry*-day?"

"Deal."

Then Gen flew into Queen Michelina's arms and held on tighter than she'd ever held before.

The queen held just as tightly back.

"Maybe when you're ready," Gen whispered, with her face buried in the queen's neck, "we can go to that secret bunker in the hedge maze and look through my mom's things together?"

"You know about the bunker?" Then Queen Michelina laughed while still hugging Gen. "Of course you do. Yes, we can go through your mom's things together, and I will tell you all the fun and silly and riotous stories of her child-hood. I would like that very much."

Gen sighed happily. "I love you, Amma."

"I love you, too, Gen. And I am never letting go."

ARE YOU READY TO PAAAAARTY?

"Are you ready?" Queen Michelina asked Gen the next afternoon as they stood inside the palace, just on the other side of the doors to the Monarch's Balcony. Gen wore the silk gown custom-tailored for today's coronation—lavender as a tribute to both the purple in Raldonia's coat of arms and the flowers the kingdom was famous for. Her elbow-length gloves were a subtle gold, with satin shoes that matched (and it turned out that they weren't uncomfortable at all!). Around her neck, Gen wore the imperial fox pendant, and she'd tucked her baby blanket neatly in the pocket of her skirt.

Gen looked up at her amma, who was regal in all her official regalia. Queen Michelina wore a cream-colored gown and matching gloves. Various royal medallions, including the imperial fox, pinned a violet-and-gold sash across her chest. The purple sapphire-and-diamond Raldonian crown nestled regally in her silver hair.

"I'm ready," Gen said, smiling.

Lee, who was standing behind the queen, spoke into her headset. "Trailblazer and Baby Fox are on the move."

Gen made a face.

Queen Michelina laughed. "We'll get them to change your code name."

Then Lee waved her clipboard in the air to signal the rest of the royal family lined up behind them. "Coronation procession beginning in ten, nine, eight, seven . . ."

Gen took a deep breath and stood tall. She'd come a long way from her roots in New York City, but she was proud that she was still the same determined, resourceful girl as she was before. Except with nicer clothes.

"Three, two, one . . ."

The Raldonian Symphony Orchestra began to play the national anthem, filling the air with the sound of majestic horns and stately drums. Monka smiled at Gen. She'd been wrong to suspect him, too. Like Lee, Monka was always *everywhere* because he truly was dedicated to the kingdom and the royal family. And in fact, he'd been the one to pick up Hill and his family yesterday as soon as they were released from jail.

Now, Monka and another Imperial Guard opened the doors to the Monarch Balcony. Midday sunlight streamed in, and the applause of the adoring Raldonian crowd in the gardens and courtyards below flooded the palace.

Queen Michelina led the way onto the wide marble

terrace, and people began to cheer. Monka nodded at Gen right before she crossed the threshold. "Go get 'em, Your Highness," he whispered.

And then Gen stepped onto the balcony. As soon as the crowd saw her, their cheering crescendoed into a thunderous roar, and a wave of love and acceptance and belonging swept over Gen like she'd never felt before. Raldonia wasn't just about being with her amma. Raldonia was home.

She grinned and waved with a tiny bit more excitement than might be deemed proper. The sea of people below went wild and started waving back ecstatically.

The rest of the royal family—all the uncles and aunts and cousins (other than Duke Charlemagne, obviously)— filed out onto the balcony and assumed their seats on the edges. But Queen Michelina and Gen remained in the center, standing on a carpeted dais so that everyone below would be able to see them.

When the Raldonian Symphony Orchestra finished the national anthem, the crowd hushed.

Queen Michelina began to speak, her voice projected across the gardens and courtyards by microphones cleverly positioned on the inside of the balcony railing.

"Today is a historic day for our kingdom," the queen said, "for we welcome home one of our own whom we believed was lost. For years I carried a hole in my heart. It was penance for breaking the bonds with my daughter, and I feared that a part of me—and a part of Raldonia— would always remain empty.

"But across the ocean, a jewel of a girl lived on. She is bold and clever like her mother, compassionate and strong-willed like her father. I have the greatest honor to be her grand-mother, and to crown her today as princess of Raldonia.

"Now, as tradition dictates, we shall have a recitation of a Raldonian poem."

This had originally been Duke Charlemagne's part in the ceremony, since he was one of only three living speakers of Raldonian. Since he was in jail, though, Queen Michelina would have to do it.

Gen, however, stepped forward. "May I?"

Her amma looked at her with confusion.

"It's a coronation day surprise," Gen said, both to the queen and the entire audience. "On my first day here in the palace, someone very unwise suggested that I wasn't smart enough to learn Raldonian. So I set out to prove him wrong. I found my mom's old Raldonian textbook, and I've been quietly teaching myself when no one was around. I'm not fluent—yet—but I plan to be. For today, though, I have a classic Raldonian poem for you, by none other than Bronze Leopold, I mean, Leopold Schumfeld."

Gen stood tall like there was a string running through her spine and her neck. She held her arms slightly away from her body (just as Professor Régles had taught her), and she began to speak Raldonian, with beautifully rounded vowels and soft consonants.

The poem was about the four seasons, and how, even when winter seems to bring only cold and barren trees, spring is always around the corner. Lavender will grow, birds will sing, and the sun will shine brightly again.

When Gen finished, Queen Michelina's hand went to her heart, and proud tears brimmed in her eyes. The audience in the courtyard below mirrored her and held their hands to their hearts, too, in silent awe of their soon-to-be princess.

Gen looked out at the sea of faces, and what was happening truly sank in. She'd found a real family, not only in the queen but also in Hill and her new friends in the palace and the town. After so many years of being rootless and alone, Gen had finally found home.

She couldn't resist a fist pump of victory and shouting out, "I love Raldonia!" in a Bronx accent.

Queen Michelina laughed and nodded her approval. Princesses *should* be spunky and tenacious and smart and proud of their accomplishments. The idea that girls could only be quiet, obedient dolls was more outdated than the duke's PalmPad.

The chief justice of the Raldonian Supreme Court made his way onto the balcony and presented the queen with a cherrywood box. She opened it to reveal a platinum tiara on a bed of dark-purple velvet. Diamonds and rubies sparkled all over it.

Gen gasped.

Queen Michelina picked up the tiara. "By the grace and power vested in me as monarch, and with the good people of Raldonia as witnesses, I hereby declare you—Genevieve Illona Caliste Aurelie of the House of Claremont-Sun—Princess of the Realm, Defender of Faith, Sincerity, and Justice!"

She set the tiara on Gen's head. Suddenly, the crowd below exploded in applause and whooping and shouting. The orchestras struck up the official Imperial Family Symphony, a resplendent song that was only allowed to be played for the monarch and direct descendants of the throne.

Gen smiled and touched the tiara, and then the Imperial Fox at her throat. Being princess was pretty cool. But even better? Defender of Faith, Sincerity, and Justice. Just like a detective. A PI . . .

She liked the sound of that.

That evening, the palace ballroom glittered in celebration. Gold silk draped across the ceilings like shimmering canopies, the crystal chandeliers sent twinkling light over the dance floor, and colorful aquariums full of Raldonia's rejuvenated sea life graced every dinner table. An invitation to the Coronation Gala was the most sought-after ticket in Europe, and the room brimmed with presidents and prime ministers and other important dignitaries, as well as every member of the Raldonian Palace staff. (It was Gen's night, after all, and the queen made good on her promise to make all the employees feel appreciated and had invited them as VIP guests.)

Chef Brillat-Savarin—happily restored to his job—had outdone himself. Shiny silver stations around the ballroom featured Gen's favorite foods in hors d'oeuvre form.

Some were American (tiny pots of macaroni and cheese, and pepperoni pizza bites), some were Cantonese (scallion pancakes and shrimp dumplings), and some were Raldonian (raldonberry jam-filled pretzels and lobster crackers). The biggest hit, though, were the miniature paper cartons filled with french fries. That, and the dessert table loaded with every type of cake and pie imaginable, plus a chocolate fountain and a machine featuring moon-drop-grape-flavored cotton candy (another culinary creation by none other than Hill).

He bounded up to Gen with his plate stacked high with scallion pancakes. "These are amazing!" he said, mouth stuffed so full, he looked like a chipmunk.

"It's a recipe I learned when I worked in a dim sum restaurant," Gen said, smiling.

"You worked in a dim sum restaurant before? Cooool! Dad's gonna go nuts. I want you to teach us everything you know." Hill crammed another crispy wedge of scallion pancake into his mouth.

Gen cracked up. "You're getting crumbs all over your nice suit!"

He grimaced. "I hate fancy clothes."

"I did, too," Gen said, thinking about when the royal tailor first presented her with her "new and improved royal wardrobe." But now as she looked down at the beautiful purple velvet dress that the tailor had made for the Coronation Gala, Gen said, "I think I'm getting used to them, though. As long as they have pockets."

Lee smiled as she walked by. Tonight, she was in a

rainbow-colored dress that made her look like an elegant circus tent. (Not easy to pull off, but Lee did.)

"I'm glad you're growing accustomed to the formalwear, Your Highness," she said. "Because the diplomatic envoys from South Mallanthra will be visiting in a week, and that means event after event after event."

The news of more princess duties didn't daunt Gen as much as it would have in the past. She felt surprisingly excited for the challenge.

Then she registered the rest of what Lee had said. South Mallanthra was where her dad was from. And *his* dad—Gen's grandpa—had been the South Mallanthran ambassador.

Her heart beat faster.

Was her grandpa still alive? Would Gen get to meet him?

"Why are they coming?" Hill asked Lee.

"Our treaty on trade is up for renegotiation. It'll be . . . interesting, to say the least. We need trade more than ever, after the damage Duke Charlemagne did to our own industries. And relations between Raldonia and South Mallanthra have been a bit shaky ever since Gen's parents had their rift with Queen Michelina." Lee looked around to make sure no one was listening, then whispered, "But the queen is optimistic and has a secret weapon in her arsenal."

"What is it?" Gen asked, leaning in.

"A priceless artifact from the Raldonian Museum of History. Queen Michelina will present it as a gift of good faith. Hopefully, it will make trade discussions much smoother."

Oh. Gen had been hoping that the secret weapon was

something more exciting than an antique vase or whatever. (Okay, to be honest, she'd kind of been hoping the secret weapon was her. Like, *Surprise! Your granddaughter is here! Now don't you want to offer us awesome terms for our trade agreement?* But on second thought, Gen decided that she'd rather *not* be a bartering chip for negotiations. Still, she was looking forward to meeting the South Mallathran delegation!)

At that moment, the Norwegian delegation rolled in on an enormous ice sculpture of a Raldonian shrimp. They were accompanied by Cleo, who announced she was going to make Brillat-Savarin Dairy's famous frosty creams, including one with extra toppings called the Princess Genevieve Special.

"Frosty creams?!" Lee practically drooled onto her headset. (Yes, she was still wearing her headset even though she had the night off. Gen wondered if it was surgically attached.)

Lee practically sprinted toward the line already forming in front of Cleo.

"Whoa, I've never seen Lee so relaxed," Gen said.

"Me neither. But frosty creams will do that." Hill laughed. "Anyway, before Lee showed up, you were telling me you had pockets in your dress? What for?"

"Oh, you know, normal stuff. Extra cookies, lock picks, and this . . ." Gen pulled out a sleek glass device the size of her hand. (Acquiring a high-tech tablet was the other favor she'd asked of Agent 34. However, it was actually Agent 43 who'd gotten this beautiful next-generation device. She'd pulled some strings with her contacts in a development lab in Silicon Valley. Agents 34 and 43 had gifted it to Gen after the coronation ceremony—with the queen's approval, of course, because they didn't want to breach palace IT guidelines section 4.07[b], subsection [iii]—and Gen had immediately uploaded her artificial intelligence program onto it.)

"Hill, meet Hopper," Gen said.

"Hopper?" Hill asked,

"Me, obviously," a high-pitched, robotic voice said from the device. "An incredibly advanced artificial intelligence program that's ninety-eight point thirteen times smarter than you."

Hill pulled back in surprise. "Did your computer just insult me?"

Gen shrugged apologetically. "The personality is still in its beta phase. I'm working out the kinks."

"That's what you say. I'm perfect already," Hopper retorted.

"Sassy," Hill said, grinning. "I like it."

"Thank you," Hopper said. "I like you, too, even though you're named after a naturally raised area of land."

Gen snickered as she stashed Hopper back into her dress pocket.

"Oh hey," Hill said, "there's Cara, Lilah, and Callan waiting for frosty creams. Come on, you can finally meet them!"

Just before Gen and Hill reached the line, though, a royal messenger sprinted into the ballroom and ran up to Lee, breathless. She immediately left to speak with him privately.

Gen cocked her head, her curiosity piqued.

"Save me a place in line," she said to Hill.

"Where are you going?" he asked.

But Gen was already slipping away. She followed Lee and the messenger to the back corner of the ballroom. Gen ducked behind a cart stacked with dirty dishes so she could eavesdrop.

"What's going on?" Lee asked.

"The South Mallanthran artifact," the messenger said, still trying to catch his breath. "It's gone."

"What do you mean, gone? It was locked up in the palace vault, and—"

"Stolen," the messenger said. "And not a trace of evidence of who or how they did it."

Lee swore under her breath, then the two of them ran off to report to the queen.

But Gen stayed crouched behind the cart and smiled. "This sounds like a job for . . . *Princess* Private Eye!"

ACKNOWLEDGMENTS

I grew up with Disney princesses, but never in my wildest dreams did I think I'd get to create a new one. It's been such a delight to bring Princess Genevieve to life, and I want to thank the entire team at Disney for this incredible experience:

In Editorial—Brittany Rubiano, Kieran Viola, and Christine Collins;

In Design—Art Director Joann Hill, Design Intern Alice Moye-Honeyman, and cover artist Whitney Lam;

In Production—Marybeth Tregarthen and Jerry Gonzalez;

In Copyediting and Managing Editorial—Guy Cunningham, Sara Liebling, Jody Corbett, and Mark Amundsen;

In Marketing—Matt Schweitzer, Holly Nagel, Danielle DiMartino, Dina Sherman, Bekka Mills, and Maddie Hughes;

In Publicity—Ann Day, Crystal McCoy, and Christine Saunders;

In Sales—Monique Diman, Michael Freeman, Amanda Marie Schlesier, Mili Nguyen, Kim Knueppel, Vicki Korlishin, Meredith Lisbin, Lia Murphy, and Loren Godfrey.

You are all amazing, and I am so lucky to work with you!

Heaps of thanks to my agent Thao Le, whose unparalleled

understanding of me and my writing has brought my career to amazing new heights.

As always, thank you to all the incredible booksellers, librarians, booktokkers, booktubers, bookstagrammers, bloggers, and my fans—both those who have followed me from my very first novels and those who are new to my work—it is for you that I write these stories.

And last but really, always first—thank you to Tom and Reese for believing I can do anything, and for loving me even when we have to eat reheated leftovers for the third night in a row because I've been writing instead of cooking. I love you with all my heart.